Ensenada File

PHIL RIBERA

ISBN-13: 978-0-9962103-7-9 (e-book)
ISBN-10: 0-9962103-7-7 (e-book)

Published by Phil Ribera

Learn more about the author by visiting: www.philribera.com

MY LOVE . . .

IF YOU ARE READING THIS LETTER, THEN THEY HAVE ALREADY KILLED ME.

WORDS CANNOT EXPRESS HOW SORRY I AM FOR WHAT YOU MUST BE GOING THROUGH, NOW THAT THE LIFE WE HAD TOGETHER IS OVER. I ONLY HOPE THAT YOU CAN STILL FIND HAPPINESS IN A FUTURE WITHOUT ME.

WE NEVER KEPT SECRETS FROM ONE ANOTHER DURING OUR MARRIAGE, BUT THAT ALL CHANGED WITH BERNICE. I FOOLISHLY HID THE TRUTH FROM YOU, AND IN AN ATTEMPT TO ATONE FOR MY IGNORANCE, I TRIED TO MAKE THINGS RIGHT ON MY OWN. APPARENTLY, I FAILED.

MY HEART WAS IN THE RIGHT PLACE, BUT I REALIZED TOO LATE THAT I HAD STUMBLED INTO THE MIDDLE OF SOMETHING "OUTSIDE OF MY WHEELHOUSE," AS THEY SAY. AND UNFORTUNATELY, IT COST ME MY LIFE.

IF I'VE ACCOMPLISHED ANYTHING AT ALL, IT IS THE EVIDENCE THAT I'VE GATHERED AGAINST THOSE WHO ARE BEHIND THIS WHOLE SCHEME. IN DOING SO, I HOPE THAT I HAVE ALSO PROVIDED PROOF OF WHO KILLED ME.

AGAIN, I AM SORRY FOR LEAVING YOU LIKE THIS.

FOREVER,

~ D

* * *

He set his pen down and stared at the letter. There was so much more he wanted to say, but time was running out. Folding the note, he closed his laptop and stepped outside into the cool air. The color was already draining from the chromatic sky, and he knew that they would be coming for him soon. He gazed out at the horizon and realized that this would be the last sunset he'd ever see.

CHAPTER 1

Ten Days Earlier

Sleek and classy, her style and nice contoured lines drew me to her from the beginning. A tad wide at the beam, perhaps, but I've always thought that her build was more for comfort than speed. Not too big and not too small, she's the perfect body type for a man my size. I was fortunate enough to get a deal on *Wanderlust*—my thirty-two-foot Island Packet sailboat—and to date, she's the only thing that I actually own outright.

I sat on her deck, drinking coffee and scrolling through my emails. The morning fog enveloped the marina like a soundproof cloak, and I realized that *peaceful* doesn't even begin to describe the place. Only a handful of liveaboards are allowed at the Buena Vista Yacht Harbor, and I'm one of them.

My online calendar flashed SUNDAY, FEBRUARY FIFTEENTH—SINGLES AWARENESS DAY. A time for single people to "celebrate their singleness," it said.

I happen to be well aware of my singleness already, thank you very much.

Refocusing on my blissful surroundings, I was distracted again, this time by the Harbormaster, as he hustled across the dock like a guy with a case of the crabs. He waved enthusiastically, and continued toward me—too spry for the early hour, I thought. *He must want something.*

"Mr. McKenna," he called with labored breaths as he stepped up to the side of my boat. "I need a favor."

I smiled. "And a good morning to you, Cliff."

"Morning," he wheezed. "Have you noticed the BAIA sixty-three over on dock twelve?"

I squinted across the water to the other side of the marina.

"Something's going on with those guys," he said.

"Seem pretty quiet to me." I sipped my coffee. "Then again, I've only been here a couple of months."

"Odd comings and goings," he continued. "Always got the lights off and the windows covered. I'm thinking drugs."

I'd actually noticed the peculiar residents a couple of weeks after I moved into the marina. It was early in the morning when one of the boat's tenants arrived in a white Ford van. He traded keys with the other tenant, who took off in it. By itself, nothing. But then I noticed the same vehicle swap the next morning, and then the morning after that. Though I didn't admit it to Cliff, I had to agree—something was a bit off.

"I hadn't really noticed," I said. "With their boat being all the way across the harbor and all."

Cliff shook his fleshy jowls as if I had somehow let him down.

"Can I ask why you came to me with this instead of the cops?"

Cliff's eyes widened. "I don't know nothing for certain. Plus, I figured you've dealt with this sort of thing before, being that your application says you're a San Francisco policeman."

"*Was*," I said, thinking that I should have put down a different occupation on the slip rental paperwork. Bartender, shoe salesman— anything other than *cop*. Even an *ex-cop* isn't likely to go unnoticed in a place like this.

"And the term police-*man* is no longer politically correct," I said. "Anyway, I left the force a few months back. For me, it might as well have been a lifetime ago."

He stood awkwardly, shifting his weight from one foot to the other. "Yeah, I get it."

I wasn't about to go into the drama of my career, and I sure wasn't going to tell him that I was now a private investigator. It might have been different if Cliff was hiring me to check into the suspicious yacht, but he wasn't offering and I wasn't volunteering. I still had my pride— at least for another month or so, when the money would run out and my fledgling PI business would probably fold.

CHAPTER 2

I didn't put much stock in Cliff's sense of urgency. To him, laundry left unattended in a washer portended the same doom as a nuclear attack. Still, I felt that there might be some substance behind his suspicions.

I'd never worked narcotics when I was with the SFPD, never conducted surveillances—not in the traditional sense anyway. The only undercover work I ever did was for the police chief, and it ended in disaster. But like I told Cliff, that was a lifetime ago.

But as I sat there observing the "suspect" boat, I realized that it didn't fit with the other trawlers, weekend sailboats, and cabin cruisers. The Italian yacht looked like something out of Miami Vice—sleek, fast, expensive, and built for partying. Never mind that these guys never entertained, didn't socialize with other residents, and hadn't even taken their boat out of the marina. Other than coming and going in their white van, these two were a couple of ghosts.

But what the hell did I care? This was exactly the sort of thing I had happily left in the past. Having already paid my dues on the force, I'd suffered through my share of backstabbers, career-climbers, and narcissistic bosses.

Though if I were to be completely honest, I still longed from time-to-time for the cat and mouse game. I missed the ebb and flow of information, and piecing together the elements of a good case. I guess something deep in my psyche still needed to figure out fact from fiction and truth from lies. It wasn't exactly like sports, but it was competition on a more cerebral level. Sadly, solving cases was the only yardstick by which I could still measure myself.

A porthole curtain drew back on the drug boat, pulling me from my reverie. A silhouette moved inside, a wisp of steam vented from an open hatch, and that was all it took—I was back in the game. *Who are these guys and what are they up to?*

I thought the simplest way to proceed would be to check their liveaboard application. But I'd have to go through Cliff, which would generate questions, and worse, he'd think that we were partners.

One of the drug guys suddenly poked his head out of the cockpit, venturing a look around before emerging onto the deck. He was fit looking, in his thirties, and had dark skin; Black, Puerto Rican, or maybe South American. The distance between our boats made it difficult to tell. The man glanced around the harbor for a minute, then vanished below deck as quickly as he had appeared.

That was another strange thing about these two. You never saw them lounging around in shorts or sweatpants, or bathing suits for that matter. Always fully dressed and almost always below deck.

A sudden flash of movement caught my eye, one dock over from the boat I was watching. A fleshy wedge unzipping itself from a vinyl cockpit enclosure. A bend, a half turn, a fold. *Was I looking at a thigh? An ass? Maybe a breast? Hopefully, it was a woman.*

Finally, she bounded onto the deck, the last vestiges of flesh being tucked into a terrycloth robe. Clearly an attractive woman, her blonde morning hair rumpled just enough to look as if she'd just had sex. At least in my mind.

Discreetly watching from behind my sunglasses, I felt as inconspicuous as a seagull. Just a fellow yachtsman enjoying his coffee and checking his emails.

She bent down to gather something in her arms—towels, maybe— and another quiver of peach peeked through. Straightening up again, the woman turned in my direction and offered a cheery wave before frisking back inside.

Imagining my head bobbling like a dashboard ornament, I realized that sunglasses notwithstanding, my surveillance skills left a lot to be desired.

By the time I turned my attention back to the drug boat, the guy had closed the hatch and pulled the porthole curtain tight.

Finishing my coffee, I headed up the ramp with an armful of dirty clothes. I dumped them into one of the washers in the laundry room, and after fishing six quarters from my pocket, started the cycle. Then I strolled out the gate into the parking lot, where I used my cell phone to snap a photo of the van's license plate. Good timing, because I passed one of the men as I coded myself back through the gate. It was the other guy—the white surfer-looking dude. He dipped his head, allowing his mushy yellow hair a single bounce in response to my "good morning." And then he got into the van and drove off.

It was another odd thing about them; they were never gone at the same time. It was as if they were waiting for a delivery, or perhaps one of them always had to stay aboard to guard their product.

Back in the laundry room, my clothes thrashed around like fruit in a blender. I'd long ago given up separating whites from colors, and delicates from permanent press. It seemed like such a waste of time and money. So, ever since Doris kicked me out, towels and underwear and slacks and dress shirts were all one big happy family. Even my knee brace, which I figured also deserved a washing now and then.

"Hey Danny!"

I was stuffing the dripping bundle into the dryer when I turned to the voice behind me. He was another resident, whom I'd met briefly a couple of weeks prior. In the same place, in fact. Nice guy—friendly, easy to talk to. Only, I couldn't remember his name.

"Dylan," he said.

We shook hands. "Dylan, sure, I remember." I tossed the rest of my things into the dryer, fed it the last of my quarters and pushed start. "You and me must be on the same laundry schedule."

Dylan smiled.

"The bane of the single man," I continued. "Wash clothes every two weeks whether they need it or not."

He forced a laugh then told me that he was actually married. Said that he and his wife also live at the marina.

Who would have known? Does his own laundry. I suddenly wondered if my Ward Cleaver domestic attitude had anything to do with my marriage problem. *Problems*, I should say.

Dylan and I talked awhile as we waited for our wash. Turns out that he graduated from Cal a couple of years behind me. Claimed to remember seeing my name in the football programs, but who knows? My sports career ended with a blown out knee only two games into my sophomore season, and I suspected that Dylan was just being polite.

My clothes stopped turning at twenty minutes, but I was out of cash.

"So, Teddy and I are barbecuing steaks tonight," Dylan said. "How about joining us for dinner?"

Teddy? His wash had stopped, giving me a minute to consider my answer while he transferred his clothes to the dryer. I'm usually uncomfortable in social situations, and stupid things occasionally slip out when I run short of conversation. Doris used to carry that ball for me.

"We're in the Grand Banks fifty," he said, motioning down the ramp.

It was a nice yacht. The same one I'd seen the half-naked blonde on earlier. *Awkward!*

"Sure," I heard myself answering. Then, turning with an armload of soggy laundry, I asked, "What can I bring?"

"Boxer shorts."

"Huh?" I nearly dropped my clothes.

"Your boxers," he said, motioning toward the dryer door where a pair of my skivvies had snagged. "Come by around six."

I figured I should bring something. *Red goes with meat, right?*

I hadn't agreed to join them just because of Teddy, exactly. She was his wife, for Chrissake. It was because I needed to get out and meet more people.

At least that's what I told myself.

CHAPTER 3

It was nearly six, and I wondered why I had accepted the invitation in the first place. Pouring myself a healthy tumbler of scotch, I drank it down quickly, hoping it would be the shock absorber to smooth any conversation potholes.

I headed over to Dylan and Teddy's yacht wearing a damp button-up shirt, damp Levis, deck shoes with no socks, and carrying a twenty-nine-dollar bottle of Cabernet Sauvignon.

The deck boards creaked under my feet as I turned toward their slip. I gave a quick glance across the water at the drug boat, but saw no sign of life on deck. At least one of them was inside, I thought, probably watching me. In a moment of mindlessness, I stopped and faced the sleek cruiser. Sweeping off my sunglasses, I stared at the smoked porthole glass—giving my best war face. If someone was in there watching, I wanted them to know that I was watching back. Why? I had no idea. Bravado, boredom, too much liquid shock absorber... Who knows?

After a few seconds, I donned my sunglasses and continued to my hosts' boat, feeling a little like a kid who had just taunted a vicious dog from the safe side of the fence.

Dylan was at the aft gunwale tightening the clamps of a stainless steel barbecue to the taffrail. He had a half-drunk cocktail sitting next to him, confirming my original impression: I really liked this guy.

We'd only been talking a few minutes—just long enough for Dylan to pour me another drink—when I heard his wife coming up from the galley. Like a giggle working its way out, the woman bubbled onto the deck overloading my senses with her blonde hair, blue eyes, and pink lips. Teddy's shapely figure was barely contained inside a rainbow sundress. A heartbeat later came aromas of berry or melon or carrot cake, I wasn't sure. Whatever the fragrance, it fit nicely with the rest of the package.

I dumbly held out the bottle of wine, but she swept past it to hug me as if we were already old friends. I self-consciously glanced at Dylan, who eased the bottle from my hand with a carefree grin. I suddenly wished I had been as confident with Doris.

The talk was a lot easier than I had expected. They were equally pleasant—Dylan with his varied interests, and a subtle intellect that never came across as boastful. And Teddy, who talked about everything from her recent diet and weight loss, to her affinity for black and white movies and her collection of Michael Bublé songs. She was giddy and touchy, and she complimented me endlessly throughout the evening. I always like that from a woman.

They said they'd voyaged to Mexico a few times on their fifty-foot yacht. Spent a week spearfishing in the Sea of Cortez once. Said that Cliff had told them about an annual trek to Los Cabos, which they had recently returned from. Along with an armada of other boaters, the flotilla had made their way along the coast to spend a week partying in Mexico. The *Baja Ha-Ha*, I think they called it. Said I should sail my boat down with them in the fall.

I didn't want to admit that I was a relative newbie when it came to sailing, and that I was still barely comfortable maneuvering my sailboat around the bay. I told them that I wasn't a fan of international travel, but that I'd definitely think about it. In any case, it was nice to be asked by friends that I'd actually made on my own.

Teddy had served appetizers of Langoustine—little shrimps wrapped in bacon. "Poor man's lobster," she called them. And a salad, baked potato, and a perfectly barbecued New York steak smothered in sautéed mushrooms. Dylan's drinks seemed to keep coming, to the extent that we never made it to my wine.

Somewhere during the evening, I opened up a little about my current situation on the home front—heavy on the *good dad*, and light on the *bad husband*. I even showed them a photo of Bridget, taken just after she'd gotten the braces off of her teeth.

Around ten o'clock, Teddy announced that she had had enough of the food and drink and was going to bed. Backing her way down the hatch, she blew wild kisses at both of us. But again, Dylan didn't seem bothered.

We were alone on deck, and I was suddenly out of conversation. It crossed my mind to ask Dylan about Cliff's drug boat. By then, I'd probably had too many drinks to think rationally. "So," I said, kind of out of left field. "What do you know about those two guys in the BAIA sixty-three?"

He looked surprised. "Why do you ask?"

"Just don't see them around much."

Dylan studied me for a second, like he was weighing how much of an opinion to give. He finally surrendered an ambivalent shrug. "Who knows? Lots of crazy stuff going on these days."

A weird answer for sure, and it did nothing to help my little *pro bono* investigation. I wondered if Dylan had some suspicions that he wasn't willing to share, or if he was simply uncomfortable gossiping about the neighbors. I immediately wished that I hadn't overstepped.

"Anyway," he said, changing the subject. "You don't seem eager to travel much."

"My dad was in the military, and I saw enough exotic places as a kid to last me a lifetime. I'd rather read about foreign countries than actually visit them."

"Hmmm," he said. "I just finished a book you might enjoy. It gave a very different perspective of international travel." He handed me a paperback. "Give it a read when you get time. I think you'll enjoy it."

"*Sadhana?*" The cover bore the sepia image of a guy wearing a backpack on a desolate road. Dylan had clearly taken my comment literally. "Thanks," I said, thinking that I wouldn't be cracking open the book anytime soon.

He just smiled.

As the night wore on, the two of us talked lightly on deck. After putting on a down vest, Dylan broke out a couple of Cuban cigars. We talked and drank, and enjoyed one of the Bay Area's notoriously mild winter evenings.

CHAPTER 4

One... two... three...

I woke to condensation dripping from the boom vang onto the hatch cover—every drop sounding like a gong in my hungover brain. Steadying myself against the bulkhead, I got up and drained off some of the previous night's liquor.

Fragments of the evening slowly floated into my consciousness like flotsam from a scuttled ship. It had been a good night; I remembered that much. And other than my bomber headache, I felt good about my new acquaintances. Dylan was definitely a guy I could see myself hanging out with. As for Teddy, she was a sultry little thing who seemed to enjoy playing the flirt. Not that I minded. But there's a line I would never cross, and it's another guy's wife. Which kind of got me thinking about my own situation and whether or not I'm still technically married. And maybe more importantly, I wondered how Doris sees herself in this conjugality? Shelving that subject for the time being, I realized that Dylan was quickly becoming a friend. And for that reason alone, I pushed any further thoughts of Teddy from my mind.

Slipping a bathrobe over my shorts, I took my cell phone and a bottled water with me topside. The cool mist felt invigorating, and helped to tamp down the headache.

A couple of bars finally appeared on my cell, and I called the office.

"McKenna Investigations."

"It's me, Sha Nay Nay. Any calls?"

"I keep tell'n you, I go by *Shanay* now."

"Forgot, sorry. Doris didn't call?"

"No. And all due respect, but that woman's chump'n you. She done kick you out yo own house--"

"Anyway," I cut her off. "No new clients?"

"Nope."

"That bites."

"Yep."

"So, I need you to get in touch with my old partner, Linh Phú. I heard she was transferred out of Homicide, but I don't know where she landed." There was silence on the line, which I hoped meant that Shanay was writing it down. Then I heard cooing sounds and realized she had brought her baby daughter into the office—which was fine, I guess. Daycare is expensive, and I'm sort of like a godfather to the kid, anyway.

Shanay took down Phú's cell number and then I texted her the van's license plate. I could have called Phú myself, but I wanted to avoid questions she was sure to have about my life since leaving the police force.

"Ask Phú to check the registered owner. Citations, accidents, any criminal connections she can find."

"Got it." Shanay paused. "So, does this mean we finally got us a case?"

"Let's just say I'm looking into something for someone."

"Humph. Don't sound like no pay'n job to me, McKenna."

"Just get that license number to Phú." I hung up before my secretary, or assistant, or whatever she is, could come back with another snappy remark.

Sha Nay Nay Moore had been my street informant when I worked the Bayview-Hunters Point beat back in the day. She's got a record going back to her early teens, and those are just the things we knew about. But the girl somehow found her way through the rabbit hole and out the other end in one piece. More importantly, she had my back at a time when it mattered most. For me that was the reset button.

Shanay, as she likes to be called now, has been clean and sober for almost two years and is raising a daughter on her own. I figured the least I could do was give her a job.

My phone buzzed, and I saw that I missed a call that had gone to voicemail. I pressed *PLAY*.

"Good morning, Mr. McKenna. My name is Claudette Higginbotham, with Marin County Family Court Services. In reference to a petition for custody of Bridget McKenna, I'm calling to schedule a home visit with you..."

It was all *Doris'* doing—the legal separation, and now the custody thing. It was her way of showing that she was still pissed off. *Why should I justify myself to some court appointed hack? I'm a good father!*

12

I mashed my finger into the delete button, as if Doris could somehow see me erasing the woman's message. Then, after a second or two, I realized that my little tantrum wasn't going to get me what I really wanted. If I had any hope of spending time with Bridget, I'd have to play their game. I went to dial the woman back, but realized that in my anger I had also deleted her phone number. *Son of a bitch!*

I sucked in a deep, restorative breath and let it out slowly—the way meditating yogis do. I couldn't sit cross-legged because of scar tissue in my knee, so I just hung my legs off the deck and closed my eyes.

With the suddenness of a roadside bomb, a wailing scream pierced the calm of the marina. The high-pitched shrill echoed off of the water and boats, seemingly from all directions. It was a painful, grieving howl that ended with a sobbing, "Oh my God!"

My eyes sprang open and I scampered on all fours, trying to get to my feet. People had come out, looking and pointing, but I still couldn't tell where the horrific cry had originated. An older couple stood at the end of their slip, the man motioning toward the water and the woman covering her mouth with one hand and gripping him with the other. I followed their line of sight past the end of the slips, into the gray-green water of the navigation channel.

Focusing my eyes through the mist, I finally saw the body.

Not much more than a bundle of clothes, bobbing gently and rhythmically to the beat of a song no one else could hear. Then I made out the head, arms and legs. A man, judging from the frame, floating face down like a skydiver waiting for his parachute to open.

I leapt onto the dock and ran toward the slip closest to the body, still a good fifty yards out toward the seawall. Taking the turn too fast, I lost my footing on the wet boards and came down hard on my bad knee. It hurt like a son-of-a-bitch, and pissed me off, too.

Unfurling to a painful standing position, I unconsciously glanced toward Dylan and Teddy's yacht. Teddy was standing topside, and I gave her a self-conscious *all's okay* wave. Continuing a little slower, I yelled to her over my shoulder: "Tell Dylan to call nine-one-one!"

When I got to the end of the dock, I threw off my robe and dove into the frigid water. Besides freezing my balls off, I hadn't swum in years and could only remember a backstroke I'd learned as a kid. So, I flipped over and sort of back-floated out to the tottering body.

Instead of an emergency professional rendering lifesaving aid, I felt like a fat sea otter floating through a tide pool. By the time I got there, I was humiliated and wished that I hadn't chosen such a slow and feminine swimming stroke.

Once I reached him, there was no doubt in my mind that he was dead. Had been for a while. The back of his neck was as gray as the bay, and all his extremities were discolored and covered in gooseflesh. Everything was swollen from water absorption—his thick playdough ears, purple lips, and sausage hands with a ring finger strangled by a wedding ring.

Remembering my short tenure as a homicide inspector, I gently rolled the body over, careful not to disturb any forensic evidence. Dogpaddling now, I stopped suddenly as I stared into the dead man's face. Vague familiarity came in unfocused waves. The eyes looked different—just pudgy little slits—and the shape of his head was off. There was no symmetry, and one side was concaved like a deflated football. A gunshot wound, I realized. Close range into the right temple.

But the context was wrong, and the recognition took a minute for me to process. I looked at the face again, took inventory of the clothes, and thought back with a clearer mind than when I saw him last.

"Holy shit," I said under my breath. "It's Dylan."

CHAPTER 5

The Old Man and the Sea. That's what I felt like, dogpaddling with one arm as I dragged Dylan through the water toward the dock.

All eyes were on me, not the least of which were Teddy's. I couldn't bear a glimpse, but I felt her standing there watching. *Did she know it was her husband?*

The elderly man who had been observing from the dock came over to help me, and I noticed Cliff huffing his way toward the commotion. The three of us struggled to hoist Dylan's flaccid corpse onto the dock, the skin on his arms literally sliding off like a glove when Cliff tugged them.

I remembered reading about the phenomenon when I was studying for the police inspector test. It's called maceration—the same process that takes place with grape skins during winemaking. This took me back to the section of study about drowning victims. And although I never investigated a drowning case in San Francisco, it's pretty much a certainty that a human body—which is slightly heavier than water—will sink. At least initially. Only to resurface several days later when decomposition creates gasses. But Dylan couldn't have been dead longer than six or seven hours. He should have still been submerged.

As I climbed onto the dock, I noticed drops of water that had beaded on Dylan's vest. Staring at them for a moment, it finally dawned on me that the water resistant material had trapped air within its feather-filled chambers. I realized that his vest had acted as a life preserver—which of course, might have actually worked had he not been shot in the head.

Sirens sounded in the distance. I found my robe, and covered myself with it. As I stood up, something made me look across the marina at the drug boat. For a second I thought I saw movement through the porthole window, but then there was nothing. Which was also interesting, since by now everybody else in the marina was out—watching, gossiping, tweeting, texting, or recording the incident with their phones.

My eyes finally got the courage to sweep around to Teddy's boat. No longer standing, she had crumpled into a heap on the floor of the cockpit. Only her head was visible—tousled blonde hair, but not like the first time I saw her. Instead of sexy and amorous, her face looked red and blotchy. I figured that waking up to a murdered husband will do that to a woman.

A fire engine and several police cars barreled in, clogging the parking lot. Cliff, who was already a frenzied mess, fumbled to prop the gate open for them. There wasn't much they could do for Dylan, but I guessed they'd be giving CPR to ol' Cliff before long.

The cops took down our names, asked who had moved the body, and peppered the group of us with questions about whether we'd seen or heard anything suspicious leading up to the time we found him. One cop was already eyeing me, so I was glad that Cliff gave them Dylan's name and liveaboard info. I wasn't going to say anything. That is, until they got something wrong.

"Must have just happened," said a sergeant to his guys as he folded Dylan's right leg and straightened it out again. "Barely any rigor at all."

Rigor mortis, or stiffening of the body, starts within the first two hours and is fully engaged six to twelve hours after death. But not always. I clenched my jaw as long as I could, then finally piped up.

"Temperature alters the rate of rigor mortis."

They turned to look at me—the sergeant with a deepening scowl. "Excuse me?"

"Cold conditions can slow the rigor mortis process," I said. Then, nodding my chin toward the bay. "Like being submerged in fifty-degree water."

"And you are?" asked the sergeant.

One of the cops stepped forward, thumbing a pocket notepad. "Name's Daniel McKenna, Sarge. He's the one who fished the body out."

"I... I used to be in law enforcement," I said.

Eyeing me up and down, he stopped at the dripping hem of my bathrobe. "That right?" He turned his back and continued speaking with his guys in a quieter voice. I took it as my cue to leave. For a minute I thought about going over to check on Teddy, maybe ask if there was anything I could do. But Cliff was already leading a brigade of cops over to her boat. Unfortunately, it didn't appear that he'd told them anything about the suspected drug boat—which still looked deserted.

So, who killed Dylan? I stopped at the foot of my slip and looked around the formerly peaceful marina. My little slice of heaven. The place where I could enjoy life and forget my past. *Could Teddy have done it? Dylan's giggly little wife? Why would she? They seemed so relaxed together, so comfortable in their relationship.*

I was suddenly struck with a terrifying thought. What if the drug guys had shot Dylan because of me? Because of the hard looks I gave them on my way to dinner. After all, Dylan and I are roughly the same age, same coloring, and same height—though I'm a tad heavier. Could they have taken my stupid stare as a threat, and then confused the two of us in the dark after I'd left Dylan's boat? *Am I responsible for my friend's murder?*

Later that afternoon, I was on the cabin sofa icing my knee. The curtains were closed and I lay in the dark, thinking, trying to make sense of what had happened to Dylan.

"Mr. McKenna!" called a voice from the dock. "You in there? Detective Sal Grassi, Alameda Police."

Pulling back the curtain, I saw that some cops—both uniformed and plain clothed—had gathered next to my boat.

I slipped on my shoes and climbed topside. Stilted introductions were made, and though I wasn't listening to their names, my mind was cataloging and indexing the group. There was the uniformed sergeant who already didn't like me; a thick, middle-aged white man in a brown suit—probably the lead detective, Grassi; a slightly younger Latino man who was similarly dressed—clearly his partner; and a stout, bookish redheaded woman wearing a beige pantsuit and carrying a clipboard—a representative from the district attorney's office, I guessed.

I invited them aboard, and toweled the dew off the cockpit seats as they ineptly climbed in. All except the woman from the DA's office, who chose to stand on the dock within earshot.

"Always keep one hand on the ship and one hand to steady yourself," I said, parroting an old sailing colloquialism that I'd learned as a kid. Nobody seemed to appreciate it.

The older suit took the lead right away. "Can you give us an account of your last twenty-four hours?"

"Okay, sure..." I leaned back against the pushpit rail. "Starting yesterday morning, I got up and had my coffee. No, strike that, I took a leak first and then had my coffee."

"We just need to know where you were and who you met with."

"Did my laundry between nine and ten in the morning," I said. "Drove to the market in the afternoon, picked up a few things, had dinner..."

"With?"

I tilted my head. "Since you've just finished interviewing Dylan's wife, I think you know that I spent the evening with them."

"Uh huh." He nodded, his tongue pressing the inside of his cheek. "That was it?"

I thought for a second. "That's it."

"Didn't go out of the marina for any other reason?"

"Nope."

He wrote something down on his notes. "Can you explain why your code was used to enter the security gate at 9:13 a.m.?"

"Oh, well yeah, I went out for a minute. I forgot."

"Went out, where?" They all waited for my answer, as if they had me cornered in some little web of lies.

"To the parking lot," I said brusquely. "I needed to get something out of my car." Good one, I thought. Came up with that in a hurry. Decided now was not the time to tell them of my little drug boat investigation, or that I had actually gone out to get the license number from their van.

He nodded again, mouth still open and tongue still pressing. "Funny thing, don't you think?"

"That someone was killed? No, I don't think that's funny."

Ignoring my remark, he said, "I think it's funny that you were the last person to spend time with Mr. Langdon last night, and the first person to see him this morning. And in between those two meetings, he was murdered."

I stretched a kink from my neck, realizing that I'd never heard Dylan's last name before. Langdon. "See that sixty-three foot BAIA over there?" I pointed out across the water like an Irish Setter. "You ought to be questioning them, not wasting your time with me."

He nodded, mouth closed finally. "Let us worry about who we talk to."

"Whom," I said. "We'll worry about *whom* we talk to."

I'd pissed him off. "Do you own a firearm, Mr. McKenna?"

"Yes, I used to be a--"

"We know what you *used to be.*" He flashed a wiseass grin. "You can voluntarily hand over your weapon for a forensic examination of the ballistics, or we can come back with a search warrant and get it ourselves."

"That won't be necessary." I went below, then returned with a black zippered case. It held the 9mm Glock that I'd bought when I started on the force.

After nodding to the younger detective to take my gun, the lead guy flipped out a business card as if doing a magic trick. *Nothing up my sleeve.* "Feel free to give me a call if you remember anything else."

He turned to leave, followed by the younger detective, and then the uniformed sergeant. As they made their way down the dock, I noticed that the woman with the clipboard remained there.

"Was there something else you needed?"

"Nope." She stepped over a dockline to hand me a business card. "I think I've got everything I came for."

I watched the woman make her way up the ramp to the gate before glancing down at her card.

CLAUDETTE M. HIGGINBOTHAM–COUNTY OF MARIN FAMILY COURT SERVICES.

"Son of a bitch!"

CHAPTER 6

For a couple of days following Dylan's murder, the marina looked like the scene of a school shooting. Uniformed cops and plainclothes detectives up and down the ramp, forensics people coming and going, and spools of yellow crime scene tape left fluttering in the breeze. They had even brought in scuba divers to comb the bottom of the channel. It was the source of excitement among the boaters, all except the probable drug dealers—now probable murderers. Those two were as quiet as a couple of bilge rats.

Nobody but me seemed to notice the absence of activity on the drug boat. I spent most of my time sitting outside with my sunglasses on, just observing, waiting for them to make a mistake.

One dock over, Dylan and Teddy's yacht was also eerily quiet. Although I never actually saw Teddy leave, I could tell the boat was empty. Curious to know where she had gone, I thought about asking Cliff but then decided against it. I had attracted enough suspicion as it was.

Later that evening, I finally got a call back from Linh Phú. Turns out that my former partner had not left the homicide detail of her own volition, but had been transferred out by the police chief. It was most likely payback for the help she'd given me during my final days on the force. Which made me feel even worse now, asking her to help me yet again.

"I ran the license number," she said. "Sorry it took so long, but I was out of the office on a case."

She had ended up in the drug suppression task force, which for anyone else would have been a brass ring. But for someone with Phú's talents, the transfer out of homicide was clearly a demotion.

"The good news is," I said cheerfully, "I'm investigating a couple of possible drug traffickers."

"Hmm." Papers cluttered in the background. "It doesn't fit with what I'm seeing on the license plate printout. Newer model Ford Econoline van, right?"

"Yeah."

"Comes back registered to Cybernetic Systems on Viewridge Avenue in San Diego. It's listed as a small startup with less than twenty employees. No debt, no tickets, no criminal history, and they pay their taxes on time. Clean, as far as I can tell."

I thought for a minute. "Sounds almost too clean."

Then Linh had to ask how my PI business was doing. I lied, told her I could barely keep up with the work. She sounded doubtful, and I immediately suspected Shanay's big mouth. After a few pleasantries, we promised to meet for lunch soon.

I called Doris, but she didn't answer and I didn't leave a message. Then I called my daughter.

"Hello?"

My heart jumped. I hadn't spoken to her in three weeks. "Hey, Bridge."

"Yeah?"

"It's me, Dad. How's everything going? I haven't talked to you--"

"Gotcha! You've reached Bridget McKenna. Leave a message and I'll call you back."

Is it possible to be embarrassed and annoyed at the same time? I almost didn't even leave a message.

"Bridge, yeah, it's me, Dad." I took a breath. "So, we haven't talked in a while and I wanted to make sure we're okay—you're okay. And your mom—I hope she's okay, too. I haven't spoken with her either... anyway, I--"

The phone beeped and the line went dead. I hadn't even gotten a chance to mention the home visit from the family court lady. My status as a dad was pretty much on hold until the woman decided whether or not I could see my daughter.

About to throw the phone across the room, I settled instead for a robust toss onto my bed. It buzzed in mid-flight, and I scrambled to get it.

"Bridge?"

"No Danny, it's Doris."

I recognized my wife's voice, but for some reason I still looked at the screen for confirmation. "Doris... hi."

"Why do you keep calling, and calling, and calling?"

"Okay Doris, I get it. I just want to, you know, ask you not give up on us."

"Isn't it a little late for that?" She phrased it like a question, which gave me a modicum of hope.

"You're still my wife." She groaned but I continued, "And Bridge is still my daughter. Nobody's going to take her away from me."

Doris was quiet for a minute. "Nobody's trying to, Danny. But you seem to be doing it to yourself. I heard about Mrs. Higginbotham's visit, and the trouble you're in. It's like déjà vu with you."

I calmed myself. "First off, the guy who died happened to be a good friend of mine. In fact, I'm the one who jumped into the bay to try to save him. And now, I'm what? I'm the bad guy? This is somehow my fault? Because this Higglebottom woman decides I'm a lousy father, I can't see my own daughter?"

"Look Danny, I don't think anybody said you can't see Bridget. I was angry after the whole SFPD thing, but it's been a few months now and I've moved past it. Or, I'm *moving* past it. Trying, anyway. I was actually going to call and ask you to watch Bridget next week."

I sat there stunned, swallowed a bubble of air. "Yes. Yes, of course! Why didn't you say so?"

"Because I was hoping to could get someone else, but I can't."

It seemed like I was the last resort. "Are you going somewhere?"

"Uh, well yes. I'm just... taking some time away."

I was dying to know what in the hell she had planned, but I wasn't about to screw this up. "No worries. What day should I pick her up?"

"I thought it might be better, easier, if you stayed here at the house. Close to Bridget's school. Just easier."

Made sense. I wasn't crazy about leaving the boat, especially now, but I hadn't been back to the house since Doris kicked me out. Besides spending a week with my daughter, I thought I might be able to parlay this into moving back home.

She wanted me at the house by noon on Sunday. I hurried off the phone before she changed her mind.

That night I tossed and turned in the dark, waiting to be rocked asleep by the rhythmic waves. Sunday was several days away, still plenty of time to get some shopping done, maybe buy a couple of CDs for Bridge, even pick up some flowers for Doris. *Flowers might seem too eager—wouldn't want to make too much out of being invited back.* I considered getting off the bed to do some push-ups and sit-ups, but decided to get my rest instead.

I'd finally fallen asleep when the boat rocked sharply against the tempo of the waves. I froze and listened in the dark. It was the first time I'd realized that being below deck put me at a tactical disadvantage. There was no escape route.

Someone had climbed onto the sailboat and was moving on the deck. Nobody should be coming aboard at 11:30 at night.

Instinctively reaching for my gun, I suddenly remembered that it had been taken for testing. I stepped quietly through to the galley and felt around in the dark for a kitchen knife.

Above me, a shadow moved across the hatch opening. There was the tight squeak of a rubber sole on fiberglass, and I froze again. The drug dealers, coming after *me* now.

Suddenly a knock directly above me, as casual as a UPS delivery. "Hello, Daniel? It's me, Teddy."

CHAPTER 7

I hadn't expected anyone at that hour, least of all Teddy. Yet there she was, climbing butt-first into my cabin in the dead of night.

The dumb expression was frozen on my face like a wax mask. *Sure, a midnight visit from the grieving widow is totally normal.*

I wanted to ask why she was there, or tell her how sorry I was about Dylan, or maybe inquire if she's the one who killed him. But as much as I struggled to say something, not a word managed to pass through my lips.

She removed her coat and shook the wetness from it, then tossed it over the galley counter. "Sorry," she said, flopping onto the couch. "Didn't mean to get your floor wet."

Teddy wasn't as colorful and perky as I remembered. Her hair, matted from the rain, lay in flat bunches against her head. And without makeup, her eyes looked saggy and tired. But without her coat, I saw that the steamy figure was still there.

"I needed to talk to you," she said. "But I didn't know your phone number. And I couldn't come earlier; not with all the police around." She stopped talking and looked at me as if it was my turn to say something.

"Listen, Teddy." I rubbed my palms roughly over my eyes. "We really don't know each other all that well, I mean, nothing more than a casual conversation over dinner. And, I'm very sorry about Dylan. I am."

She held up a hand to pause me while she tried to address each item, like a point—counterpoint thing. But I continued.

"My life is complicated enough right now, and whatever it is that you want to tell me... whatever you're involved in... I can't afford to be a part of it. I don't even want to know about it."

Her shoulders dropped as if I'd hurt her feelings. She stared down at the water droplets on my teak floor before glancing back up. For a second I thought she was going to confess to the murder.

"I'm not *involved* in anything," she said. "My husband was murdered, and I'm heartbroken. Devastated."

"But you said you couldn't talk to me with the police around, and you're here—in the middle of the night. That's not the way innocent people act."

Teddy buried her face in her hands and began sobbing. I stopped talking and watched, trying to gauge the legitimacy of her tears. They seemed real enough.

"The police are treating me like a suspect," she finally said. "Like I'm the one who killed him."

"Yeah, I know the feeling."

Her eyes sparked. "And they asked me a lot of questions about you too, like how long we've known each other, how late you stayed on the boat that night, and if you and me... anyway, that's why I didn't want them to see me here. It seems like they're watching everything. That's one of the reasons I left the marina to stay with my sister."

I nodded. "Makes sense."

"Also, I don't really feel safe living here anymore. That's the other reason I left. It really scares me to be alone on the boat after what happened."

It was a perfect segue. "What, exactly, did happen?"

"I don't know." She looked at me with empty eyes. "I left the two of you on deck, and I went below to get some sleep. When I woke up the next morning, I realized that Dylan hadn't come to bed. I heard a scream, and when I went up to the cockpit I saw you and Cliff lifting Dylan out of the water."

I thought about her description of events. A glaring inaccuracy was that she claimed to have gone up to the cockpit *after* I was already in the water. But I remembered seeing her standing there when I slipped on the dock.

"How do you know I didn't shoot him?" I asked. "The police seem to think I did."

She cocked her head and a lock of damp hair fell across her face. "My bad for trusting you, but I'm a pretty good judge of people. And I would bet anything that you didn't do it—I mean, why would you? You're a nice man, sweet and kind. And you genuinely seemed to like Dylan."

"I did like him." I thought back to the two of us talking and smoking cigars together. I also liked that she had such a favorable impression of me. *Sweet and kind.*

"That's why I'm here," she said. "I trust you, and I need your help."

My eyes closed, and the cynical me suddenly wished I'd stuck with the *don't get me involved* platform. These things never end well for me.

"Daniel?"

"Sorry, yeah. You were saying that you needed my help..."

"I want to sell the yacht," she said. "I don't think I can live here anymore with all the reminders of Dylan."

My palms fell open. "I don't have any marketing experience--"

"No, no. There's already someone interested in buying it."

"Already?"

She nodded. "A couple down in Ensenada. Apparently, they're looking for the exact size and type of yacht as ours. Anyway, I called, spoke with the husband, and we agreed on a price—which he said he will wire directly into my account. All that needs to happen is the transfer of title, and then they can take possession."

"Oh... so, how can I help?"

"I need you to pilot the boat down to Ensenada." Her expression was a mixture of relief and gratitude, even though I hadn't agreed to anything. It was all happening a little too fast, and I was starting to feel cornered, maybe even manipulated.

"Sorry, I can't." I was proud of myself for standing my ground. Then I cracked a little. "I don't think I can take that much time off right now."

So many things didn't add up for me, and I wasn't even convinced that Teddy hadn't killed Dylan herself. On the other hand, maybe thirteen years as a cop had made me too jaded and suspicious.

I cracked some more. "Don't get me wrong. I would do it if I could, but I'm so busy at work... I mean, to sail all the way--"

Teddy chuckled. "You won't be sailing, silly, you'll be motoring. No tacking back and forth, just a straight ride on a nice yacht with really big diesel engines. Dylan always said that if the seas are calm, she can cruise comfortably at over twenty knots. That will easily get you from here to there in twenty-four hours.

I wondered if this was something that Dylan would have wanted me to do. Maybe I owed it to my him.

"And as far as money goes," said Teddy, "I would pay you fifteen hundred a day, plus expenses."

Suddenly her plan didn't sound so bad. The way the business had been going—which was not so much as a penny of income since I began—the money would definitely come in handy. And, of course, I would still be doing it for Dylan.

Then I remembered Doris' phone call. "When, exactly, would this need to happen?"

"Delivery would have to take place on Saturday," she said.

My eyes widened. *This coming Saturday?*

"Oops, is that a problem?" Teddy asked. "You could leave on Thursday, which would give you two days. That's lots of time. I'd arrange for a car to pick you up at the port, hour and a half drive up to Tijuana International, and a short flight back to SFO. Two shakes of a lamb's tail and you're home for dinner Saturday night."

It sounded almost too good to be true—which should have been a red flag. In theory, I could easily make it back by Sunday—and with three or four thousand bucks in my pocket. As much as I hated traveling, especially into another country, I was having trouble finding a downside to this plan.

"You'll love the people of Ensenada, Teddy said. "They're all very welcoming." She twisted on the couch like a cat in the sun, prominently accentuating the contours of her figure. Many things raced through my mind: scenarios, fantasies, and basically alternate plans for my future—should things get worse between me and Doris.

"Okay," I said. "I'll do it."

CHAPTER 8

Turns out that besides a current passport—which I had—a Temporary Import Permit and a current Mexican insurance policy were also required—both of which Teddy had. I also needed a Mexican Tourist Card, which Teddy helped me to apply for online. She said I'd still need to check-in at Mexican INM, immediately upon crossing the border.

I had put on a pot of coffee, which we drank while going over the details of the trip and the transfer of ownership. She had brought the title papers with her, which hinted that she knew I would do the favor for her even before I did. I had indeed been manipulated. *Whatever.*

Programming her phone number into my cell, Teddy asked that I call her once the sale was made and the money was wired. It occurred to me that she was entrusting me, a man she barely knew, with a very expensive yacht. Again, I had the gnawing presage that this thing was moving too quickly. Yet I continued telling myself that the deal would benefit me even more than Teddy, and that it was really more of a favor for Dylan.

She left my boat a little before three o'clock in the morning. I'd begun to wonder if she wanted to spend the night onboard, though I never caught a whiff of it in her manner or words. Probably a good thing, anyway. I wouldn't have to wrestle with the question of *should I or shouldn't I*, or what I imagined would have been a fair amount of awkwardness afterward. Of course, there would also have been the inevitable guilt I'd feel when facing Dylan in the afterlife. Or worse, Doris in this life. In the end, it was better for me and probably better for her that nothing happened.

Zippy with a nervous system now full of caffeine, my mind spent the rest of the night churning out problems and what-ifs. I wasn't a seasoned sailor, and my time behind the wheel of a motor yacht was even less. I could run into immigration issues, navigation screw ups, bad weather, or any number of mechanical problems. Any delay would totally decimate my golden opportunity with Doris, not to mention completely disappointing Bridge.

I went over all the paperwork and transfer documents again. It all seemed to be there. Teddy had even pre-signed the USCG Bill of Sale, releasing interest in the vessel. It was the first time I'd ever noticed the name of their yacht—*Bernice*.

It certainly wasn't her name—the signature line showed Theodora Langdon. No wonder she preferred to be called *Teddy*. Maybe Bernice was her middle name, or her mother's name. Or maybe, like my sailboat, the name was already painted across the stern when they bought it.

Which got me thinking, I've never really liked the name, *Wanderlust*. It means a strong, innate desire to rove or travel about. For me it's an oxymoron. Like I'd told Dylan the night before he died, after a childhood of moving from one military base to another, I've never, ever, had a desire to *rove* or *travel about*. Agreeing to the Ensenada trip definitely ran contrary to my personal comforts, but I still wasn't sure if it also went against my better judgment.

Stuffing the forms back into the plastic folder, I noticed several NVDC vessel forms stapled together. They included the previous Coast Guard Bill of Sale form, which showed that Dylan and Teddy had purchased the yacht through an outfit called SRRA Group in Riverside, California. Which, I guess, answered the question of who had originally named the boat.

The next day was spent preparing provisions for the trip and looking over nautical charts and maps. I wanted to hit the deep water sooner rather than later, to give myself a buffer, timewise. I also wanted to talk with my daughter without Doris listening in. Guessing that after school would be the best time, I made sure to have my preparations completed by the afternoon. But my nervous system crashed once the caffeine burned off.

I woke up to Cliff's voice calling from the dock. "Yoo-hoo, Mr. McKenna."

It was 5:37 p.m., and I felt like I hadn't moved in a week. Getting to my feet, I awkwardly climbed topside—cursing myself the entire way.

"Yes Cliff, what is it?"

"Terrible thing what happened the other day," he said. "Bad for business at the marina."

"Yeah." I resisted rolling my eyes. "I'd say it wasn't too good for Dylan either."

"Yeah, that too." He bobbed there for a second. "So anyways, I wanted to update you about the cartel guys."

Now I did roll my eyes. *Cartel guys.* "What about them?"

"Well, nothing new to report," he said.

I just stared at him. *WTF?* "Didn't you share your suspicions with the detectives?"

Cliff shoved his hands into his pockets and hung his head. "Nah, probably wouldn't do no good. Between you, me and the fencepost, I don't think they'd care about that."

"Yeah, I got the same impression."

"Oh, you told 'em?" He seemed surprised.

I nodded.

Cliff seemed suddenly rattled. "Anyways, I hear that you're taking Bernice down to Mexico. Gonna try to sell 'er, huh?"

I nodded again.

"I got a few fifty footers on the waiting list, so, any idea when you're pull'n out?"

"Tomorrow," I said. "Early."

"And that'll put you in Ensenada when?"

I shrugged. "A couple of days, I suppose."

"Okay, good." He gave me a backhanded wave as he headed away. "Nice talk'n to ya."

I checked the bars on my phone and called Bridget's number.

"Dad?"

I didn't say anything for a second, thinking it was her prank message again.

"Dad, are you there?"

"Yes! Hey Bridge, how are you?"

"Okay." She jostled at the other end of the line. "I'm..." She lowered her voice. "I'm in the house and Mom's here. That's why I haven't answered your calls. You know, she's still been pretty mad. Won't let us talk--"

"No worries, sweetie. I get it."

"But she told me that you're coming to stay with me next week." Bridget sounded happy about it, and that made me happy.

"I didn't expect it, but yeah. I'll be there on Sunday."

My daughter was silent.

I continued, "Uh, so, I'm not sure what changed or why she's suddenly okay with me coming to the house. But I'm definitely excited about it."

"Uh huh." Bridge sounded as if her mom was standing right there, and I guessed that my nap had screwed me out of any chance to talk privately with my daughter.

"Do you know why the change of heart?"

"Uh huh."

I waited for her to elaborate. "Can you talk, Bridge?"

"Not really, but there's something I need to tell you..."

"Okay, don't worry about it. We can talk more once your mom leaves on her trip."

"It's about her trip..."

"Okay, sweetie. We'll talk all about it on Sunday."

"Bye Dad. Love you."

It was the conversation I'd been waiting to have for weeks. Affirmation that I was still her dad and she was still my little girl. Exactly what I'd needed to sustain me through the long hours at the helm. Those words would get me to Ensenada and back in three days.

Bye Dad. Love you.

CHAPTER 9

Teddy had left me the keys to her yacht, as well as information about the antenna, GPS receiver, transducer converter, and a bunch of other technical stuff that I neither understood nor planned to use. I was more interested in how much fuel the tanks held, and how fast she'd go without falling apart.

I had stuffed my rucksack with beef jerky, bottled water, a toothbrush, and a change of clothes, then decided to toss in the paperback Dylan had given me—not that I'd have time for reading. It was late Thursday night, and the marina was dead quiet when I decided to stash my provisions aboard the yacht. I unlocked the hatch and descended into the home of a dead man and his wife—neither of whom were there. Suddenly overcome with guilt, I felt like I was violating the sanctity of something I wasn't worthy of.

The plush cabin was much wider than mine. It felt like a regular living room compared to Wanderlust's galley/kitchen combination, and it had a dining table that doubled as an extra bed. The cockpit was fully enclosed—a wheelhouse, I guess you'd call it. No hat or sunscreen required.

They had obviously put a lot of money into upgrades, as if the yacht needed it. A weather station, Direct TV receiver, and an RF remote control were among them. There was also a new, twelve-foot inflatable dinghy attached to the stern, and the yacht had two anchors.

I nosed around a little, wondering if I might find evidence of who killed Dylan. Opening one of the drawers in the forward stateroom, I saw the colorful sundress Teddy had worn the night Dylan was killed. Checking it for bloodstains or evidence of a struggle, I found none. Only the scent of whatever perfume she'd worn.

I wanted to delve further, but going through her things began to feel a little perverse. Besides, I knew that the cops had already been all over the boat looking for the same physical evidence as I was. The fact that they had released the boat meant that they had seized everything they needed, or they had found nothing of importance.

While walking back to my slip, I had the distinct feeling that I was being watched. Whether it was by the drug guys, the police, or both, I wondered what Detective Grassi would think tomorrow when he realized that I had left the marina in Dylan's yacht. I hoped that either Cliff or Teddy would explain the situation to him.

I hadn't planned to leave until sunup, but after a few hours my mind was still in high gear and I found myself tossing and turning more than sleeping. So, at 3:30 a.m. I called the office to leave a message for Shanay, then locked up my little sailboat and made my way across the marina to Teddy's yacht. Fifteen minutes later I was rounding the breakwater and steering *Bernice* into the tidal currents of San Francisco Bay.

It was the first time I'd been on the open water at night, and the lights of San Francisco were breathtaking. I motored under the Bay Bridge, past Yerba Buena and Treasure Islands, crossing the shipping channel to the south of Alcatraz. The Golden Gate Bridge loomed high above me, and for the first time I realized that I was actually going to pilot a fifty-foot yacht through 639 nautical miles of ocean. *There was no turning back now.*

As the bay funneled between San Francisco and the Marin Headlands, the waters roughened like a field of moguls in the snow. It would have been a jarring ride in my sailboat, but the imposing yacht commanded its way through the water in relative comfort.

But it was only a forewarning of an area referred to on the chart as the Potato Patch. Sitting just off Point Bonita, a shallow bar 30-feet below the waterline can create massive waves and treacherous conditions—even for a yacht the size of *Bernice.* The tale circulating among sailors is that it earned its name in the early 1900s when several potato boats broke apart and sunk. Determined not to become one of them, I steered the yacht closer to the south shoreline.

Mile Rocks, another charted hazard, came up quickly just south of the shipping channel. It was about then that I wondered if I'd taken on more than I could handle.

I breathed a huge sigh of relief once the water smoothed and the sky began to lighten. Prevailing winds were at the stern, and the Pacific Current also helped by propelling the yacht southward.

A couple of fishing boats crossed my path coming out of Half Moon Bay, but they quickly faded into the horizon. One other boat was out there, but she was a few miles back. Otherwise, it seemed like I had the entire ocean to myself.

By late afternoon I had traveled over 340 nautical miles. With the Channel Islands barely visible to my right and the defunct Venoco oil platform *Holly* and the coastline on my left, I began to ease the yacht eastward toward the Ventura marina—the halfway point, according to my chart. The sailing had been a piece of cake, and I was definitely making better time than I had anticipated. This was going to be the easiest money I'd ever earned.

After topping off the diesel tanks, I picked up a meatball sandwich and a beer at an Italian deli in the marina. It seemed like everyone in the harbor knew each other, and again, I had the feeling that I was being watched. A young couple on a bench whispered something to each other as I walked past, and the harbormaster seemed uncomfortable talking with me. I didn't know whether it was me or them, but it didn't really matter. I still had a good three hours of daylight left, so I fired up the engines and piloted the boat back out to sea. That's when I felt it again.

I had just passed the visitor's center, on my way around the seawall when an even stronger feeling came over me. Whether it was instinct from my years of police work or some detail that my subconscious noticed, I didn't know. But something was raising the hair on my neck.

About a mile offshore, I grabbed the binoculars and did a slow three-sixty, paying specific attention to what was behind me—the place that most boaters rarely check. Nothing.

I unfolded the canvas sun cover and stood at the shaded helm eating my sandwich and sipping a beer. When I was finished, I set the wheel on a southern heading and ran below deck to grab a water. Passing back through the galley, I noticed the bottle of wine I had brought for dinner the night Dylan was killed. Still unopened, it sat securely in a wooden rack above a small spice shelf. I hadn't spent twenty-nine dollars on wine for the Ensenada boat buyers, so I slipped the bottle from the rack and tossed it into my rucksack next to the book Dylan had given me. The one I knew I'd probably never read.

Back in the wheelhouse, I gazed out at the Pacific thinking that this was turning out to be a pretty sweet gig. Perfect, except for the recurring sensation that something wasn't right.

Picking up the binoculars, I pivoted around and this time spotted a boat. It was no more than a speck, about two or three miles back. I couldn't be sure at that distance, but it seemed to be the same one I'd noticed back at Half Moon Bay. Which was weird because it should have caught up or passed me while I was refueling at Ventura.

Maybe a different boat. Probably nothing, I told myself. But oftentimes, my mind is not my friend—constantly working against me with worst-case scenarios. And this was one of those times.

Two competing possibilities ruminated to the top of the heap: one—whoever killed Dylan was now coming after me; or two—the Alameda detectives had me in their sights as a suspect, and were now convinced that I was fleeing. Neither prospect would be good for me.

I considered checking in with Teddy about the investigation, but I had no cell coverage so far off shore. I noticed that my battery was at only ten percent, which is when I realized I had forgotten to pack my phone charger. *Son-of-a-bitch!*

According to the chart, about 170 nautical miles lay ahead of me before the Mexican border—over seven hours of travel. There wasn't enough daylight, which meant that I would be navigating an unfamiliar coastline in the dark. Maybe the worst part was that I'd be entering territorial waters of a foreign country, at night, while being followed by someone I couldn't see.

I pushed the RPMs up, increasing Bernice's speed to twenty-six knots. *The hell with it!*

CHAPTER 10

I should have checked the daylight tables.

I'd been back on the water less than ninety minutes when I remembered that sunset happens earlier in winter. With the light nearly gone, I donned my Cal Bears sweatshirt and ventured another look aft though the binoculars. Too dark to see anything. Even if the boat was still trailing me, I would never be able to discern its navigation lights from Malibu's skyline behind it.

It was six o'clock, and I had to decide whether to continue or moor the boat for the night—either east to Long Beach Harbor or west to Catalina Island. I'd finally decided on an overnight mooring at Long Beach when I saw what looked like a hotel floating out of the harbor. It was a monstrous cruise ship, so bright that it could be seen for miles. Which gave me an idea.

Pushing the throttle even further, I changed course in an attempt to get ahead of the ship before it settled into the southbound shipping lane. By staying ahead but on the same trajectory as the big liner, its hulking frame and bright lights would block my pursuer's view of me. *Good plan, McKenna!*

The decision now made to continue, all I had to do was stay ahead of the cruise ship. Only I had no idea how fast they travel, or if *Bernice* was even capable of outpacing it. Then something happened that I didn't expect; the big cruise ship continued across the wake behind me, never making the turn southbound. I had wrongly assumed that it, too, was heading to Mexico, and realized too late that it was actually on a course for Catalina Island. Had I known, I could have used it as a shield all the way there.

I was on my own again—my lights now visible to whoever was back there following me.

Another idea suddenly popped into my head. Turning out all my navigation lights would make me invisible to the stalker. But it was illegal, and the dangers were abundant. Large commercial vessels in the shipping channel wouldn't be able to see me, and neither would smaller boats like mine. And if the Coast Guard spotted me, they would immediately suspect illegal activity.

One-by-one, off went the all-round lights, the sidelights, the masthead lights, and finally, the stern lights. It took a few minutes for my eyes to acclimate, but soon I was powering through the water again at twenty-five knots. It was a clear night, which helped, and the cloud cover reflected light from the shore—as long as I stayed close.

A little over two hours had passed when I saw San Diego's brightly colored outline a couple of miles ahead. That meant that I was only an hour from the border. I was progressing well; the seas were still calm, my fuel was okay, and navigating in the dark hadn't caused me any real problems.

Feeling pretty tired, I opened the cockpit window to refresh myself and maintain focus. Still, the pitch and sway of the boat and the miles of meandering coastline had taken their toll. I must have dozed off for a second, because I opened my eyes to find the boat in the middle of a kelp bed. At least that's what it looked like. I noticed dozens of dark figures bouncing and seesawing through the waves like a school of sea lions, and immediately cut my speed to about five knots. I was trying to figure out what I had navigated the yacht into, when without warning all hell descended on me.

The yacht was awash in blinding lights, and the ear-splitting whine of a helicopter shook the boat. An amplified bullhorn from somewhere overhead blared, "Heave to! This is the United States Navy, ordering you to heave to immediately!"

I throttled all the way down and cut the engine. There I was, bobbing like a cork in the middle of the calamity when two rigid hulled inflatable boats—maybe thirty or forty feet long—appeared on either side of my yacht. Still blinded by the searchlights, I could only hear the sounds of soldiers coming aboard. Deep voices called out to one another, followed by the sweeping arcs of powerful flashlights as the boat pitched with the added weight. And all the while, the thumping rotors of a Seahawk MH-60 circled above me.

A Navy officer was suddenly standing next to me in the pilothouse, his flashlight burning into my eyes. "May I ask what in the floundering fuck you are doing?"

"I... I'm... apparently, I'm being boarded by the U.S. Navy."

"Can't you see we have a live exercise going on out here?" he said, sweeping his open hand toward the bow.

I glanced through the windscreen at a now brightly-illuminated sea. It was chock-full of what looked like frogmen, porpoising up and down in the waves. They wore black wetsuits and helmets, all attached with tiny green-glowing light sticks. Special Forces, I guessed. Probably Navy SEALS. *How could I have missed that?*

Turning slightly, I recognized San Diego Bay to my immediate left—which confirmed that I had fallen asleep at the wheel a few miles back. This was the home of Naval Amphibious Base Coronado. Stupid me, I'd seen it on the map but never considered they'd be doing a swim at night. *What could I possibly say to the guy?*

His nametag read *T. Martin*, and I had no idea what rank his uniform insignia implied. He could have been Admiral of the entire fleet for all I knew. "Sorry, Officer Martin. I must not have seen--"

"Of course you didn't see them," he said. "Your props could have chewed up my entire team."

"Again, I'm really sorry."

He shook his head in disgust, and then rotated 180 degrees as if he'd been standing on ball bearings. "That's why God made navigation lights," he bellowed. "Turn yours on now, and then get the hell out of my training exercise."

He left me standing in the wheelhouse, feeling like a complete idiot. Primarily for putting the soldiers in danger, but also because I had drawn so much attention to myself. Instead of using the cover of darkness for concealment, I'd managed to illuminate myself like a Christmas tree at Rockefeller Center. I could only hope that whoever was tracking me had also fallen asleep.

Hugging tightly to the coast the rest of the way down, my new strategy was to blend with the lights on land. After my brush with the Navy, I remained wide awake as I passed the Imperial Beach Pier and then the mouth of the Tijuana River—the last two landmarks before the border.

Crossing into Mexican territorial waters at a quarter past midnight was unceremonious, without fanfare or any attention whatsoever. According to the nautical chart, I still had another couple of hours to travel before hitting Ensenada.

Immigration rules get a little confusing, and I'd been told two different things with regard to checking in once in Mexico. Teddy had said that I should show my tourist entry form—the one she'd printed out online—at the first port of entry I come to, which in all logic would have been Tijuana. But border towns can be dangerous, especially at night. I decided to go with an internet article that said visitors may check in at the first place their boat makes landfall—which would be Ensenada.

It was just after 3 a.m. when I eased Bernice into the Ensenada Marina. Noticing a Mexican Naval base at the end of the harbor, I prayed that they weren't also doing nighttime training.

ENSENADA FILE

Two cruise ships were docked just south of the entrance, and a handful of fishing trawlers were just leaving the harbor. Other than those moored in the marina, I saw no other boats. And thankfully, the seas were empty as far as I could see behind me.

I'd made it! Exhausted after the twenty-four-hour journey, I couldn't wait to get off the yacht, shower, and get a good night's sleep. A couple of hotels stood at the end of the jetty, not fifty yards away. In the morning I would return to the dock and handover Bernice to the new owners, then catch my ride to the Tijuana airport and be homeward bound.

Bending down to secure the docklines, I suddenly felt the floating pier rock under rapidly approaching footfalls. I glanced over my shoulder to see a thick man in a tan uniform steaming toward me. With his ruddy face set in a frown and his flashlight zeroed in on me, I suspected he wasn't the Ensenada Welcome Wagon.

"Excuse me, Señor. You will come with me."

CHAPTER 11

It was a harbor within a larger harbor—an anchorage sectioned off for pleasure boats. I followed the security guard up the ramp and through the perimeter gate to a small, yellow cinderblock building. Inside was a folding metal table and chair that reminded me of Bingo night at St. Paul's, a walkie-talkie charger, and a 90s era desktop computer. The room was muggy and smelled like the seat of a Greyhound bus.

We hadn't spoken during the short walk, and I felt that I was entitled to an explanation. I started to ask a question, but he held up his hand to stop me and then called someone on his cell phone.

Understanding none of what was being said, I could only hear the tinny squawk of a man speaking Spanish on the other end. I guessed that I was the subject of their conversation, and I tried to appear unfazed by gazing casually up at the bulb dangling over the desk or out the film covered window.

Maybe I should have stopped and registered at the immigration office in...

The guard cut short my internal dialogue when he abruptly ended his call. "Do you stop at Tijuana for the immigration?"

"No," I said. "Just here."

"Your papers?" He extended a meaty palm.

I handed him my passport, Teddy's import permit, insurance policy, and a copy of the Mexican tourist application I'd filled out online. He studied them carefully, and it crossed my mind that he probably couldn't read a word of English.

Returning the import permit and the insurance policy to me, he kept the other papers—including my passport. "You stay inside boat for morning when immigration come," he said. "Not come out, y no visitor."

So much for the comfy hotel.

The guy was built like a cement truck, shorter than me but with a broad chest and beefy forearms. Even with his stupid mushroom haircut, the guy looked like he would be a nasty fighter.

"Am I under some kind of house arrest? And what about my passport? I don't feel good about leaving it with you."

His bristly mustache arched upwards at the corners in a devious sort of smile. "I helping for you, Señor. I return these paperworks for you *en la mañana.*

Mañana. Now there was a word I recognized from high school Spanish.

When I reached the yacht, I glimpsed back at the office to see the guard talking on his phone again. His wide face and gap-toothed grin pressed against the window. Something definitely didn't feel right.

Bunking in the forward stateroom on top of the bedding, I slept like a guy who'd spent the last twenty-four hours piloting a boat six-hundred miles down the coast. Weird dreams though, about frogmen, boats chasing me, Mexicans laughing behind my back, and a naked Teddy looking for her rainbow sundress. It was the only decent part of the dream.

A loud bang woke me in the morning, and I jumped to my feet realizing that someone was pounding against the side of the yacht. I heard my name, heavily accented in Spanish, followed by more pounding. "Señor McKenna!"

I climbed onto the deck and was greeted by the security guard again. "I return for to you," he said, handing me a signed tourist card and a stamped passport.

"You did this for me?" I was still trying to gather my senses. Maybe this guy really was the welcome wagon. "Thank you."

The guard nodded and then headed back toward his office. He passed a man in a fitted suit who continued onto the dock where my boat was tied. This newcomer was a lean, slick-looking guy in his thirties. His black hair was combed straight back, with little ringlets that dangled over the back of his collar.

"So very nice to meet you," he said, extending a hand adorned with bracelets and jewelry. The band on his ring finger alone would have dwarfed a super bowl ring. "They call me Ozzy."

I shook his hand, unable to see his eyes through the reflective sunglasses he wore. I surmised from the look that he wasn't from Immigration or the marina. "Daniel McKenna," I said.

"Yes, I know that." He smiled. "And you are here to sell me the boat."

I remembered Teddy describing the buyers as a *couple,* whom she'd been put in touch with. I had imagined two clean, American expats. Maybe a husband and wife, something like Teddy and Dylan. Certainly not this guy who looks like he'd get you drunk and sell your kidney.

I noticed that the security guard had stopped and was watching the guy from the top of the ramp.

"You're the buyer?" I asked.

"Yesssss," Ozzy said, drawing it out like he was talking to a child. "Potential, buyer," he smiled again. "I will have my mechanic look over the boat, just to make sure."

"Make sure of what?" I glanced at my watch. "It obviously runs well; I just piloted her all the way down here from San Francisco without any problems."

"Take the morning to enjoy my little town," he said, pressing a wrinkled wad of pesos into my hand. "This inspection won't take too long."

I didn't want to enjoy *his* little town. I wanted to sign over the papers and get the hell out of Ensenada. But what could I do? Gathering my wallet and cell phone from the stateroom, I gave Ozzy my number and asked that he call me as soon as his mechanic was through.

Cluttered gift stalls and cheap tourist shops were just opening up for the day—their peeling paint and cracked plaster accentuated in the harsh morning sun. The smell of food cooking paired oddly with the stale musk of beer piss, a lot of which seemed to have collected in puddles from the night before.

Even so, my empty stomach prodded me onward. A couple of blocks away from the harbor, I spotted a place that specialized in "American-style" waffles—whatever that was. I ordered coffee, eggs over easy, a couple of strips of chorizo, and an *American-style* waffle. After breakfast, things didn't look so bad. Except that I still hadn't heard from the buyer, and the fact that my phone now had only seven percent battery power.

I left the restaurant around 10 a.m. and saw that a cruise ship had docked. Streets around the harbor were filling with people in Bermuda shorts, white socks, tennis shoes, and baseball hats with their team logos. Tourists haggled to save a peso, which they carefully tucked into their money belts. *God, I hope I don't look like them.*

A silver Mercedes raced past me, and for a second I thought that the driver was Ozzy. I wasn't positive because I only caught a glimpse, but it sure looked like him. I'd thought that by now his mechanic would have given the yacht a thumbs-up, and I could get on my way. What I didn't expect or appreciate, was the buyer tooling around Ensenada while I waited. Maybe he was picking up his mechanic, I thought. Or maybe, I don't know, maybe it wasn't even him.

The same car came around the corner again, and again I noticed the driver's resemblance to Ozzy. The Mercedes quickly pulled to the curb at the end of the block, but I couldn't see the driver's face through the sun's reflection on the windshield. Only a silhouette sat inside, watching me. *What the hell is going on?*

I ducked into the gated doorway of a combination dress shop— fireworks store, and watched for any movement in the Mercedes. A minute later, the car pulled away from the curb and continued slowly up the block as if the driver was searching the stores for me.

After he passed, I rounded the corner onto a narrower side street where the buildings were more rundown—graffiti, broken windows, and security bars on everything. I was looking over my shoulder, so focused on the Mercedes that I nearly ran into a lighted sign that took up half of the sidewalk. *Open 24-hours*, it said, *American-style* lap dances.

Now, I could almost see the waffle thing, but I thought a lap dance was a lap dance, no matter where you were.

When I turned to look back, I saw the Mercedes make the corner two blocks west and then slowly back into an alley. With the front of the car barely poking out into the cross street, it was clear that he was trying to watch me from a concealed spot. It spooked me to think I was being followed again, and I wondered if these incidents were all somehow related. Either that, or I was developing a serious paranoia disorder.

With the rest of the buildings in the area closed, I stepped into the nightclub. It was nearly deserted at the early hour. A chunky woman wearing a cowboy hat, stiletto heels and a G-string leaned against a brass pole on a stage behind the bar. In front of her, at floor level, stood another woman tending the bar. I was the only customer in the place, and my hope was that they also specialized in *American-style* cocktails.

Taking a seat at the bar, I ordered Scotch on the rocks. A Bruno Mars song came on, and the cowgirl began gyrating slowly around the pole. The bartender was on her phone, and it took a while before she got around to pouring my drink. Meanwhile, the *dancer* performed a couple of lazy toe-touches in front of me, and something resembling a *burpee*. The only thing louder than the music was her pungent perfume.

I took a mouthful of my drink and swished it like mouthwash before swallowing it. Settling onto my stool, I leaned into the bar and finally began to relax. I had successfully evaded the little greaseball outside.

After my second or third sip, the room suddenly billowed in and out like a funhouse mirror. The stage grew dim and the music reverberated in my ears as if I were under water. I gripped the bar rail and tried to speak, but my tongue felt like the chorizo I'd had for breakfast. My hand reached clumsily across the bar, knocking my cocktail onto the floor in a shattered mess.

The bartender was still on her phone, watching me.

I felt myself falling off the stool, but I don't remember landing.

CHAPTER 12

My head pounded and my whole body ached. The air, humid and stinking of urine, carried the echo of rumbling trucks and barking dogs.

My eyes inched open, and I saw that sunset had come and gone—I'd missed the whole day. Sprawled in the dirt against a piece of rusty corrugated siding, I was covered in a gritty crust that had spent the afternoon baking on my face and lips. I spat, struggled to my knees, and instinctively checked my pockets. My wallet and cell phone were still with me and my watch was still on my wrist, but the wad of pesos Ozzy had given me was gone. Then I felt my abdomen to make sure my kidneys hadn't been removed. They hadn't.

Looking around, I saw that I was under a freeway overpass in a deserted industrial area that appeared to be far from the bars and restaurants. Fighting through the brain-fog, I tried to remember what had happened. *Someone drugged me—that's what happened.* Two sips of scotch, even bad scotch, doesn't knock me on my ass—no matter how little I've slept. And I was still feeling the effects of it.

My forearms were raked raw, which I imagined was either from being dragged or from trying to crawl—neither of which I could remember. I had to figure that after drugging me, someone had driven me there and then dumped me onto the roadway.

I tried to stand, but a wave of nausea swept over me and I vomited. The detective in me wished I had the means to collect a sample of it for testing. But what was the use?

It then struck me that I'd missed my flight out of Tijuana, which meant that I wasn't going to make it back to the Bay Area in time to watch my daughter. Which also meant that my entire life was now completely screwed.

Hobbling around on my bad knee awhile, I finally got my bearings and heading west toward the water. From there I worked my way along the shore until I saw the harbor lights.

Ozzy was on his phone in the marina parking lot as I limped up. His slick, lizard lips narrowed when he saw me. "I'll get back to you," he said, abruptly ending his call. "What happened to you?"

He seemed neither surprised nor sincere, but I answered him anyway. "I was drugged and robbed."

Shaking his head chastisingly, he clicked his tongue. "I hear that too much bad booze and bad pussy can cause such things to happen."

"Yeah, well, let's just wrap up this deal so I can get on my way."

Ozzy shook his head again. "Not so fast, *carnal*. I don't want it anymore."

"What?"

"I don't want to buy it."

"What the hell do you mean you don't want to buy it?" I felt my fist tightening into a ball. "I sailed the damn thing all the way down here because you wanted it..."

He shrugged. "*Lo siento*, my friend. That's the way it goes. Guess you had better start heading back." He turned and walked toward a steel gray Mercedes parked there—the same one I'd seen following me. As he got in, Ozzy called back over his shoulder. "I left the keys on the table inside."

I stood there speechless, banged up and smelling of puke as I watched the car speed off into the night. *The trip wasn't going the way I thought it would.*

I considered calling Teddy to break the bad news, and I knew I'd also need to get in touch with Doris and Bridget. Maybe it was a good thing that my phone battery was almost dead.

My eyes settled on the yellow cinderblock building on the other side of the parking lot. A single light shone through the window, but the security guard was nowhere in sight. Then I spotted him in the shadows, peering at me through the fence. He stood motionless, arms crossed and a deadpan expression on his face. With his stupid bangs cut straight across his forehead, he looked like one of the Three Stooges. I thought about reporting to him what had happened, but realized that he was only a useless security guard.

Even more dejected now, I skulked back over to Teddy's yacht, found the keys, and started the motors. What was I going to do? Spend the next two days navigating my way back up the coast? Even if I abandoned the boat here and caught a flight, it still wouldn't put me home in time to watch Bridget. I needed to let her know.

The call went to voicemail—the playful one that I'd fallen for once already.

"Hey, Bridge... Unfortunately, I'm not going to make it there in time to watch you. I'll try to explain everything when we talk. I hope you can forgive me. I don't think your mom will. Please let her know that she'll have to make other plans."

With the battery at only four percent, I dialed Teddy. That call also went to voicemail, but without even ringing. Which meant that her phone was probably turned off. I decided against leaving Teddy the message that her "buyer" was a damn flake. It wouldn't have changed anything, and I figured that she'd realize soon enough that no money ever made it into her account.

Getting the yacht sold was no longer my responsibility, it was Teddy's. Somehow though, I still had to get back to the Bay Area.

CHAPTER 13

I still felt like shit.

Besides being stuck in Ensenada with Teddy's yacht, I was equally pissed off about having to bring the damn thing all the way back to Alameda. On top of that, I knew that Doris would hold me responsible for ruining whatever plans she'd made. *Unreliable* and *irresponsible* are the brushes she had painted me with throughout our marriage, only this time I didn't have the police job to blame.

I undressed and got into the shower, hoping to rinse away the pallor of failure that clung to me like a peeling sunburn. When I got out, I did feel a little better—until I stepped on some kind of tack.

"Son-of-a-bitch!" I hopped backward onto the bed, cradling my foot in my hands. The sheet metal screw had been lying sideways when I stepped on it, but it hadn't pierced the skin. It hurt like hell though, and I wondered where it had come from and why I hadn't seen it before.

As I sat massaging my heel, I tried to problem-solve through my dilemma. If Teddy wants to sell her yacht that badly, she could let me leave *Bernice* with a local boat dealer. After all, there has to be a sizable market for yachts in Ensenada. In that case, I could still try to get to Tijuana tonight and possibly even catch a late flight home.

I called Teddy's phone again, but it was still turned off. There had to be a way to contact her—another number, maybe a friend or family member. Checking the cockpit for an address book, I only found more maps, charts, and owner manuals. Below deck was the same, nothing in the closets and drawers but clothes—no contact number.

Something suddenly dawned on me. It wasn't just Teddy's sundress that had been left onboard, but sweaters and pants, jackets, bathing suits, even underwear. *Could Teddy be so eager to get rid of the yacht that she's selling it fully stocked? Even her clothes?*

Slipping into clean pants and a tee shirt, I went topside to open up my mind to this whole thing. It was dark, cooling off a bit, and very quiet. I watched the hulking cruise ship pulling away from the wharf, and all I wanted at that moment was to be a stowaway on it. Riding away from all the problems in my life.

Shaking off the fantasy, I dialed Sha Nay Nay's cell.

"Yeah?" she answered on the first ring.

"Sha Nay Na... Shanay, it's me."

"I know."

"You're in the office?"

"No, McKenna, it's nighttime. I'm at home."

"Oh yeah." My brain was still a little scrambled. "Anyway, I'm in Ensenada, which is in Mexico."

"I know where it is."

"I'm kind of in a jam right now. I was supposed to be back home in time to watch Bridge, and... so, can you do me a favor?"

"That's what you pay me for, right?"

"My cell battery is nearly dead, and I need to get in touch with the woman who owns this boat." I gave Shanay the phone number, and asked her to have Teddy call me right away. I also asked Shanay to get in touch with Bridget and let her know that we need to talk. "Tell her to start answering my calls," I said.

"Back up a blip. You tell'n me this Teddy bitch sent your ass all the way to Mexico for nothin'?"

I let out a sigh. "Look, Shanay, there's more to it than that. And I don't have the battery life to explain it right now. Just make the calls for me, and--"

The phone made a strange beep and then the screen went dark.

After almost two hours of waiting for a callback, I finally gave up. Either Shanay couldn't reach Teddy, or my cell had finally died.

In a huff of exasperation, I untied the docklines and brought in the hull fenders. Then, standing at the helm, I started the boat's engines again. *Bernice* let out a low grumble, as if she was as anxious to get the out of that harbor as I was. But something held me back.

I turned off the engines.

What in the hell had I gotten myself into? There was something not right about this whole deal from the beginning. And now that I finally admitted it to myself, I was certain that it wasn't just my imagination. Teddy's rush to sell the yacht just two days after her husband was killed; the mystery boat following me all the way down the coast; getting drugged, probably by the sleazy buyer who wasn't about to buy anything. Those were not just random incidences of bad luck; they were red flags. I should have paid attention to them, and I probably would have had I not been blinded by the promise of a big payday. It was eight o'clock at night, the moon was full, and I knew in my gut that I was being played.

But there was more. Something that hadn't fallen into place. Yet, it was out there, floating around my mind, just beyond my reach—like the name of that movie, or my new password, or my wedding anniversary. I couldn't remember it at the moment, but knew that it would come to me sooner or later.

The boat had drifted halfway out of the slip, and I hurried onto the dock to retie her to the cleats. As I did, my mind flashed back to the previous night when the guard walked up on me as I was doing the same thing. I remembered his phone call, and the fact that he seemed to be expecting me.

Okay, I'm onto it now. Something about that feeling... How would he anticipate my 3 a.m. arrival? Could the boat that tailed me down here have called ahead to alert someone?

I hustled down to the forward stateroom and slid open the closet door. Reaching in, I yanked out an armload of clothes and tossed them onto the bed. Nobody sells a boat that's completely stocked with the seller's clothes. It was suddenly clear to me that Teddy had never intended to sell the boat. The story of the couple who wanted to buy it was all bullshit!

But again, why?

I was close now. I could feel it.

If Teddy never intended to sell the boat, then Ozzy never intended to buy it. They had to be involved with each other, somehow. So what was his role? And why did he follow me all morning? Even more importantly, why would he drug me? If he wasn't going to kill me, or take my wallet, or steal the yacht, then why go through all that trouble?

The boat wavered in the water, and the screw I'd stepped on rolled across the nightstand. I looked at it for a minute and then glanced down to the place on the floor where I'd found it.

Examining it on my open hand, I saw that it was maybe ½ or ¾ of an inch. A tiny metallic finishing screw with a Phillips head.

I tilted back to look at the ceiling panel, then back down at the floor. Walking slowly around the bed, I knew that the screw held the answer to my questions.

Pressing my palm against the teak-trimmed wall, I ran my fingers from one bulkhead to the next, feeling for any give. Then I saw it.

A row of identical screws ran vertically along the wallboard next to the bed. Their purpose was to hold the teak panel in place at that particular corner. But there were five screw holes, and only four screws. Somebody had forgotten to put this one back in.

I grabbed a small toolkit from the wheelhouse, found a crosshatch driver, and slowly unscrewed the remaining four screws. Moving along the center bulkhead, I unscrewed the five screws there. And finally, at the forward bulkhead, I unscrewed the remaining screws.

Gently lifting the four-foot teak wall panel, I stepped back and gazed at the final piece of the puzzle.

CHAPTER 14

I've been set up!

A shitload of cocaine stared back at me from the dead space behind the wall. Kilogram packages, taped individually in clear plastic, and then bagged together in groups of about twenty-five. They'd been stuffed into thick trash can liners, of which I counted ten. A quick computation in my head told me that I was looking at about two hundred fifty kilos. That's over five hundred pounds—a quarter of a ton. More than enough to send me to prison for the rest of my life.

It had been as obvious as the nose on my face. Only a fool wouldn't have seen this coming. The stink of deception was in the air all along. Yet, there I'd been, bumbling around like Mr. Magoo, never catching so much as a whiff of it.

Something had to be done, and quickly. I couldn't risk staying another minute on a yacht full of drugs, and I certainly wasn't about to sail her anywhere.

I thought about getting rid of it—just dumping it all overboard right there in the harbor—and then getting the hell out of Ensenada. But I knew that someone, probably Ozzy, owned all of this cocaine. I also knew that before I could even make it out of Mexico, I'd be floating face down—just like Dylan.

Note to self: Figure out why Dylan was murdered, when you have more time.

At the moment, I had to save my own hide. With my battery dead, I couldn't call 9-1-1—even if Mexico had a 9-1-1. And even if I could trust their cops—which I didn't.

A harsh rap on the side of the hull startled the hell out of me. I dropped the screwdriver and clamored up the steps.

"Señor McKenna, you are leaving today, no?" The guard's question sounded more like a statement. He stood with one hand on his hip and the other on a thick black flashlight, waiting for a response. *Yes, I am supposed to leave today, but no I'm not going to leave in this drug-filled yacht.*

I was suddenly struck with another idea—run! I could simply abandon the boat right here in the harbor and take off—find a ride to Tijuana, catch a flight home, and put this whole mess behind me. But again, someone was expecting these drugs and I didn't want them coming after me. Somehow, becoming another carcass in the Mexican desert didn't fit into my long-range plans.

As I regarded the oddball security guard again, I realized that he had actually helped me with the immigration paperwork. He had even returned them to me right away.

"Someone put a bunch of drugs on the boat," I heard myself say. "Cocaine. Lots of it."

The man's expression didn't change. He tilted his head slightly, considering me up and down. "You show me this drugs?"

I hesitated for a second, imagining being walloped over the head by his flashlight as he took the loot for himself. It had to be worth several million dollars—a dozen lifetimes of his twenty pesos-a-day security job.

But I went ahead, leading him down the companionway and into the forward stateroom. He stood back, gazing into the exposed compartment. Then he glanced around the room and then at the clothes on the bed. His flat expression never changed.

"Now do you understand what I'm telling you? Someone's trying to frame me, or get me to smuggle drugs for them. It was that guy in the suit you saw me talking to earlier. You have to help me."

"*Sí*," he said.

"See what?"

"*Sí*, I understand." He scratched through his soup bowl hair. "Why you not call to *la policía?*"

I flipped out my cellphone. "Dead battery. So, can you make the call for me or not?"

"*Sí*, I make call." He dialed his phone, said a few words, and then disconnected. "They say to lock boat and come to office."

Immediately, I worried that I had made the wrong move by telling him. Though he hadn't clobbered me over the head, I knew nothing about this guy. Didn't even know his name. But I had no friends in Mexico, and no way to contact friends back in the states. Not that I had many there, either.

I locked up and followed the guard to his drab little room. It was barely big enough for the two of us, and I wondered how the cops were going to take my statement in such a confined space. I didn't have to wait long for my answer; car headlights swung into the parking lot after only a few minutes.

Thinking back on years of suspect interviews, I knew first impressions were everything. I had to project the image of a law abiding whistleblower. Leaning casually against the chipped wall, I took a deep breath and slowly let it out. *I am innocent. After all, I'm the one who initiated the call. I should probably get a reward for doing the honorable thing.*

The door swung open and my heart dropped onto the grimy tiled floor. We stood there looking at each other for a second, and not in a friendly way.

Ozzy nodded slowly. "Mr. McKenna..."

I nodded back, and then looked over at the security guard—his mustachioed grin widening beneath his stupid hairdo.

"Thanks for that, Shemp."

CHAPTER 15

I didn't want to appear worried or afraid, but I'm not sure my face was cooperating.

"So you found my nut," said Ozzy.

I said nothing.

"Like the squirrel," he said, "hiding his little pile of... anyway, now you know the real reason you came to Ensenada. Question is, what are you going to do about it?"

"What am *I* going to do about it? I'm going to--"

"Before you answer that question," interrupted Ozzy, "I should remind you about the unfortunate tragedy that befell your friend, Dylan Langdon. Is that what you want for yourself?"

"You think I'm afraid of you?" I sucked in my stomach and stretched my chest a little. "You're nothing but a cheesy little cliché— a skinny greaseball who thinks he's a tough guy."

He smiled comfortably, tilted his head back as if he hadn't even heard me, then gave a slight nod to the guard.

It was a wild roundhouse swing, the blunt end of his steel flashlight catching me under the ribcage. The air in my lungs was suddenly gone, and I couldn't seem to suck in any more to replace it. Doubled up on the tile floor, I found myself trying to blink the sight back into my eyes. When it returned, I was staring at their shoes— Ozzy's shiny black cowboy boots, and the guard's leather sandals. *Huaraches*, I think they're called. Anyway, my gut hurt like a son-of-a-bitch.

With my hand still gripping my dead cell phone, I could have sworn I saw it light up for a second—though it might just have been the twinkle of my returning vision. I hoped, however, that the beating had somehow jarred my dying battery back to life.

"I take it you've met my friend, Sacacorcho," said Ozzy, with a nod toward the security guard. "Actually, he's known throughout Baja as *El Sacacorcho*. Do you know what that means?"

I shook my head, as I gulped my first swallow of air.

"It means the corkscrew." Ozzy paused, and I looked up from the floor. "Do you know why they call him that?"

I gulped another mouthful, and shook my head again.

"Because he will twist your fucking head like a fucking corkscrew, and you will die a slow, painful death from a broken fucking neck." He smiled. "That's why they call him that."

The guard, or *Sacacorcho*, reached over to the window and dropped the louvered blinds. I braced myself in preparation for another clobbering. Instead, he helped me to my feet and then brushed the dirt off my shirt with his porky hand. It was like the guy had a split personality, and this was the *nice* Mr. Corkscrew.

Holding the phone at my side, I slyly thumbed the camera icon and angled it up at Ozzy. With my finger on the red button, the camera ripped off several photographs. I hoped that at least one of them would capture the guy's face.

"I'm not going to smuggle drugs for you," I said, finally able to breathe. "Sorry, but I just can't do that. And there's nothing you or your stooge can do to change my mind." I slipped the phone, unnoticed, back into my pocket.

Ozzy smiled. "Nothing we could do to *you* perhaps, but I'm betting you would do it to save little Bridget?"

The Corkscrew grinned as he folded his arms across his chest.

How did these guys know about my daughter? I was suddenly out of breath again. Completely panicked. *If I could only get to a working phone and warn her. Warn Doris.*

I felt my teeth grinding. "Answer me something, will you? Is this why you followed me around Ensenada this morning?"

Ozzy nodded. "Couldn't chance you coming back to the boat before we were finished. And when you gave me the slip, I had to take it to the next level."

"That's why you drugged me?"

"Technically, it was the bartender who dropped the tranquilizer into your drink."

I thought back to the young woman behind the bar. "How did--?"

Ozzy coughed out a laugh. "I know everyone in Ensenada," he said. "I run this fucking town."

My mind was still trying to catch up, and I knew I was not in a position to bargain. I would do anything to protect my daughter, and he knew it.

"So what's it gonna be, McKenna?"

"What, exactly, do you want me to do?"

"Nothing too tough," he said. "Just drive the boat back to the San Francisco Bay."

"What about Customs and Immigration?"

"Simple. Just don't get caught—otherwise, we're going to have a whole new problem. And by we, I mean *you*."

I swallowed hard. The situation left me no way out, other than to give him what he wanted. I felt myself nodding.

"What's that?" he chided.

"I'll do it."

"Typical American pussy." Ozzy grinned. "Who's the cheesy cliché now?"

I wanted to lunge across the room and smash his head against the wall. I swear I could have killed him right where he stood, and I think he knew it.

"Just to be sure you don't try to do something stupid," he said, "El Sacacorcho will ride with you to the border." He grinned again. "You two are going to become best friends."

CHAPTER 16

Under the supervision of Ozzy and Mr. Corkscrew, I put the teak wall back in place. This time they made sure that all of the finishing screws were accounted for.

Sacacorcho watched me from Teddy's bed, where his sweaty body reclined on her clothes like he owned the place. And after the way she set me up to take the fall for this drug run, I got a certain amount of joy from knowing that her dresses and pants and sweaters were forever going to smell like a training camp jock strap.

Realizing the risks of crossing the border at night, Ozzy planned to wait until morning before sending me and Sacacorcho out of the harbor. He said that once underway, I was to rendezvous with him just before Tijuana—though he left out the specifics of where and how that would happen.

Ozzy left the boat around midnight, yet I could still feel him lurking close by. Too nervous to sleep, I spent the remainder of the night thinking on deck while Sacacorcho snored away in the forward stateroom.

I thought long and hard about my options—my biggest concern being Bridget's safety. It occurred to me that Ozzy's biggest concern was getting the drugs across the border. I also knew that once the cocaine was in the U.S., I was of no use to them and they would kill me anyway. But as long as I had what they wanted, I still had leverage. Which meant that I could not, under any circumstances, move the drugs beyond Tijuana.

Around five in the morning I nodded off, sitting awkwardly on the bench seat at the stern of the boat. I awoke to Sacacorcho standing on deck, grinning down at me. One of my legs had fallen asleep, and he seemed to get a kick out of watching me work the circulation back into it. I wanted the asshole to know that it wasn't a result of his flashlight beating, then realized that my ego would have to take a backseat to more important problems.

We casted off, floating quietly out of the marina just before sunrise. I looked back from the mouth of the harbor, hoping that it was the last I'd ever see of Ensenada.

Motoring at a slow twelve knots, I wanted to give myself ample time to put together a plan. The heavy fog gave me an excuse to keep the speed down, but it also obscured the coastline.

Fog was common in the Bay Area, but rare down south. I'd read about *advection fog*, which usually happens when warm, moist air passes over colder surfaces—like the Pacific Ocean. From what I remembered, moisture is actually drawn in to shore as warm air rises from the beaches.

Sacacorcho stood nervously watching, clearly unhappy about the weather—which, of course, made me happy. I wondered if I could somehow use the climatic anomaly to my advantage.

After another twenty minutes, Sacacorcho smacked my shoulder and pointed toward land. "Turn boat here. *A la derecho.*"

We hadn't yet reached Tijuana, and I realized that this was why Ozzy had been so evasive. He wanted to keep me in the dark as much as possible.

I checked the chart and saw a tiny harbor called Puerto Salina. Tucked into the coast about halfway between Ensenada and Tijuana, there was almost nothing around it. Only a small motel and snack bar, it was right off of the highway yet remote enough to allow our coming and going without being noticed.

"This is where I'm dropping you off?" I asked, pointing at the map.

He didn't answer.

"Corkscrew got a cork up his ass?" I said.

Sacacorcho glared at me, probably trying to figure out what I had said. He looked like he wanted to wallop me again, but at this point he couldn't. It confirmed what I already knew—as long as I had the boat and the cocaine, they needed me.

The narrow harbor entrance was poorly marked and difficult to navigate in the fog, but I finally inched the yacht into the marina. It was off to the left of the channel, and held less than forty boats. Probably perfect for what Ozzy had in mind.

The Mercedes was parked at the top of the boat ramp under a sign that read Puerto Salinas Fishing Charters. Ozzy stood beside it, the same smartass expression glued to his pointy face—like he was several steps ahead of everybody else. I decided then that I was going to take him down, if it was the last thing I ever did.

Pulling the boat up to the dock, I stepped out to secure the lines.

"Don't bother, *carnal.* You're not staying long." He motioned to Sacacorcho, who climbed out and joined him on the dock. I saw that Corkscrew held a jumble of wires and circuit boards, which he had apparently ripped from the yacht's ship-to-shore radio.

Ozzy drew nearer. His breath smelled of fish sticks as he stepped up to me, grill-to-grill. "I tell you what happens now, McKenna. You get back in the boat and drive across the border into U.S. waters. You do whatever you have to do to get the load through Customs in San Diego." Then he pulled a black semi-automatic pistol from his belt and pressed it into the side of my face. "If you say anything to them, or if you make any calls, or if you leave the boat, or if you even take a little too long, I will send El Sacacorcho to Marin and he will snap your daughter's neck."

I don't know why it surprised me that he knew where Bridget lived. It was actually Mill Valley, but Marin was close enough. I had no doubt that he'd know how to find her. Then I felt the cold barrel of the gun pressing harder into my cheek.

"Oh," he said. "And I will also have the pleasure of blowing your brains out, myself."

I eased my face away from him. "Then what? So, I get the coke through Customs, and then what? You think I'm going to haul the stuff all the way to Alameda for you?"

He studied me for a few seconds, like he wondered how much I did or didn't know.

"No," he said. "My guy says things are too hot up there right now. I got a new buyer for this load. We're gonna meet you in Oceanside, instead. It's only fifty miles north of here. When you get there, you're going to tie up at the dock next to the Jolly Roger Restaurant. I'll be there to check the product and make sure it's all *kosher*, and then... I'll let you know what's next."

I thought for a minute. There was an obvious flaw in Ozzy's plan. How would he even know if I stopped in Tijuana to report it to the police or contact the embassy?

"What if I need a repair or something, and I have to dock the boat in Tijuana? How would you even know?"

"It won't happen," he said. Then he flashed that sappy grin. "There's no harbor in Tijuana. No place for you to land this thing!" That brought on a big laugh, which was followed by a chuckle from The Corkscrew—who probably had no idea what he was laughing at.

No yacht harbors in Tijuana. Huh. That kind of screws up my plan.

I nodded as if I didn't care, but inside I was twisting in knots. He knew that once I left this little marina, it was impossible for me to do anything but cross the border. The son-of-a-bitch had planned it down to the last detail. *Maybe he actually was several steps ahead of everybody else.*

CHAPTER 17

Pulling away from Puerto Salina—sans Corkscrew—I watched the two smugglers from the starboard bow. Although Ozzy had his car nearby, I had trouble imagining him simply driving away and trusting me to follow his orders. Then I noticed an inflatable Zodiac sitting uncovered in a slip. It had a rigid hull and an open bow, much like the Navy boats. But this one was smaller, only fifteen or sixteen feet long. Which meant that it would be fast, and could easily outmaneuver me in the Grand Banks.

Bernice emerged from the harbor into an even thicker fog bank. Within a minute, Ozzy and Sacacorcho would have the Zodiac going, and be on my tail. I had to make my move now or never.

As soon as I cleared the north jetty, I jammed the throttle forward and watched the bow raise in response. She was doing nearly thirty knots, close to her maximum, directly into the fog. Like a blind man running at full speed, I had no idea what lay ahead of me. All I could do was keep an eye on my compass to make sure I wasn't heading back toward land.

I had trouble believing that Tijuana—a city of over a million residents—didn't have a yacht harbor. So I checked the navigation charts for myself, and sure enough the coastline was nothing but sand and rock all the way to the border.

Then I noticed four small islands depicted on the map, lying eight miles off the Mexican mainland. It occurred to me that by now the two stooges were probably zig-zagging through the fog, looking for me. Only they'd be searching along the shore, not toward a group of barren islands several miles out to sea. I sharply altered my course and made for the El Coronado Islands. They would be the perfect place for me to stash the yacht.

Ozzy and his sidekick were sure to be confused by now, not knowing if I had fled from them or if they had simply lost sight of me in the fog. I hoped that their uncertainty would keep them from harming my daughter, reassuring myself over and over again that their primary objective remained the shipment's delivery.

If this was going to work, I needed to hurry. Accelerating to the yacht's maximum speed, her hull bounced and hammered through the heavy waves. I still couldn't see more than twenty yards in front of me, and I prayed that there were no fishing or tour boats operating on Sunday morning. I slowed slightly as I neared the islands, closely monitoring the digital depth gauge.

Something suddenly sprang from the water on my port side, causing me to jump. Instead of Ozzy's Zodiac, I had been joined by a couple of Monk dolphins. At more than ten feet in length, they looked like small gray whales. It was as if they were escorting me to the islands, and I wished that I had something to feed them in return.

Moments later, a series of tan humps materialized out of the mist. Nothing much to look at, the largest island holding only a lighthouse and a couple of barracks—both of which were perched on a small bluff. The other three islands were flat and barren. According to the chart, a small anchorage called Puerto Cueva sat on the east side of the southernmost island.

Once I lowered and set the anchor, I went to work unscrewing and removing the teak panel from the stateroom wall. I then transferred the drugs—one trash bag at a time—onto the deck. Each bag weighed over 50 pounds, so I was thankful to be wearing my knee brace.

From one of the bench lockers, I took a blue tarpaulin and used it to wrap the entire stash of drugs into an airtight bundle—with the exception of one kilo, which I set aside as evidence. I tied the huge load of drugs to the backup anchor, or Kedge, as I'd found out it's called, and then slid the entire five-hundred-pound mass over the side of the yacht. It hit the water like a fat kid doing a cannonball, and I just stood there watching five million dollars of contraband sink to the bottom of the sea. The Kedge, of course, was still attached to the boat.

I stuffed my passport and wallet into my pocket, and then slid the single kilogram of cocaine into the pass-through pouch of my sweatshirt. It gave me a *beer gut*, but I couldn't worry about that at the moment. The tricky part was climbing from the safety of the yacht into the bobbing dinghy. Pulling away felt dangerous as hell, and without a compass or navigational instruments I wouldn't even be sure of my heading. These skiffs are only meant for short trips between protected moorings and harbors, not eight mile journeys through the fog and open sea. My overriding hope was that I wouldn't run into Ozzy and Sacacorcho out there.

The swells towered overhead, bouncing me wildly from side-to-side against the hull. The small boat rocked violently, sliding off the cresting waves like butter off a corn cob.

It took nearly two hours, but I finally spotted the Tijuana coastline through the dissipating mist. Much of the shore was marked by rocks and uneven escarpments that rose steeply to the highway, so I paralleled the shore until I found a decent spot. My dinghy maneuvered well, and put me safely onto a narrow wedge of sand set between two jutting rocks.

I was just off of Mexico's highway 1D—also known as *Escenica Tijuana-Ensenada*. A small tract of exclusive homes with large pools sat just north of me on the beach side of the highway. I decided to avoid them, having learned from my days in uniform that wealthy people never hesitate to call the police.

So, leaving the inflatable under a few handfuls of dried seaweed, I crossed to the other side of the highway where I would not stand out as much. A quarter mile further, I spotted a large restaurant or public building on a bluff just east of the highway. It stretched back into the hillside at odd angles, with a large parking area to the north. As I left the road and made my way up the driveway, I saw a sign that read *Jardín Carrizalejo*.

Decorated cars outside should have been my clue that the place was an event venue, but it didn't click until too late that I was in the middle of a wedding reception. Standing out on too many levels to count, I realized that I couldn't have been more conspicuous if I'd been skinny dipping in one of the fancy estates' pools.

"May I help you, Señor?"

I turned to see a lovely woman—several years younger than me—wearing a shapely red dress and heels. Her large brown eyes were set off nicely by her short, trendy hairstyle. Since she wasn't at one of the tables or on the dance floor, I took her for one of the staff. In any case, she obviously figured me for an American.

"Yes, hi," I said. "My, uh, my car broke down a mile down the highway and I was wondering if there was a phone I could use."

"Certainly. You're welcome to use the phone in my office."

After what I'd been through in the past twenty-four hours, I have to say that this was a treat. Besides speaking perfect English, she was friendly and welcoming, and she wasn't trying to drug me or beat me with a flashlight.

Her office was tidy and modern, and I soon realized that she was the facility's manager. A nameplate on her desk read: PATRICIA URIBE.

She motioned toward the phone. "I'll give you some privacy."

"Wait," I said. "Would you mind helping me? My Spanish is a little rusty."

Patricia smiled. Perfect white teeth, just as I imagined they'd be. "Of course," she said.

I told her that I needed a taxi cab, which she quickly arranged. And then I asked her for the address of the American Embassy. She typed something into her laptop, and then jotted a few lines onto a sticky note.

Painfully aware of my bulging stomach, I nonchalantly rested my arm across the package hidden inside my sweatshirt.

"It's actually the U.S. Consulate General," she said, handing me the note. "But here's the address and phone number."

As she turned, I caught the sweet scent of whatever perfume she wore. Strikingly more pleasant than that of my former shipmate, Sacacorcho.

I almost asked to place an international call, but wondered if such a request might be pushing the bounds of hospitality. I also doubted that Bridge would answer a call from a number she didn't recognize, especially from a foreign country.

I thanked Patricia profusely, and had just started back down the hall when a server stopped and held out an appetizer platter. My face must have registered shock, but I recovered quickly enough to grab some shrimp taquitos and slices of cheese. I left with the feeling that things were starting to look up.

I waited at the foot of the event center driveway for a long time before a black and yellow Taxi Diamante picked me up.

The driver, middle-aged and stoop shouldered, had skin the color of tobacco and the texture of armadillo hide. He turned and smiled, showing off his gold fillings. "Where you want to go, mister?" – which he pronounced *mee-ster*.

There was something else, something not quite right about him. It was his eye, I realized. He gazed back through his good eye, while the fake rolled uncontrollably—pointing everywhere except at me.

"Can you take me to *Paseo de las Culturas?*" I asked, handing him Patricia's sticky note.

He glanced at the address and then over his shoulder at me. "You going to crossing the border at Otay Mesa today?"

"No," I said. "I'm going to the American Consulate near there."

The driver turned back again, and I'd swear that both eyes were rolling around now. "You sure about that?"

I nodded.

"Whatever you say, *amigo.*"

CHAPTER 18

I asked my one-eyed taxi driver if he'd let me use his cell phone to call my daughter. "It's kind of an emergency," I said.

He shrugged, then handed his phone over the seat.

I dialed and then closed my eyes, praying that she would answer. "Hello?"

"Bridge, it's me, Dad." My worry seemed to add volume and urgency to my voice, and I probably sounded out of breath. "Are you okay?

"Yeah Dad, but Mom isn't too happy."

"Can I talk to her?"

"She already left on her trip. Remember? You were supposed to be here to watch me."

"I know, but... wait, she left you alone?"

"No, Grandma's watching me."

"Grandma's house... good, okay."

"No dad, I didn't say--"

"Listen to me Bridge, just be super safe. There's something going on, and... well, people might be looking for you."

She was silent for a minute before finally asking, "Why is someone looking for me, Dad? I didn't do anything."

"No," I said. "It's not because of anything you did, it's because of something that I... Just be extra careful up there."

"Dad, what's going on? Are you safe?"

"Oh yeah, I'm fine." It was mostly true. "So, where is your mom, anyway?"

"I don't think I'm supposed to say anything."

"About what?" I felt my throat constricting.

"She doesn't want you to know that she's gone on a cruise. With a man."

Now I was silent. My mind raced to make sense of the words. When it finally caught up, the speed and tone of my words changed. "A man? What man? What do you mean a cruise? Like they're on a cruise ship? Together?"

"Calm down, Dad. I don't like it either." Bridge lowered her voice, as if she was moving out of Grandma's hearing range—which wasn't that far. "Mom hooked up with a guy. You know, like, they've gone on dates and stuff. I don't really know him because she doesn't bring him around much. I can't even tell if she really likes him, but you know, she's still pretty angry at you."

"Yeah, I know." And me not showing up to watch our daughter was probably the icing on the divorce cake. "Bridge, I'm really sorry about all this."

"I know, Dad."

Then I thought about it for a minute. "Does your mom have her cell phone with her?"

"I think so, why?"

"No reason. Just in case."

I reminded Bridget to stay put with her grandma, and not to tell anyone—not even her best friends—where she was staying. I made her promise, and then we ended the call.

My taxi driver looked leery as I handed the phone over the seat to him. "You in some kinds of trouble, my friend?"

I sucked in a long inhale and let it out slowly. "Yeah, you could definitely say that."

He nodded sympathetically, and I got the feeling it was sincere. He didn't push for information, which made me want to trust him more. The guy seemed like he was just an honest, hardworking taxi driver. The kind of person who could be trusted.

In a moment of benevolent candor, I worked the kilo-size package out of my sweatshirt pocket and held it up over the seatback. "You know what this is?"

His good eye stared while the other shimmied. "Oh yes, I know."

He stopped the taxi on the side of the road, and leaned closer to inspect the inked marking on the side of the package. It was tiny smiley face stamp—about the size of a fifty cent piece. I'd noticed them on all of the packages.

"This is why I'm in trouble," I said. "I'm being forced to take a whole load of this stuff across the border." I lowered the package and stuffed it back in my sweatshirt. "That's why I'm going to the U.S. Consulate. I need to let them know what's going on."

The driver rubbed his bristly chin. "I think this is not a good idea."

"I have no other choice. There's no one else I can trust." Our eyes met in the rearview mirror. "Don't worry, I know what I'm doing."

He shrugged and pulled back into traffic. "Okay, *amigo*."

After about thirty minutes of winding through the streets of Tijuana, the cab passed the international airport. I imagined myself getting out there, hopping on a flight, and leaving the yacht and the drugs behind. Probably would have been the best move, but for some reason I couldn't do it.

Instead, I gazed out at traffic stopped all around us. I'd heard that the Otay Mesa was one of the country's busiest border crossings, and I assumed it was causing the gridlock.

"Some demonstrations, I think," said the driver. "Be careful when you get out."

Minutes later he pulled to a barricaded intersection with police posted around it. Some of them wore helmets with face shields, and some wore tan uniforms while others wore green. Hundreds of protesters milled around on the roadway behind the cops—many holding signs referencing U.S. immigration policies.

I thanked my driver and handed him some American dollars. He held them in his hand like a golden goose egg, and then reached across the seat with a business card.

"Call me when you need the taxi cab *en* Tijuana."

I glanced at his card, the name *Felipé Cuevas* handwritten on it.

Shielding my eyes from the glaring sun, I squinted down the block toward the American flag posted in front of the building. It was maybe a hundred-fifty yards to the consulate gate, but a lot of demonstrators and police filled the space in between.

The crowd seemed to press in from all sides as I worked my way toward the building. In my Cal Bears sweatshirt, I was acutely aware of my American-ness.

About halfway down the block, I heard commands in Spanish bellowed through a bullhorn. They were immediately followed by yelling, breaking glass, and barking dogs. I looked behind me to see not one, but two dogs coming my way at the end of police leashes. A cop with a German Shephard worked the demonstrators on one side of the street while another with a Border Collie moved toward me. I was bitten once as a kid, and to this day I'm still not a fan of dogs.

Feeling like an escaped convict in a movie, I imagined running through the Bayou, chased by a pack of bloodhounds. But instead of running, I just walked faster. I had closed on the consulate, but the Collie had also closed on me. With only a few steps to go before the entry gate, the dog leapt up with his paws on my sweatshirt—like he wanted me to throw his tennis ball. He then sat on the ground directly in front of me and barked.

The cop gave me a look of utter disgust. "Don't move," was all he said. Then he made an upward motion with a hand across my torso, and again the dog pawed and barked.

"I'm an American citizen, and I'm going into the U.S. Consulate. That's my right. You can't violate my..."

With our eyes locked onto one another's, the cop reached into the front pocket of my sweatshirt and pulled out the package of cocaine.

I was going to bring up the Geneva Convention, but knowing nothing about international humanitarian law I realized that anything I said would be a waste of time. The cop with the Shepherd trotted over from the other side of the street, and the two of them bound my wrists together with plastic zip-ties.

I lifted my head, and gazed down the block to where my driver sat inside his taxi—window open, watching me with a hurt expression.

His eye dropped as he shook his head, and I could almost hear him muttering, "I told you this was a bad idea."

CHAPTER 19

The cops shoved me into the open bed of a Toyota truck where a dozen other prisoners sat. A couple of them were bloodied, one had thrown up on himself, and another lay motionless. He could have been dead for all I knew. Two military-clad guys with machine guns stood on the rear bumper, each clinging to the truck with their free hands as it wove through the dusty streets—lights flashing and siren blaring.

The route took us under an elevated freeway and past a Costco store before turning onto a street that paralleled a salmon colored wall rising twenty feet straight up. It was solid brick, with peeling paint and no windows, and it seemed to go on for blocks. I saw no signage, only guard towers spiraling up another thirty feet into the air—one every couple of hundred yards.

The truck suddenly stopped at a huge unmarked gate topped with coils of razor wire. Still, no sign to identify the building.

"Where are we?" I asked aloud to no one in particular.

Nobody answered at first, and then one old man lifted his head. "Penitenciaria de la Mesa," he said. *La Mesa Prison.*

As the gate closed behind us, the yelling and whistling started. Prisoners clamored over one another, monkeying their way up an interior chain linked fence to view the newcomers. More catcalls, and words in Spanish that I assumed to be derogative and threatening.

We were herded inside a large hollow room with solid concrete floors, walls, and ceilings. An order was given and the rest of the new arrivals began undressing. I followed along.

Once completely naked, we were directed at gunpoint to face the far wall—which I also did. A momentary image flashed through my mind, of being gunned down like the *Saint Valentine's Day massacre.*

Instead of killing us though, they made us squat, lift up our balls, and bend over. Not sure if that was better or worse than being gunned down. Meanwhile, another couple of cops or guards or whatever, went through the discarded clothes—pulling out knives, money, drugs, and any other contraband that they decided to take. When they finished, they ordered us to put our clothes back on. I guess that's how they save money on prison overalls.

Our group was herded down another hallway, past jail cells and more jeers, to a large enclosure with floor-to-ceiling chain linked fencing. The back and side walls were solid concrete. No bunks, no benches, no nothing. Just floor... and a single aluminum toilet sitting openly in the corner. And there was already a line to use it.

I took a seat as far away from it as I could, which, apparently, is considered prime real estate. Two beefy men covered in tattoos and sweat, wasted little time coming over to let me know. One of them knew enough English to communicate this to me by saying, "Get the fuck off my floor, *pinche gringo.*"

I realized that there was a pecking order, and I was the peck-ee, not the peck-er. So, not wanting to be killed just yet, I agreed to relinquish my spot.

I'd spent a night in jail once before, but this place was definitely worse. Those who still had money or jewelry bribed their way to getting a blanket. Others, like me, had only the cold, hard, and often wet, floor under us. The odors were a pungent, stomach-wrenching combination of feet, ass, and onions—all overlaid with the constant stench of urine.

Having plenty of time to go over all of my decisions up to this point, I realized in hindsight that I was an idiot. But even more than the disastrous predicament I had gotten myself into, I was most troubled by the news that Doris was dating. It ate me up inside to picture it, yet it was all I could think about. I needed to find out who this guy was, and what liberties he'd taken with my wife.

Several times during the night, I squeezed into a space against the fencing and thrust my passport through the tiny diamond shaped spaces. "U.S. Embassy?" I'd say. "American Consulate?" or, "Phone call?" I was ignored each time.

Being the only white-skinned guy, it was already a given that I was an American. The guards who had done their best to avoid me, talked among themselves and pointed in my direction. Had I paid more attention in school, I might have understood what they were saying.

In the morning, one of the guards—probably a higher up—walked to the fence and motioned me over. I'd hoped he was going to release me, or at least get me to a phone. But he leaned close, and in adequate English said, "You will go to see the judge for the trial tomorrow."

That wasn't good. I needed time, a postponement, a lawyer, bail money. I'd need to make some phone calls. They'd say they caught me with drugs, then they would put the kilo of cocaine on display, and then they'd throw away the damn key.

"Can I talk with someone from the consulate?" I asked.

He shrugged, like, sure, if you happen to see a diplomat from the consulate walking by your jail cell, you can talk to him.

"I need to make some phone calls." I held up my passport. "Those are my rights."

He shrugged again, wavered there for a minute, and then said something to another guard. The door opened, and he escorted me down a hall to a black wall phone—the kind we had at home when I was a kid. Only this one was warm and sticky, and the numbers were worn off.

"One phone call," he said.

It was almost like one of those logic riddles: You're in a Mexican prison and you need a lawyer, bail money, and an embassy official. But you only get one call.

I tried to remember the number, which I always had on my speed dial. Then I realized that calls from Mexico to the U.S. required a couple of zeros and a one before the number... I think.

After I dialed, a series of beeps and buzzes sounded and then a strange ring.

"Hello?"

"Doris, It's me. Dan."

CHAPTER 20

Doris didn't say anything, but I thought I heard her teeth grinding.

"Don't hang up," I said. "I need to talk to you about something *very important*." I wasn't sure if the hook worked or if I needed a bigger one. "Bridget's life may be in danger."

"Danny, why would you say such a thing?"

"It's a long story, but I'm not exaggerating." I paused, thinking about how to explain the rest.

"I'm listening."

"I already talked to Bridge," I said. "And I know that for the time being she's safe with your mother."

Doris snarled, "Since I couldn't depend on you to--"

"The reason I couldn't make it back in time has to do with this case I'm working, you know, through my private investigation firm. It's way too much to go into right now, but I want to let you know...and...well, I could really use your help right now."

She paused. "Help, how?"

I paused. "So, did I hear you're going on some kind of trip or something?"

"Danny, get to the point!"

"I only ask because..." I sighed. "Are you seeing someone else?"

"Damnit, Danny. Yes, I'm *trying* to enjoy a cruise with my friend."

"You're on a cruise, right now?"

She sighed. "Not that it's any of your business, but we left yesterday. In fact, we've only just arrived at our first port-of-call in Ensenada."

I nearly inhaled the receiver. "You're in Ensenada, Mexico? Right now?"

A man spoke in the background. He seemed comfortable with her—cozy even.

"Who was that?" I stared into the phone. "Was that him? Is he there with you, now?"

"Yes, Danny, that was my friend, Mike."

"Mike? His name is Mike? Do I know him?"

"Yes, he says you know each other. No more, Danny! This is none of your business. You and I aren't together anymore, and my therapist says that I need to move on with my life."

"Is it that same therapist lady who never liked me?"

"I'm hanging up now."

"Wait!" As tormented as I was, I knew I'd have to postpone the third degree. "Listen Doris, I really do need your help right now. Fact is, I'm in Mexico, too. Actually, not too far from you. Seriously, if you could do a couple of little things for me, I'd be really grateful. And I promise not to bother you again. Ever." Which, of course, wasn't true.

"What... What do you need?"

I switched hands, and wiped the phone grime on my pants. "First, I need you to call the American Consulate in Tijuana. There's an American citizen being held illegally in La Mesa Prison. They need to check on him and get him out."

"Who is he?" Doris asked. "Is he your client?"

"Not exactly," I said. "But if the consulate can't help, then you need to send some money. This guy needs cash to either make bail or bribe the guards."

Doris was silent again, and I knew she was balking.

"I'll pay you back," I promised.

She'd probably have to leave the ship and catch a cab to Tijuana. Sadly, cruise over for the lovebirds. But I doubted that she would do that for me, let alone some person she doesn't even know.

"You would be saving my client's life," I said, "and quite possibly the life of our daughter." It was a bit of an exaggeration, but I gave myself creative license now that I knew Bridget was safe at her grandmother's house. Doris' mother lived in Pioneer—a town of about a thousand residents in the Sierra Nevada foothills. Ozzy may have been able to find Mill Valley, but Grandma Abrams was just about off the grid.

I continued my plea, "Getting me out... getting *him* out of jail is the only way to really guarantee Bridget's safety. Like I said before, it's complicated, and there are a lot of moving parts to this case. I'll explain it all later."

"Did you just say '*me*'?"

"You?"

"No. '*Me*'. Didn't you just say, 'getting *me* out'?"

My silence was probably just as good as an admission, but I couldn't think of anything to say. Finally, I broke. "Yes! Okay? Yes, Doris. It's me. I'm the one in the Tijuana jail. But it's not what you think, so don't go jumping to conclusions again."

"Then tell me why you're there. What did you *allegedly* do?" She had overemphasized the word allegedly, which was a telltale sign of where her head was at. It definitely wasn't with Team Danny.

"Okay, so I took this yacht down here for, kind of like, a friend, and I was meeting a couple who were supposed to buy it off me. But instead of a couple, it was a guy named Ozzy. And instead of buying the yacht, he had someone get me drunk and slip me a Mickey Finn. Anyway, Ozzy's sidekick has a weird Spanish name I can't pronounce, that means corkscrew, because he does this, like, twisting thing with peoples' necks and..."

I heard only silence on the other end.

"Doris?"

There was a click, and then the line went dead.

Son-of-a-bitch!

I started to redial the phone, and a thick, calloused hand came down over the top of mine. "Hang up," said the guard. "I told you, only one call."

My unrehearsed story had crashed and burned, and I had only myself to blame. By trying to wing it, I had blown my only phone call, and, probably, my only chance of getting out.

Lying in the cell the rest of the afternoon gave me time to think about my situation—which had worsened, along with my marriage and my life. But I couldn't stop replaying the background voice—Doris' new BFF. She had probably told the guy everything I'd said, which made me sound like I'm some kind of schmuck. Mike... Someone I know named Mike. Mike Gibson? Mike Kavanagh? Mike Sagorsky? Mike Sandsmark? No, his name is Mark. Whatever.

Why couldn't the guy's name have been something like Delmer? I only know one of them.

More pressing, I guess, was my pending trial. I knew if I didn't get myself out before court in the morning, I'd be toast. Which got me thinking that I hadn't eaten since the wedding appetizers. Losing a few pounds wouldn't have been killed me, but I was starting to feel my backbone through my stomach.

Late in the day, a nicely dressed Latin man was buzzed through one of the security doors. He carried a brown leather briefcase and wore a laminated card from a lanyard on his neck.

Stopping in front of the cell, he called out, "Daniel Patrick McKenna, passport number V840217876."

Like an idiot, I pulled mine out to check the number—as if there might have been two of us in there. I said, "That's me. I'm McKenna."

He signaled the guard, who opened the door and let me out.

"Come with me, please." The man with the briefcase led me down a hallway, past the phone, and into a tiny room with a table and two chairs. He sat, then I sat.

"I'm Delmer Sanchez." He handed me his business card.

Now I know two Delmers.

Glancing at the card, I saw that he was not a representative of the United States Consul General.

"I'm with the American Citizen Services Unit," he said. "We typically get involved when a U.S. citizen is arrested here. This afternoon we were contacted by someone on your behalf, asking that we look into your situation." He glanced at his notepad.

My heart leapt in my chest, thinking that Doris must have at least cared enough to call someone to help me.

"Who is Tom Halliday?" he asked.

I shrugged, trying to read the writing on his pad.

"What about Jonas Rourke?"

I shook my head.

Sanchez's eyebrows furrowed together as he set his notes aside. "Interesting. Anyway, I've obtained a copy of your arrest report." He removed it from his briefcase and set it on the table.

I held up my hands. "I know, I know, it looks pretty bad. Believe it or not, I was actually bringing the cocaine to the consulate when I got arrested. You'll see in the report that I was stopped just a few feet outside the gate."

"Why would you bring drugs to the consulate?"

"It's a long story."

"That's why I'm here." Sanchez slid his chair back and folded his hands. "If I'm going to help you, I'll need to hear it."

Forty-five minutes later I was nearing the end of my saga. Surprisingly, the guy had taken several pages of notes—which I imagined said things like, *what a dumbshit!* But his face remained non-committal, and he kept his comments to clarifying questions.

When I finished, he nodded and put away his notepad. "These sound like some pretty heavy drug traffickers you've gotten yourself involved with. Fact is, right now this city is in the midst of a drug war between rival cartels. We're talking nine-hundred plus homicides in Tijuana over the past year. I would suspect that this Ozzy character and his buddy are major players, which means that you're lucky to be alive instead of hanging from an overpass."

I unconsciously rubbed my neck.

He asked a few more questions before signaling for a guard. "I'll work on getting you out of here, but in the meantime don't mention the drugs to anyone in here. These guys are all connected. It'll take me a couple of hours to file the necessary papers, so just be patient."

"Okay, thank you." We shook hands.

"My advice..." he said. "As soon as you leave this place, take the first flight out of Mexico. Leave the yacht, your clothes and any personal belongings, and just go. Contact the local PD when you get home, and have them step up patrols of your residence—just in case the traffickers try to make good on their threat."

I swallowed hard knowing that Bridget would still be out of my sight at times. She was a teenager, with school and friends and whatever. Besides, I knew that *stepping up patrols* was nothing more than a panacea that cops use to put citizens at ease.

As grateful as I was for Sanchez's help, I couldn't see myself just running away and leaving the drugs, the boat, and an angry drug lord. I would be leaving my family's safety to chance.

CHAPTER 21

More than a couple of hours had passed, and I was still sweltering in the cell without any word from Sanchez or the consulate.

The guards had fed us, which, again, there was a pecking order to. I was last in line to receive a paper plate, upon which sat a glob of scrambled eggs, a glob of refried beans, and a cold tortilla. I watched the other guys use their tortilla to scoop the eggs and beans in the absence of silverware. *Huh.*

It was dark outside, judging from the grate-covered windows above the guard station. I was beginning to think that Sanchez had failed me, when suddenly one of the guards motioned me over to the door. Without saying anything, he unlocked it, slid it open, and motioned me out.

I followed him down the same hallway, past the greasy phone, to the same tiny interview room. Relieved to be getting released soon, I stepped into the room with an enthusiastic lilt.

"Well, well, well. So, here we are again."

I stared across the table into Ozzy's reptilian eyes, as he sat back comfortably with his boots up and a cigarette in his mouth.

"Sit."

I saw no sign of Corkscrew, which was good, but the guard stepped out and locked the door, which was not so good.

"I said, sit!"

I sat.

"You want to die a slow and painful death... is that it?"

Nothing came out of my mouth. Even though I did not wish to die a slow and painful death, my mind was busy thinking about how I could spin this thing. Some way that I could maintain the leverage of still possessing the drugs.

Suddenly another Mike sprang to mind. Mike Bishop. No, Doris couldn't be dating him—he moved to Utah six months ago.

"No, I don't want to die," I said. "And I still have the coke."

Ozzy shook his head. "No you don't. Me and El Sacacorcho found the yacht out by Islas Los Coronados. Smart thinking, running into the fog and stashing the boat. But not smart enough."

"You've got it all wrong," I said. "I wasn't trying to outrun you, I got lost in the fog. Your boy Corkscrew messed me up by ripping out all the navigation wires."

That gave him pause. Apparently, Ozzy wasn't familiar enough with the GPS system to realize it had nothing to do with the two-way radio his partner had disabled. I had him doubting himself. *Good!*

"What about the load?" he said. "We went aboard and unscrewed the wall. There was nothing there."

"I... I took it." Thinking as fast as I could. "I took it off of the boat, because I didn't want someone to snatch it."

"Bullshit! You can't carry a half-ton by yourself. Where is it?"

I sat there for a second, stretched my neck, then leaned back in the chair. "Look, Ozzy. I'm telling you, I still have it. And I may be stupid, but I'm not stupid enough to just hand it over to you. I know that my life's worth nothing once you have your drugs."

He glared across the table, pinched his lips around his cigarette and took a final long drag. Then he flicked it against the wall and fiery embers flickered in all directions.

"If you're lying to me McKenna, I swear I'll not only kill you and your daughter, but I'll kill everyone in your family, all of your friends, and your friends' families. Got that?"

I nodded. "Yeah, I got it. And I've also got your drugs." Something suddenly dawned on me. "So, how did you know I was here, anyway? In fact, how did you even get into this place?"

Back came his cheesy grin. "I told you, I know everyone. Someone on my payroll recognized the package you got caught with—*Pendejo!* The stamp is the distributor's trademark. You ever hear of CJNG?"

"No."

"Cartel Jalisco New Generation," he said. "We're taking control of the border."

"I thought our government was cracking down on--"

Ozzy coughed out a loud, cracking laugh. "Don't kid yourself, McKenna. Tijuana is wide open. Whoever controls the pipeline, owns the drug trade in your country. Right now, that's me and my people. *Entiendes?*"

"Uh huh." We still hadn't gotten to the next move in this little cat and mouse game. So, I waited silently for him to blink.

"Okay," he finally said. "I'll give you one more day. Twenty-four hours from right now." He looked at his watch. "At seven o'clock tomorrow night I'll be waiting on the Oceanside dock for my product."

"Same place?" I asked.

He nodded. "In the harbor near the Jolly Roger."

"I'll be one kilo short, since they took the one I had."

He smiled. "No worries, they already gave it back to me."

"What if something happens, and I'm delayed?"

"Fuck you, McKenna. No more delays!" Ozzy leaned back and took a breath. When he spoke again he seemed calmer. "I already pushed the transfer back far enough. Money has changed hands and I've got buyers waiting for it. You get the coke to me by seven o'clock, or the McKenna house is going to be a goddamn bloodbath."

After Ozzy left, they put me back in the cell—but only for a few minutes. Sanchez must have sent the paperwork over with a courier, because I was abruptly taken to the opposite end of the building and shoved though a pedestrian gate onto a street called *Los Charros*.

Several people milled around in the dark, including a family with several small children, a pregnant woman who sat on the curb, and an old man sleeping on a blanket. Two women—maybe a mother and daughter—stood at an information board where several printed sheets were stapled.

A taxi pulled to the curb down the street, and I started toward it. Realizing that I was out of money, I stopped and watched as a man and woman got out and the cab drove away.

I pressed my grimy palms into my forehead. *Twenty-four-hours to get to Oceanside, but I've got no money, no cell phone, no friends, and--*

"Danny?"

I turned toward the woman who had just gotten out of the cab.

"Doris? You came?"

... And you brought MIKE?

CHAPTER 22

I squinted into the dark street where Doris' *"friend"* loitered uncomfortably behind her. I didn't immediately recognize *Mike,* but knew he wasn't one of the friends I had speculated about.

"Danny!" Doris sidestepped in front of me, blocking my view of the guy. "What in the hell are you doing out of jail? I thought you were in real trouble."

"I was." I leaned further into the street, trying to get a better look at him. "The consulate people got me out."

"So, I came all the way here for nothing? Do you have any idea what it took to disembark halfway through a cruise, have our luggage forwarded, and find a cab to bring us all the way here? Not to mention getting a bank in Tijuana to give me the cash?"

The guy took a step into the light. "Michael Prowse?" I said in a hoarse voice. "Are you kidding me, Doris? Your *friend* is Lieutenant Prowse?"

Prowse approached in his Margaritaville shirt and Docker shorts, then put his hand on my wife's shoulder. "I told you it was a mistake to help him, Doris." Then he looked at me and said, "Last time I saw you, McKenna, you'd also just gotten out of jail. Seems like things haven't changed much."

I felt my Irish boiling up inside, and I was about to unleash on the jerk. Not just for his wiseass comments, but for touching Doris like she belonged to him.

"He's right," said Doris, easing herself between me and Prowse. "I should never have listened to your sob story. Now the vacation we'd planned is totally ruined."

I rolled my eyes. *Vacation.* A million questions were stacked bumper-to-bumper in my mind: How long have you been seeing each other? Has he spent the night at my house? Does he drink my good Scotch and watch TV in my recliner?

Prowse checked his watch. "It's probably too late to get out of this Godforsaken place tonight."

My eyes rolled again. *Couldn't she see that Prowse was just trying to get her into a hotel room?*

Doris walked away, muttering. "Now what are we going to do?" Her flailing arms punctuated her words. "We won't get our cruise money back, you know. And now we have to find a way back to Long Beach."

"Long Beach..." I was trying to figure that one out when Prowse answered.

"Yeah. Not that it's any of your business, but Long Beach was the original departure port. We drove down from the Bay Area and parked the Jag there."

The Jag. I had to stop rolling my eyes every time this guy opened his mouth. I turned my back to him. "Listen, Doris. You coming here wasn't for nothing, I still need help."

She cocked her head and folded her arms.

"You need help alright," said Prowse. "*Non compos mentis.*"

I glared at him, knowing that whatever he'd said wasn't a compliment.

"It means you're mentally ill, McKenna."

Raising my palm toward him, I took Doris by the arm. "Mind if I speak with *my own* wife in private for a minute?"

We moved to the other side of the street. "I didn't want to tell you this Doris, but these guys I told you about? They're very dangerous men. And..." I glanced back at Prowse. "Seriously, Doris? It's bad enough that you're seeing someone I used to work with..."

"My social life is none of your business, Danny."

"Yeah, I know. But an Internal Affairs stiff? The guy's an idiot."

"Michael is not an idiot. He's got his law degree, and he's number one on the captain's promotional list."

I squinted at his beltline. "He wears a fanny pack."

"One more crack about him, just one, and I'm leaving."

"Wait, okay," I said. "I really do need your help. In fact, ...did you happen to bring your phone charger?"

Now she rolled her eyes. "C'mon Mike, let's get out of here. This *was* a mistake."

I watched Doris turn on her heels, take Prowse's arm, and walk away. After a few steps, she abruptly turned back, whipping Prowse around with her. "What did you say on the phone about a boat?"

I scratched my head. "Uh, yeah. I told you that I brought a yacht down here for someone."

"And?" She took another step toward me with Prowse in tow. "And, what happened to it? Where is it now?"

"I have it parked somewhere," I said.

"Parked. Like what, is it on a trailer?"

I was still scratching my head. "Not parked. I have it anchored out by some islands. Why?"

"Because Mike and I need a ride back up to Long Beach, that's why."

"Oh no, no, no. That clown isn't stepping one foot on my yacht. Besides, this case I'm working on is too dangerous. I won't expose you to that kind of risk."

"Right." She looked up at the night sky. "I don't know if I can believe anything that comes out of your mouth anymore. Regardless, Michael is a cop and you're a cop—or an ex-cop—and I'm sure we can make it safely to Long Beach."

"Bad idea," said Prowse. "The less time we have to spend with your ex, the better for all of us."

I had to agree with the asswipe, though not about being Doris' 'ex'. At least not yet. But he was right about it being a terrible plan. For one thing, I hadn't even decided whether to return to the yacht. Besides, the delivery was supposed to take place at the Oceanside Harbor, which is eighty miles *before* Long Beach. That meant that Doris and Prowse would be with me during the drug transaction. And since Ozzy had already threatened to kill my family, I would be leading my wife right to him.

"You owe us that much, Danny." Doris strode right up, looking me square in the face. "You completely trashed our cruise trip, and you've cost both me and Mike thousands of dollars. It's the least you can do to make it right."

My head slowly nodded as I agreed to the ridiculous notion. "But we won't be able to make it to the yacht tonight. We'll have to stay the night in Tijuana, then leave first thing in the morning."

CHAPTER 23

I hadn't paid much attention to it while handcuffed in the back of the truck, but I remembered passing a hotel close to the prison.

I led Doris and Prowse around the corner and down a street marked by warehouses and auto body shops. It wasn't the best area to begin with, and it looked even worse at night. Another block over, I found a hotel—though it wasn't the same one I'd seen.

With peeling pink paint and a partially lit neon sign, Hotel Los Jacuzzis boasted clean rooms for *190 pesos*—the equivalent of about fifteen bucks.

It was the type of place that would disgust Doris. I knew that she would be so creeped out, in fact, that she'd never even think about getting into the bed. *Sorry Prowse.* The place was perfect!

"Probably has bedbugs," said Prowse.

"Really? Ya think?" Doris looked sick, and mad, and tired.

I laughed to myself. *That'll seal it for Doris.*

Prowse took hand sanitizer from his fanny pack and squeezed it onto his hands. Then he turned toward me and said, "The dump is probably a step up for you, eh McKenna?"

I chomped down on the inside of my cheek, trying to ignore him. "No, no, this won't do at all," I said, knowing everyone was exhausted. "It won't take more than a couple of hours to find a new place. Thirty or forty minutes, tops, to get a taxi, and then another forty-five minutes to drive across the city to find a Marriott or Hyatt."

I smiled to myself, content that there wasn't a chance in hell they'd go for my suggestion. It was almost ten o'clock, and we all had to be up early. I had painted myself as the good guy, willing to do whatever it takes to make Doris comfortable. But I knew she'd end up spending the night on a chair in Hotel Los Jacuzzis with a coat wrapped tightly around her.

As I started toward the registration office, I heard Prowse say, "The heck with it. Let's do it, Doris. The jailbird can stay in this scumbag place if he wants, but you deserve better—better than him, and better than this Jacuzzi dump."

The son-of-a-bitch had called my bluff! He had trumped my Mr. Nice Guy by playing the benevolent suitor card. Doris looked relieved, and my efforts to appear considerate went down the toilet.

The desk clerk at the hotel called a cab while me, Doris and Prowse sat smooshed together on a loveseat in the tiny lobby. I tried to ignore their inane chatter, turning my back to them as I used Doris' cord and charger to juice my dead phone.

Prowse blathered on about the great deal he'd gotten on his *"accessory pouch."* I let out a snicker, and he turned to me as he motioned toward its zippered pockets. "I'll have you know that you'd pay a heck of a lot more for this kind of hand-stitched leather at someplace like Brookstone."

I continued thumbing through a soccer magazine I couldn't read. The whole time, I was thinking about how much I didn't want to ferry Doris and Prowse up the coast, and how much I didn't want to stay in a hotel room right next door to my wife and another man. And though these weren't the worst of my problems, they were definitely a distraction from them.

My real problem was the shipment of cocaine that I still had to smuggle across the border, and the cartel guys who would kill me and my family if I didn't pull it off.

When the cab finally showed up, I gave the phone charger back to Doris and told the two of them to go ahead without me. "Text me the location of your hotel, and I'll meet you there in the morning," I said. "I've got a couple of things to do tonight."

Doris looked suspicious and Prowse looked relieved. In any case, they got into the cab and left.

My phone battery was only at seventeen percent, but at least it was better than before. I knew that 11 o'clock was later than I should call, but I hit speed dial and woke her up anyway.

"McKenna, why you call'n me so late?"

"Sorry, Sha...nay. Just wanted to let you know that I'm still down here in Mexico, but with any luck I'll be back in the Bay Area in a few days."

"Uh, huh. So I guess you finally figured out how to turn on your phone."

"My battery was dead. Why?"

"I been try'n to reach you, that's why. What you got yourself into now?"

"I told you, I'm working on something for that woman at my marina."

"Well, whatever it is, you got some drug cops sniffing 'round the office. Came in yesterday and axed a bunch of questions, like where you are and what you been doin'."

"Drug cops... What did you tell them?"

"I said you was visiting your sick ol' aunt in Canada."

"Good girl. Thanks."

"One more thing, McKenna. I called your daughter to see how's she's gett'n along. You know, she kind of looks up to me like I'm her big sister."

I closed my eyes. Her kind of *big sister,* Bridge didn't need.

"Anyway, I found out that yo wife is goin' on a vacation trip with some dude. Just thought you should know."

"Thanks Shanay." My jaw tightened. "He's an Internal Affairs lieutenant with the SFPD."

"Not that clown who tried to get me to swear out a statement against you."

"Yep. Same guy."

She thought for a minute. "Yeah, he kinda' seemed like he wanted a piece o' her back then. I tol' you McKenna, don't trust that woman."

"Okay, yeah, thanks for the advice." I said. "Back to the drug cops; were they Alameda PD?"

"Nuh-uh. They was federal." The phone clattered in my ear, like she had reached for something. "Here's the dude's card. Thomas Halliday, U.S. Drug Enforcement Agency."

"Holy shit. How do they know?"

"How do they know what, McKenna?"

I ignored the question. "Now the DEA is looking for me?"

"Yep, I guess so. The other dude was kinda hot. He look like Elijah Kelly—the one in Red Tails and that other movie about a butler. Try'n to remember his name... Jonah somethi'n."

"Jonas Rourke?"

"Yeah, that's it."

After I got off the phone with my assistant, or secretary, or whatever Shanay was, I replayed the conversation with Sanchez—the American Citizen Services guy. He had asked me if I recognized those same two names. Which meant that despite whatever Shanay said to throw them off my scent, the DEA must have figured out that I was in Mexico. That also meant that they probably suspected me of being a drug courier.

So, besides being murdered by the cartel or thrown in a Mexican jail for the rest of my life, I now had the option of going to federal prison in the U.S.

Door number three seemed like the best of them, but I still had a way to go before deciding. For starters, I needed to find a ride to the coast, and then figure out where I'd stashed the dinghy.

Then I thought of Patricia Uribe, the beautiful event center manager, and how nice it would be to see her again. Better yet, use her to get even with Doris...

Stay focused, McKenna!

I fished through my wallet, finally locating the business card of my one-eyed taxi driver. "Felipé Cuevas," I said aloud as I punched in his number. It was a stroke of luck that he was on duty, and even though he was fifteen minutes away, he was coming to pick me up.

I waited on the curb out front, thankful to be in the cool night air instead of a stuffy cell. It had been a wild couple of days, and I needed time to figure out my next move. Ozzy had surprised me, showing up in the jail and knowing where my family lived. But he hadn't gotten to them yet, probably because I still had his drugs. As long as I was in possession of the cocaine, I believed that my daughter and my family were safe.

Then there were the two DEA agents waiting for me back in the Bay Area. They were yet another wrinkle that I hadn't anticipated. Thankfully, I still had the benefit of time—after all, the agents were up there and I was still down here.

First thing in the morning, I thought, I'll get back out to the yacht and pull up the load of cocaine attached to the anchor.

"Stay right where you are," said someone behind me.

Then another voice. "Keep both hands where we can see them."

Whoever they were, they were Americans and they sounded like cops. So, I did what they told me and didn't turn around.

Finally, I asked, "Who are you guys?"

"Tommy Halliday and Jonas Rourke," they answered. "U.S. Drug Enforcement Administration."

CHAPTER 24

"Am I under arrest?"

They were still behind me. Neither answered, and I imagined them looking at each other. Finally, one of them said, "Not yet."

"Not yet. What does that mean?" I twisted my upper body around and looked up.

"It means we have no arrest authority in Mexico, but you'll be taken into custody as soon as you set foot on U.S. soil."

So much for my options.

"Wait a minute." I used a hand to stabilize my knee as I pushed myself to a standing position. "I know you! You guys live at my marina in Alameda. You're the drug dealers who stay on the Miami Vice yacht."

"Drug dealers." They both laughed.

"Undercover surveillance," said the dark guy. "Been living on that boat for five months... watching."

"Watching who?"

The blonde surfer, Tommy Halliday, thrust his DEA identification in my face. "Watching someone who actually *is* trafficking drugs."

Two things finally made sense. I now understood why these guys were so mysterious, and also why the Alameda detectives hadn't bothered following up with them. Detective Grassi must have already known that these guys were federal cops working a major case.

"Want to tell us what you're doing down here?" It was the other guy asking. Jonas—the one that Shanay thought was "hot".

"I'm vacationing." Then, remembering that they probably saw me leaving the harbor in Teddy's boat, I added, "Trying to sell a friend's yacht."

"Tell us about the drugs," said Rourke.

"What drugs?"

Having no idea how much they already knew, I wasn't about to volunteer information. So, it went on like that for several minutes; them asking questions, and me pretending that I didn't know what they were talking about. Surfer Boy finally got fed up and put it out there.

"Look, McKenna, we're not stupid. We didn't just decide on a whim to come down to Mexico, and then happen to run into our neighbor in front of the..." He looked up at the sign. "The Hotel Los Jacuzzis."

"We're talking about the drugs on Theodora Langdon's yacht," said Rourke. "Her husband was killed over this shit, and from our perspective you're not far behind him."

"If you guys are surveilling the Alameda yacht harbor, then you must have been there the night Dylan died. Do you know who killed him?"

My question had thrown them off their game, and it was clear I'd struck a nerve.

"What the hell?" I pressed. "You saw it?" I was nodding now, an incredulous, finally understanding the picture, nod. "You two sons-of-bitches sat there on your boat and watched him get murdered, didn't you?"

"It wasn't like that," Halliday said. "We weren't sure what--"

"Never mind that," interrupted Rourke. "We've had a tracker on the Langdons' yacht since you left the marina, and we followed you all the way down here. We know you're involved, so quit playing games."

"If you have a tracker on the boat, then you know where I anchored it."

Rourke nodded.

"And you must have already searched it."

Rourke nodded again.

"And if you searched it, you saw that there were no drugs on it."

Rourke cocked his head. "You're right. The drugs weren't on the yacht. The entire load of coke was tethered to your Kedge anchor, seventy feet underwater. So, now can we dispense with the bullshit, McKenna?"

I tried to swallow the knot in my throat, but couldn't. I was as good as dead without that cocaine in my possession. Finally, I asked weakly, "Did you take it?"

"Of course we took it," said Halliday. "We hauled it up, weighed it, tagged it, and now it's safe and sound in an evidence locker at the Imperial Beach Customs and Border Protection Station."

"All except two kilos," added Rourke. "The one you took off the boat and so dutifully brought to the embassy..."

I could barely look up. "And the other kilo?"

"We'll get to that," snapped Halliday. "Right now we want to know how much they're paying you."

Sighing, I said, "Look boys, the only money I'm making is what Teddy's paying me to sail her yacht down here and sell it. She's a friend, and I can use the money. There's nothing more to it."

"So why isn't it sold?" Rourke picked at his nails, as if he didn't care one way or the other about my answer.

"The supposed buyer said he'd changed his mind."

"And you, an ex-cop, weren't suspicious?"

"Suspicious about what?"

Halliday leaned into my space, his blonde mop falling over his eyes. "Suspicious about why a recently widowed woman would be in such a hurry to sell the yacht she lived on. A yacht worth upwards of half-a-million dollars."

"Not really. She seemed legitimately afraid to stay at the marina after her husband was killed."

"What about the name of the boat?" asked Rourke. "That didn't make you wonder?"

"What about the name? Bernice?" I thought for a second "You mean because her name is Teddy?"

They both rolled their eyes in tandem. "No, numbnuts." Halliday crowded me again. I didn't like the space-invader to begin with, and the *numbnuts* crack just about pushed me over the edge.

Rourke raised an arm between us, easing his partner back. "Bernice is a slang, a synonym, you know, like a code word on the streets for cocaine."

"You were a cop and you didn't know that?" said Halliday.

"Hey, I never worked narcotics. And the cocaine snorting crowd didn't spend much time on my Tenderloin beat. So, no, the name of the damn boat didn't seem suspicious. And as far as having ulterior motives, I don't. These Mexicans drugged me, beat the shit out of me, and threatened my family. So, both of you can go screw off."

Their questions had been a test of sorts, and whatever I'd said seemed to tame them a bit. I guessed they needed be certain that I wasn't involved before hitting me with their terms and conditions.

"So, here's what's going to happen." Jonas and Rourke sat down on the curb next to me, like suddenly we're all partners. "First thing in the morning, you're going to get back out to the yacht and sail her back up to the harbor in Alameda. You'll do the hand-to-hand exchange with our suspect, and our case will be airtight."

Something didn't make sense. If they had removed all of the cocaine from the yacht, what was I was supposed to exchange—*hand-to-hand?* "You said that you already seized the drugs."

"All but one kilogram," said Rourke. "That's two-point-two pounds of pure cocaine. We replaced the rest of the packages with lookalikes filled with flour. In order to bring charges against our suspect, we have to have at least some real product transacted—enough to prove intent to sell."

"The authentic package will be easy for you to spot," said Halliday. "It's on the top of the load, and there'll be a tiny 'x' penned on the package right next to the smiley face stamp that's already on it."

I wavered for a minute, trying to decide whether I should tell them about my other problem.

"The guy who was supposed to buy the boat in Ensenada," I said, "He's the one responsible for drugging me and then hiding the cocaine on the--"

"Yeah, we know their drill," said Rourke. "But our only concern is what happens to the coke once it gets to the Bay Area."

"But he expects me to deliver the shipment to him in Oceanside, otherwise, he'll said he'd kill my--"

Rourke was already shaking his head. "Just bypass Oceanside and continue north to Alameda. We'll take it from there."

It was clear that Halliday and Rourke weren't interested in who drugged and beat me, or who packed the yacht full of cocaine and threatened to kill my family. They were invested in their part of it—the Bay Area connection, and only that. Front page headlines no doubt, and probable promotions for these two.

"So, you're telling me that the entire shipment of drugs is phony? And only one of the kilos of cocaine is real?"

"That's right," said Rourke.

"And you want me to pass off a bunch of flour to your suspect in Alameda?"

"Right again."

"What if I refuse?"

The agents glanced at one another, and then Halliday answered. "We still have over 500 pounds of cocaine in evidence, with your name listed on the report as the suspect. It's cocaine that you smuggled into the U.S., on a boat that was under your control. We can paint a pretty compelling picture of you—disgraced ex-cop, life in shambles, struggling financially, sees an easy opportunity to make some big money..."

"Believe me," said Rourke. "It's an easy case to prosecute, and that doesn't even count international transportation and conspiracy. If you don't do this for us, you'll be looking through steel bars for the rest of your life."

I felt a cold, insincere pat on the back.

A car horn sounded, and I looked up to see that my ride had arrived. There sat Felipé Cuevas, smiling at me through the window of his yellow and black taxi cab.

CHAPTER 25

The two agents surged from both sides as I walked to the taxi—coercing me to "do the right thing," and then threatening me with prison if I didn't. As I reached for the door of the cab, Rourke made his final pitch. "We'll be tracking you all the way up the coast, and at no time will you be in any danger."

Felipé stared straight ahead, but he eyed me in the rearview mirror as I slid into the back seat. Halliday leaned through the window and added, "So don't worry. We've got your back."

I barely nodded my response, and then Felipé eased the cab away from the curb. These are the same two guys who just sat there and watched Dylan get murdered, I thought to myself. How could I trust that they'd have my back any better than they had his?

"Where you want to go, *amigo?*" Felipé asked, his good eye still on me.

"Danny." I reached over the seat. "Danny McKenna."

We shook hands. "*Mucho gusto, Donny.*"

It was the best he could do with my Irish name, but somehow his pronunciation made me feel even more of a kinship. He studied me in the mirror like a dad who didn't want to watch his kid make a huge mistake. Or maybe he was just waiting to be told where to go.

My cell phone rang for the first time in a while, and I saw Doris' number on the screen. She started talking before I even got out a *hello.*

"Mike and I got a room at the Marriott, which, FYI, is much nicer than that sauna place of yours. Anyway, just pick us up here in the morning."

A room. Not like I really thought they'd get separate rooms, but hearing about it just pissed me off more.

"Look," I said. "I've got to meet a friend in the morning, so how about you and Prowse come to me?"

She hesitated, probably trying to figure out who I was going to meet. "Well, I guess that's okay," she said. "I'll need my coffee anyway, and we'll probably do the breakfast buffet, since it's free with the room."

I sighed. That bumped us out to at least 9 a.m., a good three hours later than when I wanted to leave. And even then, I still wasn't sure where I'd be heading. I only knew that before I left, I was going to find a way back to the banquet facility to see Patricia Uribe. With the gut-punches I was taking from my wife and the IA dweeb, Patricia had become a beacon of hope that I, too, could have a relationship. Even though the logical me knew that the woman had only let me use her phone, and may remember neither me nor the gesture.

"I'll call you in the morning to let you know where to meet," I said before disconnecting. Then, looking up at Felipé, I asked, "Do you know the Jardín Carrizalejo?"

"*Jardín Carrizalejo?*" He wrinkled his brow. "I'm sorry Donny, but this place is for *los matrimonios*. The weddings. Is not open so late in the night."

"It's okay," I said weakly. "I need to find a woman I met there, and I also need to search along the shore for my inflatable boat. Her name is Patricia Uribe."

"A beautiful name for a boat," he said.

My words had come out like a punch-drunk fighter, but I hadn't the energy to straighten them out.

Felipé continued driving in silence through the Tijuana night, with only an occasional glance over the seat to check on me. He stopped once at an all-night market, but I was in deep thought. Suddenly materializing with two cups of coffee, he started the cab and continued driving to a place on the western edge of the city called *Puente La Joya*.

He pulled into a lot just off Highway 10, and parked overlooking a field of crashing black waves. Felipé turned in his seat and took a sip of his coffee. "You are a visitor to my country, and I don't need two eyes to see that you are in some kinds of trouble, Donny. I will help you if this is possible, but even if I cannot help, I can still listen."

It was 2 a.m. when I began telling Felipé my story. I began all the way back in November of the previous year, when my career with the SFPD ended in disaster—thanks to a scurrilous police chief and an ass-kissing Internal Affairs lieutenant.

I recounted my failed marriage, described Dylan's murder, and told Felipé about my efforts to sell Teddy's yacht in Ensenada.

When I got to the part about Ozzy and Sacacorcho hiding cocaine on the boat, Felipé's paper cup paused at his lips. If he recognized the two names he didn't show it, and he continued listening without comment.

He nodded almost imperceptibly at Ozzy being given access to me in the prison. I kept talking, uninterrupted, for what seemed like hours. Doris' flowering relationship with the man who ended my career didn't seem to surprise my driver, but I detected a rueful shake of his head.

It was almost daylight when I wrapped up my pathetic tale. I had purged myself of all my sins, my stupidity, and my poor choices, yet there would be no Hail Marys to release me from the consequences of my actions.

"So, I can bypass the cartel waiting for me at the Oceanside Harbor, and then have them dispatch someone to kill me and my family. Or, I can deliver the cocaine shipment to them and face the rest of my life in a U.S. prison."

A sigh emitted from my driver as he digested the hopelessness of my options. Finally, he said, *"Me sorprende que, siendo un gato, no sepas atrapar ratones."*

Seeing me shrug in the mirror, he winked his good eye. "It is a Mexican proverb, my friend. It means, I'm amazed that being a cat, you don't know how to catch mice." Then he let out a hoarse smoker's chuckle.

It took a minute for its meaning to permeate into my emotionally wracked brain. He was right. I had been a cop at one time, a homicide detective, and a pretty good one. In Felipé's mind, I was a cat and all the others were mere mice. None of them had my level of knowledge, experience, or training. These *mice* hadn't defeated me; I had defeated myself. And just as I had gotten into this mess, I was also capable of pulling myself out of it. Marshalling my natural skillset into a clever plan is all it would take, and perhaps a little luck too.

Feeling something suddenly changing inside of me, I told myself that one way or the other I was going to regain control of my situation. And control of my life, as well.

CHAPTER 26

Felipé continued driving on the highway after our talk, following my directions to a sandy pullout near where I had stashed the inflatable. Climbing down the rocky bluff, I was relieved to find the dinghy still there—hidden beneath a bunch of dried seaweed.

I climbed back up the bluff and got into the cab. Taking me across the highway, my driver veered onto an access road that led up the hill to the Jardín Carrizalejo. I handed Felipé the little bit of cash I'd borrowed from Doris, and I thanked him for his help.

"You are a good and honest man, Donny." Felipé gripped my hand. "The *right thing*... It isn't what drug agents say for you to do; it is what you feel inside." He put his fist to my chest. "*Tu corazón.*"

I'd been naïve and foolish up to that point, relying and confiding in the wrong people for all the wrong reasons. And though I knew that I'd probably never see Felipé Cuevas again, he was on a very short list of people in my life who I trusted.

Standing on the side of the deserted highway, I savored the early morning air and thought about my plan to get out of this mess. But overshadowing the drug smuggling, the DEA indictment, and the cartel's death threats, was my torment over Doris and her boyfriend. Whether it was because of my heart or my ego, I knew I'd have to fix that problem as well.

Easing open the double glass doors, I stepped inside the event center. Unlike the last time I was there, the building was eerily quiet. I looked around and then guessed my way back to Patricia's office. Her door was partly open and a wedge of fluorescent light fell across the Saltillo tiled floor in front of it. It was like an arrow, urging me forward.

A subdued conversation was taking place inside as I tapped lightly on the doorframe.

"Sí?"

I eased the door open and smiled. "Good morning." Aware of another person sitting off to my left, my eyes were locked on Patricia. "You probably don't remember me, Miss Uribe, but a couple of days ago you--"

"Yes, of course I remember. You made a call for a taxi."

"That's right." I copped a quick glance to the left before stepping in. My immediate sense was that there was no threat, although I hadn't soaked in any more information than an old man sitting on a chair and holding some kind of vase on his lap. Back to Patricia. "Well, I never got the opportunity to thank you."

Her face looked puzzled. "You came all the way here so early in the morning to thank me?"

I nodded. "Sounds ridiculous, I know. But I was in a really bad spot, and your kindness helped me more than you can imagine. Anyway, I was just down the road picking up my boat, and I wanted to stop by and thank you."

Her big brown eyes smiled along with the rest of her face. She flashed a self-conscious look at the man in her office, then back to me. "I don't remember your name."

"I'm Danny," I said. "Danny McKenna. I don't think we got that far the last time."

She stood up behind her desk and said something in Spanish to the old man in the chair. Then, gesturing in my direction she ended the sentence with, *"Señor McKenna."*

It sounded formal—like an introduction—so I extended my hand to him.

"This is my father, Jorge Uribe." The slightly built man gripped mine with a calloused hand—weathered from hard work.

"Mucho gusto," I said, hoping that the borrowed line from my taxi driver was the appropriate response.

They both smiled, but her father's was anemic and forced, as if he could have just as easily broken into tears.

The vase was not a vase, but an urn. I was playing catch up now, with no words and few clues. Only an urn and a sad expression, which wasn't really that difficult to put together.

"My mother." Patricia motioned to the urn. "She passed away three months ago, and it's only my father and me now. We are going to scatter her ashes today."

"I'm very sorry for your..." I was beginning to sound like every impassive cop I knew: *Sorry for your loss, now how about breakfast?* "Please accept my condolences," I tried again. "As well as my apologies for interrupting."

"No, please," she said, "Can I get you some coffee?"

A moment later, the three of us sat in a semi-circle in her office, sipping from our steaming mugs.

Most of the conversation was between Patricia and me, but she occasionally translated something or other to her father. I felt a little guilty for intruding on their somber task, and even more so for taking advantage of Patricia's time and generosity.

Her father finally spoke to Patricia. It was a gentle monologue filled with soft words and long empty gazes. She was quiet for some time afterwards, then turned to me.

"My parents were married for thirty-four years," she said. "Since they were seventeen. He was just reminiscing about their courtship, when they would row his boat out to the Islas Los Coronados and catch fish."

"The Coronado Islands?" I eased forward. "Is that where you're bringing your mother's ashes?"

"Oh no. We don't own a boat," she said. "We will find a nice spot along the beach, or perhaps scatter them from the hillside over the water."

The idea had already formed in my mind, and now all I had to do was find the right words. "You know, I've got a dinghy right here at the shore, and I'm taking it out to my yacht."

"You own a yacht?"

Yes, and no. Yes, I do, in fact, own a sailboat—which you could hardly call a yacht. And no, the yacht I mentioned does not belong to me.

"Yes," I heard my voice answer. Telling myself that it was simpler than trying to explain the whole thing, I continued, "It's a fifty footer, and I have it anchored out at the Coronado Islands." My mouth was out of control now, with an apparent mind of its own. "And I am more than happy to give you and your father a ride out to scatter your mother's ashes. I mean, wouldn't it mean more to your dad to do it at her old fishing hole?"

Something about that last part hadn't come out right, but I hoped Patricia could see past the subpar wording.

She conversed with her father for a minute while I sat there sweating. I couldn't visualize how this was all going to work if he agreed to it. The one thing I did know for certain was that Patricia was breathtakingly beautiful, and her presence would drive Doris batshit.

Mr. Uribe nodded, and Patricia turned to me.

"Yes, thank you so much for your generous offer. We would love to do it."

CHAPTER 27

Doris answered on the first ring. "Danny? Where are you?"

"I told you last night, I had to see someone."

She paused. "Well, now that we've finished breakfast, where are we supposed to meet you?"

"Take a taxi south on Highway 10, to Jardín Carrizalejo. It's a short walk from there to the boat."

"What's it called?" Her voice sounded like a parrot. "I can't even pronounce that."

"Then write it down, Doris. It's an event center outside the city. Cab drivers will know where it is."

"Why do we have to meet there? Why can't we just go straight to the--"

I hung up, and boy did that feel good.

Forty-five minutes later their taxi stopped at the foot of the driveway. Patricia and Mr. Uribe followed me down the roughly paved road to greet them. I tried to hang back, walking as close to Patricia as possible and wishing that her dad had opted out of the trip.

Doris' face went blank, and I caught Prowse's eyes giving Patricia the once over. Pretending not to notice, I offered a brief group introduction starting with Patricia. "Patricia, this is Doris and Mike. Doris and Mike, this is my *very* good friend Patricia, and her father, Juan Uribe."

"Jorge," said Patricia.

"And the boat is right this way." I waved an arm over my head like a field sergeant leading his troops. The little platoon followed me along the side of the highway; Doris, then Prowse, then Patricia, and finally Mr. Uribe with his urn.

We veered off the road just north of the rocky outcropping, and I left the group on the gravel beach. After several minutes of picking off the foul smelling seaweed, I started the motor and maneuvered out and around the escarpment to the beach.

Doris stood with her hands on her hips. "Do you mean to tell me that this little thing is supposed to take us all the way to Long Beach?"

"No Doris, it's called a dinghy." I stepped into the surf and tugged the boat onto the sloping bank. "It's how one gets from the beach to one's yacht." Then I turned to Patricia. "Come Patricia, let me help you onto the inflatable."

I assisted her and her father onto the dinghy, and then I got on, letting Doris and Prowse bumble in together. *So far, so good!*

Unfortunately, I hadn't anticipated the destabilizing weight of five adults in a tiny 4-person skiff. It was an agonizing eight-mile trek through the surf, and by the time we made it there my crew seemed as if they were all on the throes of death—especially Mr. Uribe, whose frail body clung to the urn as if it was a life preserver.

But Bernice looked radiant, moored at the cove near the largest of the four islands. Long and sleek, she seesawed gently in the placid surf. I caught Prowse doing a double take, while Doris sat beside him—her mouth agape.

Prowse leaned into Doris and whispered, "The thing is probably stolen. You watch, he'll get us all thrown in jail yet."

It was then that I noticed the small round patch behind Prowse's ear. *Ha! Seasickness!*

Doris tried to stand, thinking she would be the first to step aboard. But I took Patricia's hand and helped her over the starboard gunwale and onto the yacht. Assisting Mr. Uribe next, I held the urn while he climbed aboard. Then I followed, again letting Doris and Prowse fend for themselves.

After securing the dinghy to the aft platform, I offered to stow the urn in a safe place. I put it on the bed in the forward stateroom, and then brought the Uribes some water.

Doris watched through pinched eyes, as if trying to find the tiniest flaw in the spectacle playing out before her. She finally asked, "How, exactly, do you two know each other?"

I stepped to the side of the old man. "Mr. Uribe is Patricia's father. That's how they know each other."

"Not them," snapped Doris. "You! You, and, and, Patricia." She nearly spit the 'P' out of her mouth.

"Oh," I said, feigning bemusement. "We met during a wedding at the event center—the place on the hill where the cab let you out. One thing led to another, and, anywho..." Turning back to Patricia, I asked, "Can I get you or Dad anything else?"

Patricia's expression was one of confusion, and I realized that the "*Dad*" reference may have gone too far. Moving past the stalled conversation, I stepped into the wheelhouse and started the engines.

"Prowse," I called out. "Secure the anchor for me, if it's not too much trouble."

"Uh, okay, what do I do?"

I let out an exasperated sigh. "Never mind, I'll do it."

After taking care of the anchor, I asked everyone to take a seat as I began motoring out of the cove.

The clouds and fog were starting to burn off, and I was hoping for pleasant weather. I made my way around to the leeward side of the island, where we would be protected from wind while depositing Mrs. Uribe's remains. But as I brought the yacht around the point, I saw an approaching boat—the Mexican flag flying above a machine gun turret.

I'd been so wrapped up in my little jealousy charade that I hadn't given my contraband cargo any thought. Now it was all I could think of.

I watched the military boat for a second, hoping that they were just out for a training run and would change course. But when it was clear that the gunship was headed directly toward us, I panicked. Came completely unhinged.

"Take the wheel, Prowse!"

He looked at me with shock, like I'd handed him a scalpel and ordered him to remove the tumor.

"Take the damn wheel!" I jumped down the hatch, grunting loudly as I wrenched my bad knee. Then I called up to him, "Just head away from the islands, and do whatever you can to avoid that boat."

Turning in circles, I frantically tried to figure out what to do next. Limping into the forward stateroom and around the far side of the bed, I saw that the two DEA morons had left the screwdriver sitting out in the open on the nightstand. I used it to quickly unscrew the three vertical sets of finishing screws holding the teak wall in place.

Someone was making their way down the steps, probably Doris or Patricia, but I needed more time. I yelled, "Stay up top. I'm using the bathroom."

Nearly spiraling into a grand mal seizure, I violently tore into the heavy trash bags holding the packaged kilos of fake cocaine. They all looked the same.

Vibrations from the other boat's motor echoed off the hull, as the waves from its approach pitched me back and forth. I knew they were nearly on top of us.

Which one of these was the real cocaine? I couldn't remember what Halliday had said. *Was it the one with the smiley face stamp on it? No, they all had the stamps.*

I found one marked with the X sitting right on top. It was the key to the DEA's case against their suspect in Alameda, but I knew it was about to be the key to the Mexican government's case against me.

Speaking of the DEA, where in the hell are those guys? I thought they said they'd have my back.

Grabbing a pillow from the bed, I whipped off its outer case. Then I tore open the authentic drug package and poured the cocaine into the pillowcase. The genuine coke was snow white, pure and shiny, like finely ground salt. I had to get rid of it, quickly.

Now what?

Spotting the urn full of ashes on the rumpled bedding, I had a sudden inspiration. An idea that would make me both a genius and an asshole at the same time.

Cranking the lid off, I started dumping Mother Uribe into the empty cocaine wrapper. The ashes were chunky and gray, and they left a powdery haze lingering in the room. I felt really badly, as if the old woman was somehow watching me desecrate her remains. Trying to pour the rest of her into the bag with reverence, but also quickly, I think I was only able to accomplish the latter.

In my frenzied angst, I had inadvertently torn the hell out of the plastic casing—but there was little I could do about it now. I hobbled back up to the wheelhouse to find some tape. Prowse was up there doing his best, under Doris' direction, to keep the yacht straight and away from the island's shoreline. He looked about as ashen as Mrs. Uribe, and I could tell that his seasickness patch was no longer doing the trick. *Good!*

By that time the military boat was upon us. A blaring squawk emitted from a bullhorn, as the boat drew abreast of the yacht. I found some tape in a utility drawer and quickly hobbled back down to the stateroom.

I could hear Patricia telling Prowse to shut off the engines before they started shooting. Praying for another minute or two, I worked furiously while trying to stay on my feet. It also crossed my mind that Prowse might have trouble figuring out how to power down the engines, and I hoped that if the gunboat did start shooting they would aim for him.

Slapping a wad of silver tape over the feeble looking kilo of human remains, I wedged it back into the stack with the others. Not only was Mrs. Uribe not going to be scattered over her favorite spot in the sea, but she was going to spend all of eternity duct taped in a plastic bag behind the cartel's smiley face stamp.

As I heard the engine shut down, I knelt on my good knee and furiously tried to screw the wall back into place. Sweat dripped from my head as the soldiers boarded the yacht directly above me. I still hadn't gotten them all in.

Fumbling with the last of the screws, I listened as they moved toward the companionway.

It was too late.

CHAPTER 28

Heavy footsteps trudged down the companionway as I drove the final finishing screw into the hole. I quickly tossed the screwdriver under a pile of clothes, then dove across the room.

Crashing onto the bed, I rolled to face the door just as the officer rounded the corner. I yawned and stretched, as if I'd been woken from a nap.

"Hi there," I said. "Is there a problem?"

"Is this your vessel?" His English was clear.

I explained that I'd piloted it down to sell for a friend, but that the deal had fallen through.

"Who are these other people on the boat?" he asked.

"Just friends." I smiled politely.

"Papers." He said, glancing around the cabin. "Passport, Mexican insurance, tourist card, and temporary import permit."

My mouth was as dry as if I'd eaten a cigar. I was afraid my eyes might unintentionally glance at the false wall and give the whole thing away. "They're in the wheelhouse," I said, guiding him back up the stairs.

Two younger soldiers stood guard over Doris, Prowse, and the Uribes.

The officer glanced at the papers and then at the two women. "Which one is the owner, Theodora Langdon?"

"Mrs. Langdon couldn't come," I said. "Which is why she asked me to sail her boat down here."

He looked at me as if more of an answer was required.

"Uh, unfortunately there was a death in her family." *Always keep your answers as brief as possible*—a rule I learned as a rookie testifying in court. The officer stared into me, waiting. "Her husband died, and he was also a good friend of mine."

I hadn't broken my rule too badly, but it was definitely more than I'd wanted to say. He made the sign of the cross, lowered his eyes and said, *"Mi más sentido pésame."*

Lowering my eyes too, I tried to look distraught.

"His remains are in the urn down below deck?" the officer asked.

My stomach lurched again. I was sure that my eyes or my mouth were somehow going to give this thing away. *No, sir. The urn actually has 2.2-pounds of cocaine in it.*

Patricia said something to the officer, thankfully redirecting his attention onto her. He seemed only too happy to talk with such an attractive woman. They conversed in Spanish, and I supposed that she was explaining the loss of her mother. Patricia even introduced her father, and again, the sign of the cross and condolences were offered—although only the gestures were intelligible to me.

The soldier suddenly went below deck and returned with the urn, again throwing me into panic mode. With a bow, he handed it to Mr. Uribe and a long conversation ensued. I fully expected that at any minute he would order the urn to be opened.

A tense few minutes passed. Doris and Prowse sat wordless while Patricia and the soldier conversed. Patricia must have seen my expression of worry, because she halted the discussion so that she could translate for me.

"He's saying that they can't allow my mother's ashes to be emptied into the sea. Anti-pollution laws prohibit such actions without a permit."

"What about all those pipes emptying raw sewage into the ocean?" I motioned toward the coast. "How come the Mexican military isn't so concerned about them?"

"These men are not actually military," Patricia said, completely missing my point. "Their Coast Guard detachment is here on the island. Officially, they are called *Search and Rescue Unit*."

I thanked them, and then told Patricia, "Let them know that we don't need rescuing."

The English-speaking officer frowned while Patricia translated for the younger soldiers. A lengthy discussion between the three soldiers followed, during which someone set the urn on the deck. It wobbled and teetered with each wave, and I wondered which would give out first, the urn or my heart.

Unable to handle the anxiety any longer, I burst across the deck and grabbed the damn thing before it toppled over. Then, cradling it against my sweatshirt like a recovered fumble, I looked around at the hushed group. "I didn't want it to break," I said meekly.

Patricia and her father seemed thankful for my efforts, but Prowse and the Coast Guard officers looked at me like I'd gone crazy. Doris, on the other hand, watched me in dubious silence.

As I sat against the bulkhead cradling the urn between my legs, I realized that I was drawing too much attention to myself and the urn.

In a cold sweat, I watched as more negotiation ensued between Patricia and the ranking officer. At one point Patricia took some pesos from her purse and passed them to the officer. He nodded at her, and she nodded to her father. Realizing I'd just witnessed how things are done in Mexico, I struggled to my feet and handed the urn to Mr. Uribe.

Again my heart lurched, as I became aware of a faint powdery dust on my sweatshirt and pants. Apparently, cocaine shavings had stuck to the rim of the urn when I'd mashed the kilogram block into it. As slyly as humanly possible, I tried to brush them off as I moved to the bow. Still trying to bolster my image with Patricia, I solemnly held the urn as her father removed the lid.

Everybody, including the three soldiers, gathered around him in reverence, but I felt like I was suffering a massive stroke.

Queasy from the anticipation of what was about to go very wrong, I steadied myself against the bowsprit to keep from collapsing onto the deck. The rest of them were completely engaged, with the exception of Doris, maybe, who eyed me the entire time.

Patricia said a few words, first in Spanish and then repeated them in English. "Those who have lived a good life do not fear death, but meet it calmly, and even long for it in the face of great suffering."

Mr. Uribe then made a comment, which I assumed was a tribute to his wife, but I didn't understand it and it was not translated. The ranking officer and his two minions put their hands over their hearts as Mr. Uribe, steadied by Patricia, held the urn over the bow.

Slowly, a few powdery crystals fluttered into the water. Not much more than a tablespoon though. Patricia's father lifted the urn higher, and finally upended it all the way.

With a hallow *whump*, a large rectangular loaf of crystalline white powder slid out the end of the urn and plopped into the sea.

The soldiers' eyes all widened and their mouths dropped open as they watched the snowy blob drift on the surf beneath us. I wanted to grab a boat-hook and dunk the damn thing, but instead I had to stand there in silence, about to pass out.

The Coast Guard men pointed and jabbered excitedly for a second. Probably about the shape, consistency, and whiteness of the dead woman's ashes. Maybe they'd seen enough of the stuff to know exactly what it was. After what seemed like several minutes, the cakey block of cocaine dissipated into a cloudy wave and was swept away forever.

I quickly placed my hand on Mr. Uribe's shoulder. "She must have led a pure life," I said. Then, clasping my hands together, I turned to the rest of the group. "And so she returns from whence she came."

I'd heard it once at a service, and it seemed the perfect wrap-up for the occasion. I mainly wanted to hustle the Coast Guard guys on their way.

It seemed that something had given them pause though, and the soldiers were not as eager to leave as I would have liked. The senior officer made a call, and then used a turned shoulder to shield us from his conversation. Considering all of the possibilities, I realized that it could only be bad for me. Something about the way he was gesturing and then glancing in my direction... it was getting worse by the minute.

Maybe it was my own paranoia, but I had the distinct feeling he was talking with Ozzy. After all, the asshole did claim to be connected with everybody down here.

The officer ended the call and turned toward us—looking over the group as if assessing a class of recruits. Nobody but me seemed to notice that the vibe had suddenly changed.

"Atención!" He barked the words, and I knew my goose was cooked. "Señors y señoras, I am sorry to inform you that this boat is being seized for inspection on authority of the Mexican government."

Whether the urn's contents or the suspicious phone call had triggered the change of heart, what seemed to confuse the rest of my crew was crystal clear to me. The soldiers knew what I was up to.

Now, what was I going to do about it? We were close enough to smell freedom—only a few nautical miles shy of U.S. territorial waters. So close in fact, that the Coronado Islands are often mistaken as U.S. territory.

I'd seen a documentary a few years back about L. Ron Hubbard—an American Naval officer and later founder of the Church of Scientology. Under the mistaken belief that the barren archipelago belonged to us, Hubbard got himself into hot water when he and his crew mortared the holy hell out of the place. Cost him his job, I think.

A low murmur circulated through my guests as they tried to make sense of what was happening. Meanwhile, I tried to come up with a quick plan of action. We were outgunned and outmanned, and I knew that the Coast Guard vessel could move a lot faster than Bernice.

The two young soldiers followed the officer across the jumbled knot of lines lying on the deck, and climbed over the port bow onto their patrol boat. They had tethered our two boats together, and it was difficult to tell my docklines from theirs.

The senior officer spoke to Patricia in Spanish, then glanced at me again before getting behind the wheel of the Coast Guard boat.

Patricia looked up somberly. "We are to follow them to a port on the mainland immediately."

A brilliant idea suddenly played out in my mind's eye, but only a narrow window of opportunity would exist to put it into action. And that narrow window was opening right now.

"I'll untie your docklines," I yelled to the officer as I sprung up and over toward the port bow.

That's when I made my move.

CHAPTER 29

Working quickly to untie their line, I listened as the officer snapped commands to his two underlings. I sensed everyone's eyes on me as they started their motor.

"One second." I held up a hand. "The lines are all tangled." Which they were, but I was also using it to my advantage.

I'd noticed the Kedge line laying among the mess of rope. The DEA duo had apparently left it in a heap after they pulled up all the cocaine. It was easy to differentiate from the other lines, because it had a distinctive blue strand woven through its braiding.

Hurrying to tie the Kedge line to the Coast Guard boat's dockline, I turned to Doris and Prowse. "Pull up the main anchor." I pointed with my chin toward the stern, where a single ½ inch white line snaked over the aft transom. "Quickly," I added. An electric wench can easily raise the anchor with the flip of a switch in the pilothouse, but I wanted them to lift it by hand.

"One more second," I shouted to the Mexicans. Then I made like I was coiling all their docklines, which was really just buying more time. I chuckled to myself as I heard my wife and her idiot friend grunting with each tug of the water saturated line.

The senior officer was getting more irritated by the minute, as I could tell that whatever he was saying to his men was full of red hot expletives—some of the same words that I'd heard Ozzy and The Corkscrew saying about me.

Finally, I saw the chain *rode* of the anchor line, and I knew that Doris and Prowse were down to the last few fathoms.

"Here you go," I said, tossing the coil of dockline over to the patrol boat. It was a load of rope, and I hoped they wouldn't notice that one end of it trailed over their bow into the water. From there, it dipped below the waterline before snaking up and onto my boat.

Unknown to anyone else, I had tied the loose end of their rope to my Kedge anchor. With my main anchor now being lifted over the gunwale, and the Coast Guard boat starting to pull away, I quickly hefted the Kedge over the side and dropped it into the sea.

One of the junior soldiers spotted his coiled dockline rapidly unraveling at his feet, and his eyes grew wide. He stood in shock, watching the line play out as their patrol boat retreated. I saw his perplexed expression as his eyes followed the line across the water to the splash of my Kedge anchor. It was like a funny social media video: *Wait for it...*

But I didn't have time to wait for it. Even though it would take time for them to haul up the anchor and all the line, my little ruse was no more than a banana in the tailpipe. They'd figure it out and come after me.

Bolting across the deck and into the pilothouse, I fired up the engines and dropped Bernice into gear. The power of the duel diesels nearly threw Doris and the sock monkey over the back of the boat, while Patricia clung tightly to her haggard father. None of my crew had the slightest idea what I'd done, but they soon would.

I cranked the wheel hard to the portside, heading northbound toward the retreating fog bank. My mind raced to figure out the Coast Guard's next moves. Would they try to pursue me with the Kedge anchor dragging along the rocky bottom? Or would they spend the valuable minutes trying to raise the anchor, hand-over-hand? I figured the entire *rode* to be close to 50 fathoms, which meant that the two young goons would have to pull up 100 yards of wet rope. It would take even longer if the anchor had set itself on the bottom. *But how long would it take me to get us into U.S. waters?*

As the Coast Guard patrol boat faded into gray, I was again left to navigate blindly in the fog at high speed. If I didn't slam into one of the islands or another boat, I'd probably run into Ozzy or the DEA.

"What in the hell are you doing, McKenna?" Prowse tried to sound assertive. "Didn't you hear them? We're supposed to follow their vessel to the closest port."

I looked back at my passengers and saw on their faces that it had finally sunken in. They may not have understood the reason I was fleeing, but they definitely knew I was making a break for it.

Patricia's usually soft voice came with a decisive warning. "These men have guns, Mr. McKenna, and they won't hesitate to use them."

Holding up a palm to calm everybody, I said, "Don't worry about that. I did something to slow them down and give us time to get across the--"

My sales pitch was interrupted by the bark of heavy gunfire. It was close, too, and I couldn't figure out why. Dragging the anchor should have bought us more time. Then it dawned on me that they had simply cut the line and continued after us.

How could I not have seen that coming?

"Danny!" screamed Doris as she pointed over the starboard bow.

Ahead and off to the right, the dingy water roiled foamy white, as if a school of sardines had surfaced. But the bubbles weren't caused by fish, they were bullets. And then came the horrifying realization that even in this thick fog they could track our exact location on their radar. *Son-of-a-bitch!*

"Do something," Doris cried.

"I am." Pushing the throttle as far as it would go, the forward bow tilted a few more degrees into the air as the yacht lurched ahead.

Doris hollered, "I meant go back. Turn yourself in before we're all killed."

"That's why McKenna took all of us along," yelled Prowse. "We're his human shield!"

I wanted to bitch slap the guy, but I needed both hands on the wheel due to the vibrations. The hull slammed hard into each swell, and the pounding felt as if the yacht would disintegrate—but I wasn't about to go back. My head ached and my jaw shook so hard that I thought I'd chipped a tooth. Poor Mr. Uribe looked as if he was about to join his wife. They were all yelling at me, but I couldn't make out the words over the screaming engine and the wild surf.

"Where in the hell is the border?" I mumbled to myself, sounding like the kid in my second grade class with a speech impediment.

Ping! A round ricocheted off a metal cleat right next to me. Then a thud against the fiberglass roof. I glanced up and saw the murky sky through a pencil sized hole in the roof. Cranking the wheel sharply, I began a zig-zagging maneuver, hoping to evade the shower of bullets.

Glancing back, I saw that my passengers were okay. Banged up a bit, but at least nobody had been struck by gunfire or had gone overboard. They clung tightly to the railing, except Prowse, who was working his way toward the cockpit. I noticed that he had picked up the *priest*—a wooden mallet that fishermen use to clobber fish. Only he was clearly coming to clobber me. A real life mutineer, right here on the Bernice.

"Stay back," I yelled. "Or I swear I'll knock your ass overboard and leave you to the sharks."

"Get back here Michael," yelled Doris. That felt good, like maybe she was taking my side. But then she added, "Danny's crazy enough to do it."

"Doris!" I yelled. "Throw that thing overboard."

Tossing the mallet into the water, she closed the storage locker where Prowse had found it, and slid the seat cushion back into place.

Prowse, looking dejected, settled back into his spot next to my wife. I wondered if he really had the guts to attack me, or if his sudden flash of *cojones* was just another act to impress her.

Meanwhile, the Uribes looked like a couple of kidnap victims. I figured that at any moment, the urn would come crashing down on my head. I tried to mouth *I'm sorry* to Patricia, but she ignored me and continued tending to her father. Doris had witnessed my silent apology to Patricia, and she turned away as well—though with a tad more malice. I couldn't explain any of this to her, or to Patricia for that matter, without telling them about the drugs and the rest of the story.

"Behind us!" Doris bellowed. "They're catching up!"

Without looking back, I weaved the boat again. *We should have reached the border by now.*

More bubbles erupted in the water around us, and what sounded like an ice storm pelting the roof and deck. I finally stole a quick glance over my shoulder, just in time to see the dark hull of the Coast Guard patrol boat bearing down on us from the fog bank.

Running from these guys might not have been one of my better ideas, I thought. Somehow, I had miscalculated the whole thing—the Kedge slowing them down, the distance to U.S. waters, and even the cooperation of my crew. At that point, I considered throwing in the towel.

Then Prowse bellowed, "Look out!"

CHAPTER 30

The monstrous blue and white trawler emerged from the mist like a giant iceberg, seemingly motionless—taking up my entire field of view. My foot automatically stomped on an imaginary brake pedal, which of course, wasn't there. Then I throttled back on the engine and cut the steering wheel hard to the right. A more seasoned pilot would have known that a boat needs forward motion in order to turn. Another dumbshit move on my part.

Slamming the throttle forward again, my yacht lurched hard to starboard. The sounds of falling bodies and shattered glass crept into my awareness, but I had no time to check my passengers. My eyes were fixed on the huge fishing trawler that I was trying to avoid.

Everything suddenly went into slow-motion, and I could almost hear the lookout calling from the Titanic's crow's nest: *Iceberg, dead ahead!*

My eyes must have bugged out of my head as I peered over the bow, following my boat's trajectory as it buzzed the trawler with only inches to spare.

The Mexican Coast Guard guys must have seen the fishing boat on their radar, and had already slowed their speed. It gave me a few more seconds of lead time, but I knew that wouldn't be enough. The gunship would be back on top of me in less than a minute.

Taking a quick glance back at the fishing vessel I had narrowly missed, I saw the boat's name stenciled in big black letters across its stern: SEAS THE DAY.

The cleverness of the name was lost on me. I cared less about seizing the day, and more about just living through it. Then it dawned on me that the boat's name was an Americanized play on words. Which meant that it was a U.S. fishing boat. Which also meant that we had crossed the border into U.S. territorial waters.

Looking over my shoulder, I saw the pursuing Coast Guard captain had also figured out the boundary line and was turning back. The fishing trawler sat placidly, oblivious to its role in nearly killing us and then saving us.

"We're all good," I called to my passengers.

Doris and Prowse were in a dogpile on the deck, and Patricia had a death grip on her father. The decorative urn that once held Mrs. Uribe's remains was in pieces—the only real casualty suffered during the incident. That is, other than the damage to my shriveling respectability.

I saw in their eyes that whatever trust they may have had was gone—swallowed by my frenzied escape, the hail of bullets, the near collision, the bumps and bruises, all of it. The shattered urn only symbolized my failures, and there was no way to rebuild my reputation without telling the truth about my pact with the devil— Ozzy, and his cartel. But I couldn't do that. And in the end, ensuring that my daughter was safe with her grandmother carried more weight than the fuzzy affirmations of my rebellious crew. Still, I had to come up with something, a reason as to why I felt compelled to run.

We were moving slower, more comfortably, and bits of sunlight had started to peek through the clouds closer to shore. "I owe you all an apology," I said, turning to my disgruntled shipmates. "I know you are all wondering why we had to take... evasive maneuvers."

"Evasive maneuvers?" repeated Prowse, as if he was about to lay into me.

"Pipe down, Prowse." I pointed a finger at him. "I've got the floor." Then addressing the others again, "I know firsthand the way things work down here. No disrespect to Patricia and her father, but the Mexican police have already framed me once for something I didn't do. I wasn't about to let it happen again. Not to me, and not to the rest of you. Other than bringing dear Mrs. Uribe to her final resting place without the proper permits, we've done nothing wrong."

Doris rolled her eyes.

"May I speak?" Patricia raised a hand. "I know you mean well, and my father and I appreciate all that you've done, but we've now crossed into the United States, and that makes us illegals."

It was a fair point, and one I hadn't considered.

"I've already thought of that," I lied. Then, thinking quickly, I added, "And I have a good friend in the U.S. Customs. She will be able to help with all of that."

"Help with all of what?" Patricia looked confused.

"Help getting you and your father into the country legally, at least on a temporary visa or something."

Her brow arched sharply and then came together. "We don't want to go to the United States. Isn't there some way you can return us to Jardín Carrizalejo where I work?"

Now I was confused. "Why would you want to go back there?"

"Because that's where my car is parked." Patricia's expression was one of innocence, of faith, of loyalty. I knew that out of everybody onboard the yacht, she was probably the only one on my side. "And, if I could add one thing, Mr. McKenna. I overheard those Search and Rescue men talking among themselves, and they seemed to have evidence that you are a drug smuggler."

Humph. Little Patricia isn't quite as faithful and loyal as she comes off. I waved my hand dismissively. "See? What did I tell you?" I glanced around at all of them. "Framed again. This is exactly why we had to--"

"I don't know about the rest of you," interrupted Prowse, "but I don't buy a word of this bullshit. I'm keeping a list of each and every violation of maritime law, McKenna. And I'm getting off at the first port we come to so I can report it all to the federal authorities."

"Whatever." It was all I had the energy to say at that point.

Steering the boat northeast, I worked my way on a course that took us closer to shore. Emerging momentarily into the sunlight, I realized that the scant border demarcation indicators were just behind us and to my right. The only real landmark was an ugly timber and chain linked fence that meandered down the sandy dunes into the ocean. Just beyond it, directly off our starboard side, sat a dismal coastline parcel called *International Friendship Park*. It appeared neither friendly nor parklike, but at least I knew that we were now officially in the United States.

"Please, Mr. McKenna," Patricia pleaded. "Take my father and me back."

I wanted to help her return, but I wasn't going to risk crossing back into Mexico to do it. "Do you think between you and your father you can manage the skiff?"

"The what?"

"The little inflatable boat." I pointed to the dinghy tied onto the stern.

Doris piped up. "You're not thinking of leaving the poor girl and her father out here in the ocean to fend for themselves, are you?"

Now my wife is on her side?

"No, Doris. I'm going to pull the yacht as close to shore as I can. They'll be near enough to motor along the coastline back to where they're going."

"What if they get caught crossing into Mexico?" she asked. "Have you thought of that?"

I let out a long sigh. "Nobody's looking for people going in that direction. Who the hell wants to sneak *into* Mexico?"

The look on Patricia's face told me that my last remark likely cost me her support. Prowse shook his head, disgusted, and Doris gave me a face that said, *Nice one!*

I ignored both of them and went about readying the dinghy. After untying it and sliding it into the water, I brought it up even with the side of the boat.

First assisting Mr. Uribe into it, I then held out my hand to help Patricia. She reluctantly took it, and then let go as soon as she stepped into the inflatable. I had hoped to have a private word with her, but it wasn't in the cards. As soon as I started the motor for them, she took hold of the throttle and began to pull away. I had to jump aboard Bernice in order to keep from toppling into the sea.

I felt a little down about Patricia leaving in such a state, especially when we had gotten along so well. But in reality, whatever connection we had was more of a fantasy to counterbalance the relationship that Doris was rubbing in my face. Still, as waves of fog dissipated along the coast, I found myself wondering if I'd ever even see Patricia again.

CHAPTER 31

Timewise, we were still doing okay. With three hours to go before Oceanside, I planned to arrive at the meeting spot with enough time to eat something before the big drug exchange—which wasn't really a *drug exchange* at all, since I had only a half-ton of flour, and wouldn't be receiving anything in return—except, hopefully, my life.

"What now?" Doris asked, rousting me from my thoughts. "Don't we have to go through Customs or something?"

The answer would have been *yes,* but I doubted that the DEA guys would risk my being boarded and searched. Hoping that they had somehow smoothed the way for me, I finally realized that I couldn't depend on their help with that any more than with the Mexican Coast Guard. *Sure, they've got my back.*

"San Diego." I pointed eastward, trying to sound sure of myself. "We have to report our entry to CBP."

Prowse whispered something to Doris.

"Feel free to get off here," I told him.

I'd seen the reporting requirements on Teddy's notes. Which, the more I thought about it, didn't make sense. If she had expected me to sell her yacht and take a flight back, why would she leave notes about reporting my return by boat? It was further confirmation that I'd been duped.

About a hundred yards off to my right, a dark silhouette emerged from behind a rocky outcropping. It was a small inflatable with two people aboard, and it was heading northbound across our path.

Prowse stood and pointed. "Isn't that your friend and her father?"

Doris squinted toward the little dinghy and shook her head. "I told you they'd get lost out here."

Doris' snarky remarks aside, I had to wonder how Patricia managed to motor five miles in the wrong direction. Regardless, it was one of those good/bad situations for me; good because I'd be able to play the part of Patricia's hero rescuer, and bad because I would now have two illegals onboard when I reported in at the Customs and Border Protection office.

I thought about simply pointing them in the right direction and hoping for the best, but by now the dinghy was probably low on fuel. At least that's what I told myself. In reality, my desire to spend more time with Patricia, and at the same time tweak Doris, nearly outweighed the risk of getting caught. Besides, having two illegals onboard was the leverage I needed to keep Prowse's mouth shut.

Gazing toward a gap of sunlight, I saw a clear path into the San Diego harbor. *Twenty minutes*, I thought to myself. That's about how long I'll have to get Patricia to go along with my scheme.

Bernice came to a bobbing stop and Patricia helped her father aboard. "I think I became confused in the fog," she said. "Are we still in America?"

"Yes." I tied off the dinghy. "And I'm so sorry that I didn't provide better directions. I've been worried sick about you making it to shore safely." I didn't look back, but I knew Doris was rolling her eyes again.

Mr. Uribe was shivering, and both were damp from the spray. "Come below and we'll get you warmed up," I said. Then turning to Prowse and Doris, I asked, "Do you think between the two of you, you can secure the inflatable to the aft platform?"

I ushered the Uribes down the companionway without waiting for a response. Once below deck, I gave them blankets and boiled some water for coffee.

"Are you going to bring us back into Mexico?" Patricia asked.

"Yes and no," I said, motioning her into the forward stateroom. "I'll explain in a minute, but first I have something to show you."

Finding the screwdriver in a drawer, I set about unscrewing the teak wallboard. As the panel came loose exposing the cache, Patricia's mouth dropped open.

Her father stepped up behind Patricia and whispered something over her shoulder.

"The Search and Rescue men were right about you," she said.

"No Patricia, they weren't. This isn't what it seems." I reached over and closed the door so Doris and Prowse wouldn't hear the story I was about to tell her.

My wife and her skin tag had secured the dinghy, and we got back underway. The fog had completely cleared, and the entrance to San Diego Bay came into view—Coronado Beach and the Naval Air Station on the nearside of the mouth, and Cabrillo Monument set high on Point Loma on the far side. I'd asked Patricia and Mr. Uribe to keep out of sight in the forward stateroom, so it was just me, Doris, and the idiot on deck as we entered the harbor.

"You really think you're going to get away with this?" said Prowse. "You're in the states now pal, and you can't bribe your way out of this one."

"He's right." It was Doris' turn to peck. "Smuggling illegals across the border won't be taken lightly if Customs find them on your boat."

Prowse shot her a look. "What do you mean *if* they find them? I'm going to lead the agents right downstairs to your little *wetback* friends."

"I don't think you want to do that," I said.

"And why wouldn't I?"

"First off, because this isn't my boat. As far as the authorities know, it could be under the control of any one of us."

"You wouldn't dare implicate me." He glanced between Doris and me. "It would be your word against ours." He gave another quick look at Doris, and I saw concern in his eyes. *Would she cave and support the ex-husband?*

I smiled. "I'm talking about Patricia and her father. They're going to tell the immigration agents that it was you who smuggled them into the country, not me. Which means, it's three against two. Or, maybe four against one." I winked at Doris just for effect, but she only glared back.

"They'll never make it stick." Prowse nervously reached an arm around Doris. "I have an alibi. We were on a cruise ship."

"But they'll still lock you up until they can sort it all out," I said. "And they'll have to notify SFPD. Which, my friend, will be a turd on your record and a stink on what's left of your career." I forced a confident laugh, like I had the whole thing figured out. "You can kiss your promotion to captain goodbye. They'll have you passing out car keys at the motor pool until the day you retire."

In truth, it was another good/bad situation I'd gotten myself into. The good was that Doris never said a word. I couldn't tell if she was on Prowse's side or not, but if her support for him wasn't clear to me, it definitely wasn't clear to him. On the other hand, Patricia never agreed to lie to the authorities about Prowse. Even after I explained how Ozzy and The Corkscrew set me up, and that I'd brought the drugs to the Embassy in Tijuana, she still wouldn't do it. "I go to church every Sunday," Patricia had said, her eyes downcast and reverent. "And I pray to the Virgin each night. It would be wrong for me to tell a lie, even to help prove your innocence."

Patricia had taken my hand and gently squeezed it. "I wish I could help you," she said. "You are a good man."

At least there was that.

CHAPTER 32

Teddy's notes said that vessels under 130 feet must report directly to the Harbor Police Dock and immediately contact CBP by dialing *82 on the dock telephone.

The sunshine and light breeze was perfect sailing weather, and along with all the pleasure crafts on the bay, there were a number of Navy boats on the water. One of them, a rigid-hulled inflatable, cruised slowly behind us as we entered the harbor.

With my stowaways hidden below, I eased the yacht up to the police dock and stopped at the section painted white. A harbor cop watched from an office window as I secured the boat and walked up the ramp to the dock phone. With each step I imagined that I was being profiled: *White male, late thirties, crossing from Mexico in an expensive yacht;* which would undoubtedly equate to a huge stash of cocaine and two illegal aliens hidden below decks.

Nervously reporting our arrival to the woman on the other end of the line, I was instructed to remain aboard the vessel until a CBP officer arrived to clear us.

Seems pretty standard, I assured myself. Probably happens a hundred times a day. As long as I don't raise any red flags, they'll just look at my paperwork, check our passports, and we'll be on our way.

A uniformed Customs officer showed up right away—a woman in her 30s. She stood on the dock beside the yacht, glancing at me, Doris, and Prowse. "Where are you folks coming from today?" Friendly, but businesslike.

I told her that we'd spent the weekend in Ensenada, opting not to complicate the answer with unnecessary details.

"Just the three of you?"

"Yep," I said, again keeping my response simple.

It seemed to work, because she breezed through the documents and checked our passports without becoming aroused.

"Anything to declare?"

"Nope." I smiled as she started to hand back my papers.

Vaguely aware of a boat idling behind me, I assumed that it was another pleasure craft waiting to report in.

"Ahoy," came a booming voice.

I cringed, not wanting to even turn around and look. It was Naval Officer T. Martin and his merry band of SEALS, in the same raft that had followed us into the bay. "Ever figure out how to turn on those nav lights?" he asked with a laugh.

Martin seemed affable enough now, unlike the night I nearly ran over his team. But his timing couldn't have been worse. I gave a terse wave, and tried to quickly wrap things up with the Customs woman.

"You know these guys?" she asked Martin, slowly retracting the hand that held our passports.

"That one," he said, motioning to me. "Not the other two. A few nights ago we had a *run-in*, you could say."

"Oh?" said the Customs agent. "What sort of run-in?"

My heart was pumping fear into every part of my body, and all I could do was stand there with a dumb look on my face.

"He was underway with his navigation lights off," Martin said. "Nearly motored over my men during a training exercise."

"Is that a fact?" She was no longer looking at me through the *routine border crossing* lens. With a frown, she asked me, "Why were you traveling into Mexico at night without running lights?" Then, before I could answer, she said, "And didn't you just tell me that the three of you traveled to Ensenada together?"

"No, no, no," interjected Prowse. "*We* were on a cruise," he said, motioning between he and Doris. "The only reason we're even with this guy is because he got himself into trouble in Tijuana. He asked us to come bail him out of jail."

Thanks for that, asshole. I had suddenly become the sole focus of everyone's attention—Prowse, my wife, the navy guy, and the CBP officer—all of whom stared at me as if waiting for a response that would clarify everything. But I had none to offer.

A childhood nursery rhyme suddenly played in my head: *Hi-ho the derry-o, the cheese stands alone.*

The CBP officer said something into her shoulder mic, and having been a cop, myself, I recognized the code requesting backup. Then, to me she asked, "So, what sort of trouble did you get into while you were in Tijuana?"

I shook my head. "It was nothing really, just little a mix-up."

She turned to Prowse, probably thinking that he knew the reason. Prowse shrugged. "For all I know, he was doing the Pee-wee Herman at a donkey show."

Out of the corner of my eye, I saw Doris elbow Prowse in the ribs. *At least there was that.*

I gave Prowse a discreet raised eyebrow and nod toward the boat. It was my silent warning to keep his mouth closed, otherwise I'd make good on my threat to expose him as the smuggler. It was a weak bluff, but it was all I had. Thankfully, Prowse piped down.

The dock suddenly rocked with the weight of a second CBP officer and his canine. My batting average with drug dogs wasn't so good, and I knew that it was about to get worse.

I've had dogs sniff me before, and everyone knows that they often go for the crotch. But a drug detection canine who smells cocaine on your pants... let's just say that the dog needed a cigarette when he was finished with me. And I could tell that the encounter, as uncomfortable as it was, left no doubt in the border cops' minds that I was Public Enemy number one. The kingpin. Pablo Escobar, right there in the San Diego Harbor.

We were immediately detained—me seated on the dock in handcuffs, and Doris and Prowse unrestrained and allowed to sit comfortably on a bench. Prowse kept shaking his head at me, but Doris just stared. It was as if she'd always thought I was a screw-up, but it never really sunk in until that moment.

The officer waved to Martin, who was still seesawing in the bay. He signaled back, and then he and his SEAL team motored away.

We were led into the Customs Office, which wasn't anything like the district stations in San Francisco. The place could have just as easily been a real estate or insurance storefront. They left me handcuffed to one of several wooden chairs that lined one wall.

The canine cop had followed us inside, and both he and the woman were checking their computers to see if I was wanted or had a record. Meanwhile, Doris and Prowse took turns giving me dirty looks while they enjoyed free coffee and a selection of magazines.

All I could think of was that my plan would have worked, had we been allowed to continue up the coast to Oceanside. Now, thanks to Prowse and his big mouth, I was about to go to jail for the second time in as many days.

After what seemed like hours, I was anxious, claustrophobic, and I had to take a leak. The dog guy moved my handcuffs to the front and then escorted me to the restroom. When I was finished, I overheard the two officers mention something about a search. Since they had already checked me stem-to-stern, I knew they had to be talking about the yacht. The woman officer had been on the phone, and I guessed she was organizing a team to do a full vessel inspection. Though I knew they wouldn't find any drugs, 250 kilos of fake coke hidden in the wall might generate a few questions.

And then there were the Uribes, still hiding in the stateroom. Finding them, would permanently seal my fate. I was certain that the feds would impound the boat and impound me.

Figuring that it was as good a time as any play my last card, I asked the CBP woman, "Mind if I make a phone call?"

"Not until we're finished," snapped the dog guy.

The woman watched me for a second, then said, "Just out of curiosity, who do you want to call?"

"A friend who works with you guys." I dipped my chin downward, toward my pants pocket. "Her number is programmed in my cell... which is now saturated in dog slobber."

She chuckled, but the canine handler just glared.

"What's her name?" she asked. "This so-called *friend* of yours?"

"Sarah Brooks."

CHAPTER 33

Sarah Brooks and I hadn't started out as friends, but we ended up investigating the same case together when I was still with SFPD. In fact, it was my last case. Along with my ex-partner, and my office assistant, and now a Tijuana taxi driver named Felipé, Sarah Brooks is on a shortlist of trustworthy friends.

I was taking a chance by mentioning Sarah's name to these CBP agents. She was hardheaded and I knew she had a marred reputation within her own organization—which is probably why we got along so well. In any case, I could tell that her name had struck a chord of recognition with these two.

"Humph," said the dog guy. "So, you know Brooksie?"

"Uh-huh."

I let the silence hang in the air for a few seconds. "We worked a big case together in San Francisco."

The two of them glanced at each other. "The Latvian cargo thing?" asked the woman.

"Uh-huh." I was feeling a little better now. Like I was finally being taken seriously. That is, until the asshole opened his mouth again.

"I know all about this guy," Prowse blurted out. "That *big case* nearly landed McKenna in prison. That's why he's no longer a cop."

I glared back. "Are you guys really going to listen to an Internal Affairs guy with the police chief's Preparation-H all over his nose?"

Even Doris cracked a tiny smile at that one. "Boys, boys," she said.

Neither of the Customs officers said anything, but I sensed that my friendship with Brooks had cast me in a better light.

"Look, the reason your dog alerted on me is probably because I was drugged and robbed when I was down in Ensenada. Maybe the guys who attacked me were high on something. You know, like an evidence transfer. But if you call Brooks, I know she'll vouch for me."

Prowse shook his head in frustration, but the two agents had definitely altered course. The woman stepped away, apparently not even needing to look at my phone's contacts—which to my mind meant that she already had Brooks' number. Another check in the plus column for me.

I heard the agent talking quietly on her cell, presumably to Sarah. Though I couldn't make out the particulars, the conversation seemed light and friendly. The agent giggled at one point, and glanced over at me. What I wouldn't have given to hear that conversation.

At the conclusion of the call, the agent gave the dog handler a nod and he left the office with his pup. He didn't seem happy about it though, and I worried that he and his dog still might go back to the boat for a little covert *sniff and search* operation of their own. With all of the cocaine powder wafting around that stateroom, the dog would have gone berserk. So the fact that they never returned to the boat was about the only break I'd had during the entire trip.

Finally, the agent removed my handcuffs. I struggled to my feet, my bad knee feeling like it had been super glued. My back wasn't much better.

"So, can we go now?" I asked.

She nodded. "Agent Brooks stuck her neck out for you, big time, McKenna. My advice to you is *don't make her regret it.*"

"I hear you."

It was nearly 5:30 p.m. when Bernice finally pulled away from the police dock. I crossed the channel to top off the diesel tanks, and headed out of the San Diego Harbor.

Surprisingly, my two stowaways were still with us—having sheltered in place during the entire two-hour detention.

Prowse reluctantly climbed back aboard, though I'm sure if not for Doris he would have abandoned ship right then and there. But something about the saga seemed to have piqued my wife's interest, to the extent that she now wanted to see it through. Kind of like eyeing the gas gauge as it hits *empty*—you almost want to see how far the car will take you before it actually dies. Only in my case, I think Doris was watching to see how far my story would play out before the whole thing fell apart.

My little incarceration at San Diego Customs had set us back, and I'd have to rush my plan if I wanted to prove Doris wrong. Kicking up the power to 18 knots, we raced northward through the chop, and spray, and glare of the late afternoon sun.

As we sped along, my mind went over the details of my strategy— all of which was based on a comment Ozzy had made. He said that money had already changed hands and that his buyers were waiting. It sounded like his buyers were anxious, if not angry. To me that meant that Ozzy's ass was hanging out almost as far as mine. It was the only reason he hadn't already killed me.

My plan counted on buyers so eager for their shipment, that they would also be waiting at the harbor. But it was all about the timing, and it had to go just right in order to work. Because in the back of my mind was the other thing Ozzy had said: "You get the coke to me by 7 p.m., or the McKenna house is gonna be a goddamn bloodbath."

"I'll be glad to get off this scow," said Prowse.

"What's the matter, that little patch behind your ear running out of juice?" I shook my head as if to say, *What a wimp.*

Then Doris spoke up. "How far 'til Long Beach, Danny?"

I shrugged. "A few hours." But nobody had any idea we were diverting to Oceanside first. Not only did I have to come up with a credible reason for stopping, but I also had to get them all out of the boat long enough to make the delivery to Ozzy—and hopefully his buyers.

"We have to make a small detour," I said. "But it won't take long."

Doris groaned.

"What?" Prowse tried to stand, but fell back onto the seat as the boat pitched. "Why the hell can't we go straight through? Is there another mess you've yet to get us into?"

If you only knew.

I squinted at the diesel gauge. "We need fuel." Prowse had played right into my hand, so I slapped him with the *concerned-for-Doris* card. "And I thought *my wife* could use something to eat."

I cast my best *thoughtful eyes* to Doris. "The guide shows a couple of good seafood restaurants there."

Her face softened a bit, then she turned to Prowse. "Dinner is probably a good idea, especially if it's going to be another couple of hours."

He grunted.

"I'm just trying to make it up to you two." I was laying on as much remorse as I could fake. "Think about it. If not for me, you'd be enjoying the surf and turf on the Promenade Deck of your cruise ship right now. I just want to do what I can to salvage your vacation."

Prowse chuffed. "Yeah, like taking us to the Jacuzzi Motel?"

"Anyway," I said. "Oceanside is only a half-hour or so further. Dinner is on me."

Prowse sneered. "You're pretty generous with the bail money Doris loaned you."

It was just about dark. I envisioned myself waiting until the rest of them went below deck, and then I'd throw the douchebag overboard for the Great Whites. I could simply tell Doris that the poor sap got dizzy and fell over the rail.

"Lights," said Doris. "I see red and green lights."

"Harbor entrance markers." I felt my heart accelerate. It was nearly seven o'clock, and suddenly I was the sap about to fall over the rail.

My plan wasn't ready. There were still too many details I hadn't figured out. Too many things that could go terribly wrong. There was a good chance that I'd be sailing into an ambush of my own making.

By that time, I was fully committed into the navigation channel and it was too late to turn the yacht around. Then, just beyond the Marina Suites Hotel, a brightly lit sign came into view: WELCOME TO OCEANSIDE HARBOR.

CHAPTER 34

Oceanside Harbor was actually two side-by-side marinas separated by a rocky seawall. I steered right, toward the South Harbor, avoiding the Jolly Roger restaurant where I knew Ozzy and company were waiting. That part of my plan couldn't move forward until I first got rid of my wife, her *friend*, and the Uribes.

"Yummy," said Doris, gazing out at the restaurants. A few fish and chips eateries dotted the cove, along with a couple of fancier sit-down places—all of which were far enough from the North Harbor that my yacht couldn't be seen by Ozzy.

Tying off the boat, I surveyed the marina for any sign of cops or federal agents. Seeing nothing amiss, I went below to fetch Patricia and Mr. Uribe while Doris and Prowse deliberated about where to eat.

Getting anxious and tight on time, I hustled them all off the yacht in the direction of the Oceanside Broiler. "Why don't you folks go ahead and eat without me?" I said to Doris. "I've got to refuel, and I'm not too hungry anyway."

"What's the matter?" said Prowse. "The Broiler too fancy for your taste?" Then, turning to Doris he whispered, "I knew the cheapskate wouldn't pay for our dinner."

I realized from all their confused expressions that I hadn't sold my disappearing act very well. Even Prowse, who for all his political ass-kissing, at the end of the day was still a cop. And even he was tasting the tang of deception. He asked Doris, "Didn't we just refuel in San Diego?"

Sooner or later he'd figure out that something was up. I just needed it to be *later* rather than sooner—just enough time for me to make the delivery to Ozzy, and get the hell out of Oceanside.

Doris didn't have the experience of police work behind her, but she was a Danny McKenna expert. As such, her skepticism seemed to grow with every word I spoke.

The still-in-mourning Mr. Uribe, didn't understand English and clearly had no idea what was going on. His daughter, however, was the only one of the group who knew about the dilemma that I faced.

Our eyes locked, and Patricia's discreet expression was both protective and comforting. I felt good knowing that at least she was back on my side.

Patricia and her father were the only innocent victims in this fiasco, and I realized that their day had begun with the simple goal of dispersing Mrs. Uribe's ashes into the ocean. Since then, they'd been detained, pursued, and shot at by the Mexican Coast Guard, cast out to sea in a dinghy, and smuggled across the border against their will. Somehow, I needed to get them on a bus back to Tijuana.

The foursome continued along the winding esplanade, blending with shoppers strolling beneath the canopy of tiny white lights. I watched until they got to the top of the walkway where a line formed at the restaurant's door. I hoped that without a reservation, my crew's dinner would take quite a while. *The longer, the better.*

Motoring slowly from the South Harbor, past the separating seawall and into the North Harbor, I spotted the Jolly Roger ahead on my left. It was exactly 7 p.m., which meant that I had pushed Ozzy's timeline all the way to the limit. With his buyers waiting for the shipment they'd already paid for, Ozzy would probably be in even more of a hurry than me.

I first recognized Ozzy's spine-snapping sidekick. El Sacacorcho stood with crossed arms at the foot of the dock near the restaurant. Ozzy sat at a small table nearby. Both men wore deadpan expressions, their faces set like dogs about to fight.

I'd arrived too soon. The buyers weren't there yet, and I was sure that Ozzy would use the extra time to examine the load. He'd surely notice that I had tampered with it. He'd know it wasn't cocaine. In which case, Doris would come out of the restaurant to find my headless body floating in the harbor.

My esophagus constricted with the realization that without a weapon, I was defenseless against these two armed men. Suddenly reminded of the human *fight or flight* reaction to a threat, I eased off the throttle and the boat came to a bobbing stop in the channel.

Ozzy's eyes became tiny black bullets. He stood slowly, glaring at me without changing expression.

I scrambled through the flight scenario in my mind. Take off now, leaving my group and racing back to Alameda before Ozzy and The Corkscrew could get to Bridget. *But, what about Doris? If they all came out of the restaurant looking for me, Ozzy might see them. He might even figure out that Doris is my wife.* Any way I looked at it, I was screwed.

My heart thumped harder, and every second took an hour to pass. The sounds of laughter and music couldn't make their way through the pounding inside my head, and I was suddenly viewing the scene through the wrong end of a telescope. I had to make a decision, and I had to make it quickly.

Over Ozzy's right shoulder, I noticed two pairs of headlights sweep into the restaurant parking lot. Two black Cadillac Escalades abruptly went dark and pulled to the end of the lot. Black silhouettes sat inside while the engines idled ominously in the shadows. The buyers had come to get their cocaine.

If I took off at that moment, Ozzy would be left holding the bag—or more accurately, he'd be left *without* the bag. I wondered if he and The Corkscrew would survive. Almost as if he could read my thoughts, Ozzy's expression changed ever so slightly. Glancing from the SUVs to me—his eyes narrowed with a message: *These guys may send me to hell, but I swear that I will take you with me.*

I took a breath. The buyers' arrival meant that there would be less time for anyone to thoroughly examine the shipment. It was only a presumption on my part, but it gave me enough hope to continue. Easing forward on the throttle, I drifted slowly toward the dock.

As I closed the last fifty meters, I saw four Latino men exit the black vehicles—two from each. Two of them started down the paved footpath while the other two stood behind the SUVs. My view of the pair who stayed back was partially obscured, but the two who approached were not what I had expected. Both men were in their twenties, and both wore jeans and football shirts. One sported a replica Tony Romo jersey, and the other was in a black Raiders shirt. Both men bore inky tattoos on their arms and necks and wore shiny jewelry.

We all arrived at the end of the dock at exactly the same time; me aboard Bernice, Ozzy, Sacacorcho, and the two buyers.

I disembarked, and with jittery hands tied off the lines. In my periphery, I saw Ozzy and the buyers exchange terse greetings. No smiles, no handshakes, just a few clipped words in Spanish.

Ozzy nodded to me, and I assumed that meant to make myself scarce while they did the deal. But as I started to walk away, he called out to me. "Where the hell you going, *pendejo?*"

Damn it. I knew once someone got a closer look at the stuff, it was game over for me. It's why I waited until the last minute to show up—more of a rush on their part meant less time for verification. It was also supposed to give me time to get out before these two groups realized it was fake dope and turned their guns on each other.

I hesitated before stepping back aboard ahead of the group, wondering how many guns were pointed at my back. I motioned toward the companionway, and Ozzy flashed a *no-shit* look.

When we got to the forward stateroom, he said, "Open the wall."

The tiny room was suddenly stifling. My ears started ringing again, and my hands felt like they weighed a hundred pounds each. Ozzy was next to me, and I saw the gun bulging beneath his suitcoat. The two gangsters stood on the opposite side of the bed as Mr. Corkscrew watched from the doorway. I found myself glancing at the overhead hatch, which I might have been able to squeeze though when I was ten.

One of the other men said something to Ozzy, to which Ozzy forced a nervous grin. Then he wheeled around and cuffed me on the side of the head with an open hand. It wouldn't have hurt so much had it not been for his fucking ring.

"Open it," he said, this time a little louder.

I found the screwdriver and went to work on the finishing screws. My ear stung like hell, and I suddenly envisioned myself plunging the screwdriver into Ozzy's ear. *Now, how do you like it?*

As the final screws dropped to the floor, I felt a wave of nausea lurch inside me. My eyes went straight to the package that I'd hastily replaced with Mrs. Uribe's ashes. It looked all screwed up, poorly taped and different than the others—worse than I remembered.

Diving into the stash, I yanked one of the plastic trash liners and a dozen kilos tumbled out. "See? It's all here."

They looked at each other in confusion, said something to Ozzy, and I felt another heavy crack over the back of my head. Getting smacked is bad enough, but taking it from a scrawny weasel like Ozzy was really hard for me. I made up my mind that if I lived through this, he was going to pay.

One of the gangsters said something to Ozzy, and I braced for another crack. When it didn't come, I looked up and saw that they were pointing to Mrs. Uribe.

Ozzy scrunched his brow and stepped past me to get a better look. Then he picked up the repackaged kilo and held it up to my face. "What the hell is this?"

I doubted that the real story would translate very well, but I had to say something. "I... I..."

CHAPTER 35

All eyes burned into me. Ozzy grabbed the back of my neck with one hand and stuffed the poorly wrapped remains of Mrs. Uribe in my face with the other.

The Corkscrew made a comment from the doorway and a couple of them grumbled. Ozzy glared at him and then back at me.

"You been tasting our product, fuck tooth?" Ozzy released his grip to take another swipe at me, but I ducked it.

It was dawning on me that my piss poor repackaging job is what had tweaked them, not the contents. My pulse slowed a little with the realization that they suspected me only of trying some of the coke. It was still bad, but not as bad as if they'd found it was a kilo of human ashes. Or worse, that the rest of the packages were all flour.

"I was sailing all night." I hung my head in remorse. "And I needed something to keep me awake so I wouldn't crash the boat." *It was a good excuse, but was it enough to save me?*

One of them said the word *"adicto."*

"I'm just a recreational user," I protested. "Some nose candy once in a while. Toot. Blow. Uh, snow. A little *Bernice* every now and then. You know what I'm talk'n about?"

I'd tried to sound believable, but I don't think they followed any of it. The other three just looked at each other, and Ozzy's face twisted like he wanted to slap me again.

"I'll be happy to pay you back for it," I said.

There was some banter between them, and it sounded like the tenseness was waning.

"I ought to stuff what's left of this brick up your gringo ass," said Ozzy. The group understood enough of what he said to laugh.

Corkscrew chimed in with his two cents. "Maybe we put the whole load into his asshole, Boss."

Maybe it was the graphic delivery, but nobody seemed to think his insult was as funny.

"No worries," said Ozzy to the buyers. "I'll replace this with another one."

He then tossed Mrs. Uribe to one of the gangsters who flung her onto the bed. Ozzy then produced a new package from his coat pocket. Wrapped just like the others, I realized that it was the same kilo of drugs that I had carried to the consulate. The Tijuana Police had obviously returned it to Ozzy.

"I'll take care of this *gilipollas* later," he added with a nod in my direction.

That seemed to satisfy everyone, but I tried to grasp what it meant for me. With Mrs. Uribe's remains tossed aside, the buyers were now taking possession of a boatload of baking flour. The fuse had been lit, and was quickly burning down. I had to get out before this dynamite keg exploded.

When we came up on deck, the two men who had stayed with the SUVs were waiting on the dock. They had lined up five plastic coolers, and stood beside them with an aluminum hand truck.

I wasn't sure if they expected me to hump the load up from the stateroom, or just stay out of the way. Unless somebody told me different, I planned to quietly loiter on deck so I could run or bail overboard when the shit hit the fan.

The two men with the hand trucks were older, sturdy worker types. They immediately began moving the packages up the companionway and into the coolers. None of the patrons strolling along the marina showed the slightest interest, and I realized that it was probably a fairly routine scene—the day's catch of fish being offloaded into portable coolers. Except that there were no fishing poles and these *fishermen* were all armed.

As I stood there watching, I noticed the guy in the Tony Romo jersey pluck a random package from the cooler and walk up the ramp with it. Again my heart went into arrhythmia. The only reason he would pull a single kilo from the shipment was to test it. It was the exact worst-case-scenario that I'd been dreading.

My eyes darted around the boat, making a mental note of my situation. The five coolers were just about full, so I knew the two workers would be off of the yacht and carting the load up to the vehicles soon. Tony Romo was still stooping into the SUV's rear cargo hold. I had no idea how long his test would take, but I had to assume that the results would be quickly apparent.

Ozzy and the other gangster were on the dock supervising the last of the transfers, and Corkscrew was still aboard the boat, arms crossed, closely watching me.

As I glanced up the ramp, the interior light of the SUV went out and I heard its cargo door slam shut. Tony Romo started back toward us, one hand tucked behind his back and a look of raw fury on his face.

None of the other men knew what I knew—which was that the big red button had been pushed, the nuclear reaction had begun, and we were only seconds away from a complete annihilation.

"I gotta take a leak," I said. Then, without waiting for permission, I stepped down the stairway and into the head. Locking the bathroom door, I took out my cell phone and quickly dialed 9-1-1.

"Oceanside nine-one-one, what's your emergency?"

I took in a gulp of mostly air, then felt the bubble work its way down my throat. Maybe I should disguise my voice, I thought. Less evidence that I had anything to do with this.

"Hello?" The female call taker's voice was husky and to the point. "Oceanside nine-one--"

"Yes," I whispered. "There's a big drug deal going down right now at the marina. Two black Cadillac Escalades in the parking lot next to the Jolly Roger Restaurant. Six men, all Latino and all armed."

"Armed, you said?"

"Yes." I heard voices on the deck above me, and realized that Tony Romo had returned. "Handguns, for sure," I whispered. "But I don't know what they've got in their vehicles."

The voices grew louder above me, and I knew there wasn't much time before angry accusations aimed at Ozzy would turn to bullets aimed at me.

"Your name, sir?" asked the call taker.

I felt the boat pitch suddenly, and I couldn't tell if The Corkscrew had gotten off or the others had climbed aboard. I hoped for the former.

"Sir...?" The woman on the phone was holding me hostage. Like, either give me your name or I won't send anyone to help you.

Shouting suddenly erupted outside on the dock. Hostile sounding threats that needed no translation.

I disconnected the phone.

Easing the door open, I stuck my head out to listen. The exchange grew louder, echoing down the companionway. I heard the word *gringo,* and I knew that my time was up.

Scrunching down into the tight space, I wanted to kick myself for not losing some weight. I felt like a jack-in-the box about to spring out.

It was dark, and each passing second seemed to take forever. *Where are the cops?*

The smugglers had all stopped arguing, at least for the moment, and I suspected it was because they had a new focus. Me.

The boat rocked fiercely with the weight of the men, and this time I knew they were all coming aboard.

Heavy footfalls clamored down the companionway and through the galley. A few more Spanish words, quietly whispered among them, and then I heard one of the men jiggle the bathroom doorknob. It was locked. There was a moment of uncertain silence, then a few more footsteps as the men repositioned themselves. I assumed that they were stepping back and taking aim.

Where in the hell are those damn cops?

Like a kid hiding under a blanket during a thunder storm, I closed my eyes tightly. A second passed, and then another. Suddenly, my whole world erupted in a thunderous barrage of gunfire.

CHAPTER 36

The hull vibrated with the pounding munitions. Pieces of splintered wood, ricocheting bullets, and ejected cartridges flew everywhere. The deafening sound seemed to go on for thirty minutes, though in actuality it was probably only a few seconds. Then it abruptly ceased.

The smoky sourness of fired artillery filled my nostrils as the room reverberated in the silent aftermath. Trying to figure out if I'd been hit proved more difficult than one might think. My knee was screaming in pain, and my fingers ached from the tight grip I had on the wall. I'd held steadfastly to the teak panel, barely holding it in place during the gunfire. Still struggling against the weight of it, I was pretty certain that I was okay.

They'd fired through the locked door, thinking that I was still inside the head. Somehow, in the midst of all the calamity, no one thought to check the space behind the false wall where the drugs had been hidden.

But that had only bought me a minute or two. They would undoubtedly push open the bullet-ridden door, only to find an empty bathroom.

At any time, my aching fingers would fail and the wall would clatter to the floor—exposing me and my stupid hiding place. I supposed that they would find me in another few seconds anyway.

The sounds of reloading weapons told me that they may have already figured it out and that the gig was up. I held my breath and waited for the wall to be yanked free of my grip. Or, like the bathroom door, the killers would simply fire right through it. There would be no missing me this time, since my contorted girth took up the entire space behind the panel.

Unable to hold on to the teak façade any longer, I felt it start to slip loose. I was about to tumble out at their feet and beg for mercy when frantic shouts outside interrupted their second offensive. The two lumpers, it sounded like, calling to the others from the dock. Again, all of their words were in Spanish—though this particular discourse ended in the word, *"policía!"*

The arrival of the local cops apparently outweighed their interest in viewing my bullet ridden body on the bathroom floor. I listened with a mixture of exhaustion and jubilation as the men scrambled out of the stateroom, up the companionway, and onto the dock.

I released my grip on the teak wall, and rolled out of the hiding place with a *whomp!*

Glancing into the head, I saw that the door was a honeycombed shell of splintered wood. I found it amazing that they hadn't seen through the holes that the bathroom was empty. Or maybe they had, and were about to turn their guns on my hiding place when the police showed up.

A bullhorn blared, "Drop your weapons!"

It sounded like pandemonium outside, people screaming and running in all directions. Gunshots rang out farther away from the boat, and I imagined complete chaos as panicked shoppers dove for cover—the cops trying to discern good guys from bad guys.

I stepped up onto the bed and ventured a peek through the forward hatch. The drug dealers had abandoned the yacht, and had left a plastic cooler on the dock in the process. Red and blue lights flashed from the parking lot, reflecting off of the water in every direction. More sirens sounded in the distance, and I knew that in a matter of minutes a perimeter would be thrown up and the harbor would be completely locked down.

Slithering up the companionway and onto the deck, I stretched as far and as low as possible to untie the docklines. Snaking my way back into the pilothouse, I turned the key. The engines started with a low bubbling noise that paled against the blaring bullhorns and police sirens.

Ever so slowly, I pushed the throttle into gear and eased the yacht away from the dock. I thought for certain that the cops would notice and order me to freeze, but their attention was dominated by the chase. Uniformed and plain clothes officers sprinted in every direction. I heard police radio traffic that shots had been fired, and I knew from experience that a shooting always ups the ante for cops. They would turn the yacht into Swiss cheese if they thought I was involved.

As Bernice moved slowly and almost silently through the water, I spotted more cruisers sliding into the marina's parking lot. There were San Diego County Sheriff's, Vista Police, Carlsbad Police, and Highway Patrol. The water ahead of me was suddenly spotlighted from above, and a Sheriff's helicopter swooped down over the harbor.

Only they weren't looking for a 50-foot Grand Banks cabin cruiser, they were after Mexicans with guns and drugs in black Escalades.

To my left was the sign indicating the two sides of the harbor, and on my right was the channel leading out to sea. For a moment, I again considered leaving Doris and her idiot friend. I had done my penance for upsetting their little trip. But as eager as I was to save myself from this mess, I couldn't turn my back on Doris—no matter what she'd done to me.

The Broiler Restaurant was off my port bow, and dozens of people had gathered along the paved walkway to watch the police activity. Although most of the drama was playing out in the North Harbor, the helicopter swung low over the restaurant illuminating the area like daylight. Diners stood on the restaurant's patio as well, pointing and gasping.

I was certain that by that time Doris and Prowse had also noticed the activity. And knowing that Prowse might assume I was involved, I had to convince them that I had nothing to do with it.

My shirt was torn, my hair was a mess, and I was covered in sweat. Easing off on the throttle, I tried to slow my breathing as the yacht parried back and forth in the channel. I closed my eyes, took some deep breaths and then let them out slowly. Using what was left of an old bottled water, I splashed my face and smoothed my hair with it.

I glanced at my phone, but there were no messages. Not even a callback from the Oceanside Police. Then I checked the discreet photos I'd taken of Ozzy when he and his pal were kicking my ass. Surprisingly, the camera had actually worked. I had captured five poorly lit and poorly framed pictures; the corner of the desk, a hanging lightbulb, ceiling panels, and the top of the louvered blinds. But the last shot showed Ozzy's scrawny face. It wasn't a great image, but it was him. I quickly typed "Ozzy" into the text box, attached the photo, and sent it to my old partner Linh Phú.

Back in gear, I slid the yacht alongside the dock in front of the Broiler. Hoping that my crew would all be waiting and ready to leave, I found only my wife and the Uribes—which was actually fine with me. I'd leave the stooge behind in a heartbeat.

Doris squinted across the water toward the hovering police helicopter. Patricia and Mr. Uribe huddled close behind her—Mr. Uribe with a bag of leftovers tucked under his arm. They were probably under the mistaken belief that the cops were all looking for them. Shielding her eyes from the spotlights, Doris stepped toward the yacht without really looking in my direction. That was a good thing, because it meant she wasn't suspicious of me.

"What's going on?" I innocently asked.

"I was about to ask you the same thing," she said, still preoccupied with the searchlights. "Didn't you just come from over there?"

"Yeah, but I must have just missed it." I shrugged. "Where's the suck-up? We need to get moving."

Doris glanced back at the restaurant. "I'm sure he'll be right back."

Something about the wording didn't set right. It wasn't like he'll be out of the bathroom shortly, or he's finishing his second helping of crème brûlée. "Right back" indicated that he went somewhere.

"Right back?" I asked. "Back from where?"

"It's nothing, Danny. He just stopped to talk to an officer about what's going on."

I pressed my palms into my eye sockets and took a breath. "A police officer?"

"A plain clothes guy, like a detective or something," she said. "Relax Danny, Michael's just curious about law enforcement things—like you used to be."

"Get in the boat."

She frowned in confusion.

"Just do it, Doris." I leaned over the bow and extended my hand. "Don't ask me questions—just get in the damn boat!"

She took a step toward the yacht, then stopped. Studying me for a second, her brow twisted as she glanced back and forth between me and the flashing lights across the marina. "Danny... what in the hell is going on?"

The ringtone startled me, but it also took the focus off of Doris' question. I glanced at my screen: City of Oceanside. *Finally, they call me back.* About to answer it, I heard Prowse's voice.

"There he is detective, right there on that boat!" Prowse trotted down the paved path, leading another man and pointing toward me. "He's trafficking illegals into the country, and he's probably involved in whatever's going on across the marina."

A man in dark clothing was partially obscured by Prowse as they made their way onto the dock.

The last thing I needed was do-gooder Prowse sicking the local cops on me. Being detained again would not only screw up my plan to get Patricia and her father on a Mexico-bound bus, but it would give the cops time to connect me with the drug bust. *I should have just pulled Doris into the boat and high tailed it out of Oceanside.*

But as Prowse led the *"detective"* closer, I was able to get a better look at him.

Son of a bitch!

The newcomer slowly raised a black handgun and pointed it directly at me. "Well, well McKenna. You wanted to be a *hero*, but now you're a *zero*."

Prowse looked perplexed as he tried to understand what he had done. Doris seemed to get it before he did, and just glared at him.

I couldn't help asking my wife the rhetorical question: "This is the ass-wad you decided to start seeing?"

Then, her focus was on me. I saw in her eyes that she was about to ask how this armed Mexican knew my name, when Ozzy yelled, "On the boat, all of you!"

With his handgun now aimed at the backs of Doris and Prowse, Ozzy roughly manhandled them into the yacht with his free hand, then grabbed the back of Patricia's neck and shoved her and her father onto the boat as well.

Effectively taking control of the yacht, Ozzy stepped right up to me. "And you won't be needing this anymore," he said, snatching the cell phone from my hand.

Ozzy drove the gun barrel into the middle of my chest as his iguana face stared straight into mine. "Untie the lines, gringo. You're getting me out of here."

Thanks to that idiot Prowse, we're all as good as dead.

CHAPTER 37

"The rest of you," Ozzy demanded, "Put your cell phones on the deck!"

He tossed my phone with the rest of them and then began searching us, one-by-one. All except Mr. Uribe, who stood slump-shouldered and as lifeless as his bag of leftovers.

With his gun digging into my ribcage, Ozzy frantically checked my pockets—his clumsy, amateurish manner was so obvious that even Prowse had to realize by now that the guy was no cop.

"This is your new *detective* friend, Prowse?" I twisted my face in disgust. "Remind me to thank you when he shoots all of us."

Ozzy swung the gun around level with my face. "Shut the fuck up, McKenna." He glanced nervously toward the dock, then dipped the barrel toward Patricia. "You," he said. "*La chíca bonita*. Open that locker and get out some rope. *Cuerda!*"

"I understand English," she said softly as she opened the storage bin beneath the seat.

I wasn't sure how well Mr. Uribe was tracking any of this, but his hazy eyes sharpened as he leaned forward to peered inside the metal deck bench. Maybe it was because he, himself, had been a fisherman at one time, or perhaps seeing all the fishing tackle made him long for the days on the boat with his wife.

A police helicopter zoomed overhead, but the searchlights had been turned off. A few people still milled about near the restaurant, but the activity and excitement had abated.

"McKenna first," Ozzy barked. "Strap him to the railing, and make sure his knots are tight!"

Patricia's eyes averted mine as she knelt in front of me and tied my feet together. Ozzy hovered over her, his gun at her back, checking each of the bindings and cinching them until they ached. Patricia looked up at me with her big, brown, apologetic eyes, and I saw how difficult this was for her. The pain in my ankles and the hopelessness of my fate aside, I found our proximity and this particular position to be a tad stirring. The clandestine glance we shared added to it, and made me feel less like a loser.

My head abruptly bucked forward as Ozzy smacked me one. "Change of plans, McKenna." He yanked me onto my feet. "You're going to drive the boat. It'll look more natural, since you drove it in here."

He then had Patricia bind my hands together, just like she'd done with my feet. But as she started gently wrapping my wrists, Ozzy shoved her aside and wove the cord several times around in a figure eight. The skin blistered beneath knots so tight that I knew there was no way I'd ever be able to work myself free.

Hobbling and pogo-sticking my way across the deck, I followed Ozzy into the pilothouse where I started the yacht's engine. Then the lizard tethered my bound hands to the boat's wheel, which allowed me to reach all of the yacht's controls while still constrained.

On his orders, I pulled the yacht away from the dock and out onto the open sea. Unfortunately, my prayers that some observant cop would detain us went unanswered. The farther from shore we motored, the darker it got and the more hopeless my situation became.

Meanwhile, Ozzy had ordered Patricia to bind Prowse's hands and feet, the same as mine. Smart move, except that I doubted the Dockers-wearing IA dweeb could ever pose a real threat. Besides, the wind had definitely left Prowse's sails as everyone now eyed him as the buffoon who had led in the Trojan horse.

In any case, with me on a dog leash in the cockpit and Prowse trussed to the stern rail, Ozzy was able to move about the boat in relative freedom. He made a couple of phone calls from the bow of the boat, but I couldn't hear any of the conversations. His final call left him agitated. He stormed over to the pile of cell phones, and I heard a loud *thwack* as he kicked them—sending phones clattering in all directions.

Yelling a string of Spanish expletives, Ozzy bent over and plucked my phone from the bunch. "See this?" he said, holding it high over his head. Then he slammed it down onto the deck, and with the heel of his cowboy boot, stomped it into plastic confetti. His juvenile display now over, Ozzy gazed around at his stunned hostages with a satisfied look. Then he toed the pulverized fragments of wire and circuitry under the rail and into the sea. Scooping up the rest of the phones, Ozzy stuffed them into a canvas sack and tossed it onto the aft platform.

What in the hell was that all about? Not only did my phone have all of my important numbers on it, but now my only photographic evidence of Ozzy was sitting at the bottom of the Pacific.

My nervous mind jumped to what was coming next. The facts were clear: Ozzy had used us to make his escape from the cops and the angry drug buyers. I speculated that he was now pissed off because the human corkscrew hadn't made it out of Oceanside alive. And even though there was now one less killer I'd have to contend with, Ozzy would be desperate. The slick weasel wasn't used to operating outside of Ensenada, and now, without his lackey enforcer. But the most concerning factor in my mortality was that the cocaine—my life insurance policy—had either been snatched up by the buyers or seized by the cops. In either case, possession of the drugs had been the only thing keeping me alive. *The ocean, the sharks, no witnesses, no evidence... Why not just kill us all and get it over with?*

I heard Doris ask him, "How do you know my husband?"

Ozzy's head whipped around like lightning, his gaze moving slowly from Doris to me. Then, the grin returned. I rolled my eyes.

"Mrs. McKenna?" he said in mocked chumminess. "The real, honest-to-goodness Doris McKenna?"

Doris' shocked expression was tinged with fear—the question of how he knew me, now eclipsed by how he knew *her*.

"Mother of little Bridget McKenna?" Ozzy continued. Then he used the gun barrel to cattle prod Patricia toward my wife. "Tie her up too."

When Doris was securely hitched to the railing next to her beau, Ozzy turned to Patricia. "*Lo siento amiga*, but you're next."

By the time Ozzy had finished lashing Patricia in place next to the other two, the yacht was well past the breakwater. It was dark, and it occurred to me that my navigation lights should all be on. But instead of activating them, I left them off.

Wouldn't you know it? This time, Admiral Martin and his SEAL team were nowhere in sight. What I wouldn't have given to be boarded by them now. The farther we drifted from the coast without intervention, I knew our chances for survival dropped exponentially. Prowse, who knows nothing, was even able to glean that much from the situation.

I kept the boat heading north past Los Angeles, toward the Santa Barbara Channel. About an hour from Oceanside, I saw the Carpinteria Offshore Oil Field marked on the chart. The whole area was peppered with oil pumping platforms, standing anywhere from two to eight miles offshore. Ozzy seemed unnerved by the activity and lights as we passed between towering rigs, and he instructed me to head further out to sea. There were too many hazards in the water, so I finally gave up and turned on the running lights.

"Please," Prowse pleaded. "Take our money. We can even get more from an ATM. Take whatever you want... here, take my watch." Prowse chinned pathetically toward his bound wrists.

This generated a chuckle from Ozzy. "Yes, we'll stop at the next ATM. And, of course, your fine wristwatch. It's exactly the accessory I need."

Prowse slumped back in silence.

"I'll ask you again," said Doris, leaning past Prowse. "How is it that you know not only my husband, but my name and the name of my daughter?"

Ozzy grinned over at me. "Shut off the motors," he said. "In the interest of marital transparency, I think it's time for a little McKenna family meeting."

CHAPTER 38

The boat floundered lifelessly in the water as Ozzy unhooked me from the wheel. I hobbled to join the others on the deck, thinking the entire time that this is where he shoots us and dumps our bodies overboard. *Why not? At this point we're only a liability to him.*

We were in a semicircle—me standing next to Ozzy like a praying mantis, and the rest of them strapped to the rail.

"First of all," Ozzy said, directing his words to Doris. "I'd like to thank you for saving me a lot of time."

Doris cocked her head.

"Now, I don't have to go all the way to Marin to kill you."

Doris tried to maintain an obstinate air, but I knew my wife well enough to sense the fear beneath it.

"Mill Valley," said Prowse. "She lives in Mill Valley, not Marin."

Doris and I both glared at Prowse with identical venom. *Idiot!*

"What?" Prowse asked, too stupid for his own good. "I was just saying..."

"Yeah, I know all about their little house on Walnut Avenue." Ozzy flicked the gun past my face, so close that I felt a swoosh of air. "Whatever. None of you are going to see the place again anyway." Turning to me, he said, "First one to go is you, McKenna. But before I put a bullet through your head, I want you to know that my friend, El Sacacorcho, is going to take good care of your little girl, up there in... *Mill Valley.*"

Ozzy must have seen the skepticism in my eyes. I had hoped that The Corkscrew had been caught by the police, or better yet, shot and killed during the fracas in Oceanside.

"What is it, McKenna? You thought your little girl was off the hook? You didn't know that Sacacorcho got away too?" Ozzy spit at my feet. "*Pendejo!*"

"Damnit, Danny!" Doris screamed. "Who is this monster?" She tugged against her restraints. "What in the hell did you get our family into? You son-of-a-bitch!" Then she broke down and began sobbing uncontrollably.

The idiot attempted to whisper something comforting into *my* wife's ear. Emboldened by Doris' berating assault on me, Prowse then turned his attention to me. "Yes, I'd like an answer to that question, myself. What, exactly, *have* you gotten us all into?"

Again, all eyes were on me. Ozzy, who had been just about to shoot me, crossed his arms and smiled. He was clearly enjoying the fact that my final minutes would be spent getting bitched out by my wife and her asshole boyfriend.

I said, "Aside from the fact that it was *you* who brought Ozzy aboard... I never invited you and Doris to come along in the first place. In fact, I told her that it would be too dangerous."

"That's it?" Prowse glance around at the jury. "That's the best he can come up with to explain all of this? The last time I heard such a pathetic attempt at a defense was when the SFPD brought him up on criminal charges."

I ignored Prowse and spoke to my wife. "I could explain it better, but the less you know about this, the better."

"Oh, I think it's a little late for that strategy," she said.

Ozzy grinned. "Yeah, McKenna. You're all about to die anyway, so you might as well tell her."

Heads now turned back to me, waiting for a response that I wasn't going to give.

"Excuse me," Patricia said softly. "If Mr. McKenna won't tell you, then I will."

Doris' face said that now she had even more questions, starting with how Patricia knew a secret about me that she didn't.

"This man," Patricia motioned to Ozzy, "tricked your husband into believing he was going to buy the yacht. And then he drugged your husband and hid cocaine inside the walls of the boat."

My wife's expression was hard to read at that point, though she seemed to have been knocked back a few steps. Whether surprised by Patricia's support of me or shocked to learn what I'd been involved in, she just sat there in stunned silence.

"I must confess, it's all true." Ozzy grinned proudly. "But then your husband foolishly tried to double-cross me by turning the drugs over to the embassy in TJ. That's when the cops threw his ass in jail." Ozzy let out a greasy little snicker. "But I got the last laugh, didn't I, McKenna?"

"How's that?" I asked.

"Even though you tried to cross me a second time with all those kilos full of bullshit, I already had the money for the Oceanside deal. And thanks to you, I got away from the buyers and the cops."

"How did you know that the drugs weren't real?" I asked.

He looked at me as if I was a child. "I'm in the business, McKenna. You think I can't tell high quality cocaine from talcum powder?"

"Flour," I said quietly. "The DEA seized the real stuff."

Ozzy gazed comfortably around the deck. "Doesn't matter now," he said. "Besides, once I get rid of you people, I'll also have myself a nice party boat."

"Please, I beg you." Doris leaned forward as far as her bindings would allow. "I don't care what you do to me, to us, but please don't hurt my little girl."

Ozzy shook his head smugly. "Sorry about that Mrs. McKenna, but your husband and I had an arrangement. He didn't hold up his end, and now there's no room left for negotiation. There's got to be a price to pay." He grinned again. "Nothing personal, it's just the way we do business here."

Doris' chin dropped to her chest, and she wept. Prowse again leaned in and tried to comfort her.

"Now, I have a question for you," Ozzy said.

Doris gazed up at him, her eyes red and swollen.

"If McKenna is your husband, and you two have a daughter together, what are you doing with this clown?"

He motioned toward Prowse and I felt the slightest smile cross my lips. At least me and Ozzy agreed on one thing.

"Back at the controls," commanded Ozzy. "Can't dump your bodies this close to these oil drills. Keep heading north."

As I started the boat, Ozzy stepped back to admire his captives—three of them in bindings, and Mr. Uribe constrained only by grief and old age.

The wind had kicked up and the passengers all shivered against one another—which gave me a good dose of guilt as I stood in the shelter of the wheelhouse. Then I heard Doris asking Ozzy if she could use the toilet. After giving it some thought, he unfastened the ropes around her ankles.

I pretended not to be looking, but when I did, I noticed something twinkling on the deck just next to Mr. Uribe's foot. Caught just right in the moonlight, I realized that it was a shard of glass from Mrs. Uribe's shattered urn.

By the time Doris returned, I had the fundamentals of a plan rolling around in my head. Not a great one, but a plan nonetheless.

I leaned away from the wheel toward the companionway when I heard her coming up the steps. Then, just as she passed behind me, I whispered, "That buys us at least an hour."

Doris and the rest of them had no way of knowing that a series of islands lay just ahead. If Ozzy had been worried about witnesses, or the bodies floating up near the oil rigs, he'd definitely be concerned with the archipelago. The nautical chart was dotted with islands: San Clemente, Catalina, San Nicolas, Santa Barbara, Anacapa, Santa Rosa and Santa Cruz. In addition to those, a few more oil platforms still remained in our path. His decision to continue north would give me time to figure out my next step.

Though my long range goal was to stay alive, I also wanted to show Doris that I wasn't the loser that she clearly thought I was. A close third place was to impress Patricia enough to sweep her off her feet. My short term objectives were in some ways simpler: Free myself without Ozzy knowing it, find a weapon, and take back control of the boat.

Feasible or not, these were the elements of the plan I was about to put into action.

CHAPTER 39

I could have kicked myself for making them throw the fish club into the sea. Thinking of how handy it would have been made me curious about what other implements might be on the boat. A toolbox with a hammer had to be stashed somewhere onboard, or maybe even a fire axe or a flare gun. Before I did anything, I had to find a way out of the damn ropes.

Ozzy's back was to us. All of his attention was on Prowse, who was still trying to negotiate his release—probably by offering a pair of cufflinks or his fanny pack in exchange.

Doris had ignored what I'd just whispered to her, and asked, "What the hell happened to the bathroom door?"

"Never mind that," I lowered my voice. "Listen to me... the fact that he won't kill us here buys us a little more time." She gave me a sizzling glare.

"Work with me, Doris," I whispered. "I'm going to find a way to get out and onto the deck so you can slap me."

Her expression perked up.

"You're going to have to make it look real," I said.

She flashed a wry smile. "That, I can do."

I waited until she got back to the bench, and thankfully, Ozzy hadn't yet retied her feet together.

"Hey," I called out to Ozzy. "We've got a problem."

He did a three-sixty, glancing nervously out at the water. "What's that, McKenna?"

"A *problem* is like an uncertain or difficult situation--"

"Enough of your stupid jokes." He pulled his gun out and aimed it at me. "What...is...the...problem?"

"Up ahead," I said, realizing I'd mistimed another attempt at levity. "There are a bunch of islands. Which means more boats and more people."

He scanned the darkness. "I don't see anything."

"It shows them right here on the charts." I reached toward the chart table, then did an exaggerated rebound as my movement reached the end of my tether. "Whoa!"

Ozzy shook his head as he started in my direction. "Show me."

"There's not enough light in here," I said. "Besides, I'll need to spread out the chart so you can see what I'm talking about."

He glanced at Doris—not yet secured to the railing—and I could almost see the wheels turning as he wondered if the two of us could be up to something. But men's egos being what they are, Ozzy strode over and untied my hands from the wheel. The fact that my wrists were still bound together probably contributed to his momentary complacency.

I set the engines at low speed, and the wheel on a northwesterly heading. Walking me out to the open deck, Ozzy held the rolled chart with one hand and my elbow with the other. "Show me where we are."

Right on cue, Doris said, "What does it matter? You're going to kill us anyway."

"True enough," he said, barely looking up from the chart. "I'm just trying to figure out the best place to do it." He smiled at Doris. "We don't want some tour boat or fishing trawler finding five bodies floating out here." Then Ozzy glanced up at me and winked. "As McKenna can attest, dead men don't always sink in cold water."

Not sure why it surprised me, I must have known in my heart all along that Ozzy was behind Dylan's murder. "So, you were the one who shot Dylan," I said.

The slimy grin was really beginning to piss me off. "Dylan Langdon was a minor annoyance," he said. "Just like the rest of you."

Something about what he said gnawed at me. But before I could sort it out in my head, Doris jumped to her feet. "Look what you've done, Danny! Because of you, we're all going to be killed."

Doris' acting was superb. Played so well in fact, I had no doubt that Ozzy was buying the whole *angry wife* bit, hook, line, and sinker.

She took another step, closing the space between us. "And if that's not bad enough," Doris screamed, "they're going to kill our daughter, too!"

Bravo! I thought, as she slowly reared back, twisting like a batter swinging for the center field fence. It was then that I realized both of my wife's hands were still knotted together at the wrists. But it registered too late.

Doris' walloping right hook carried the power of both fists, and her follow-through was one for the record books.

As I lay there on the deck trying to focus my eyes through the cacophony of sparkling lights, I sensed that there had been something more in her punch. Something even beyond her Oscar winning performance.

I opened and closed my mouth a couple of times. As painful as it was, my jaw still seemed to work. Turning my head, slowly getting my bearings, I realized that I had ended up on the ground below Patricia with my head between her feet. Not the worst view I've ever had, but even so, I still needed to move myself over one spot to where Mr. Uribe was sitting.

Arching my back, I started to push myself up, then collapsed in sort of a rolling motion.

"You look like you've been kicked by a mule," said Prowse. "Good thing I'm tied down or I'd also have given you a good--"

"Violence won't solve anything," interrupted Patricia as she glared at Doris. "And furthermore, I have not seen your husband show anything but kindness and courage."

"Why don't you mind your own business?" Doris snapped.

Besides an emotional boost to me, the little repartee between the women proved an added distraction. It allowed me to surreptitiously writhe over to my objective. Quickly tucking my bound hands beneath my torso, I carefully fingered the piece of broken urn under my wrist bindings.

Neither Ozzy nor the others had noticed, with the exception of Mike Tyson. She'd been watching me slither around on the deck, knowing full well that I was up to something.

Ozzy's cell phone rang, surprising all of us. We froze as he fished it out of his pocket. While he engaged himself in a conversation that I couldn't understand, I rolled onto my back and slid up to a sitting position.

My wife watched me with curious satisfaction as I opened and closed my jaw. Eventually, I was able to mouth the words to her, "I only said 'a slap'."

The grin I got in return looked more like Ozzy than the Doris I knew.

Patricia listened intently to Ozzy's half of the phone conversation, then looked at me and shook her head. Her expression confirmed that it was more bad news for us. She leaned forward against her restraints and whispered, "He's speaking with a man called The Corkscrew. This man he has sent to... find your daughter."

I nodded, knowing Bridget was safe with her grandmother and I could focus all my attention on freeing us.

"I'm trying to get loose," I said. "Is there anything in the locker that we can use?"

Shaking her head, Patricia answered, "I'm sorry, I didn't pay much attention. Just some fishing gear, I think."

"Ask your father," I said.

She looked perplexed for a second, then leaned to the old man's ear and whispered something. Mr. Uribe nodded slightly, but as he started to answer his daughter, Ozzy's phone lost reception and his call went dead. He wheeled around, and I could tell that the conversation—whatever it was about—hadn't gone well.

"Change of plans again, McKenna," said Ozzy.

"You're going to let us off the boat?" Another of my ill-timed attempts to lighten the mood.

"Close," he said. "I'm going to kill all of you right here, before we get near those islands, and then I'm going to let you off the boat."

"Then what?" Not that I really cared, but my mind was racing through viable reasons why he shouldn't. And to be honest, nothing was coming to me.

"Then I turn the boat around and sail back to Ensenada," he said.

"My eyebrows arched as I eked out a condescending nod. "Good luck with that plan."

"What the hell do you mean by that?"

"Coast Guard Station," I said, dipping my head aft. "Looking for poachers all along the coastline." I had no idea if there were poachers, let alone a Coast Guard station. The whole thing was completely out of my ass. "Yeah," I continued. "Blue Marlin. Mexicans coming across in droves, not to sneak into the U.S., but to catch the vaunted Marlins in their gill nets."

Ozzy looked about as confused as the other four passengers. Their faces all registered the same unspoken question: *So what?*

I kept going with it. "Not only are the fish a protected species, but gill nets are illegal in this country."

Their eyes all shifted to Ozzy. Nobody moved, except Mr. Uribe. He quietly slid across the storage bench until he was directly over the hasp.

"So fucking what, shithead?" Ozzy reached beneath his blazer and pulled the gun from the middle of his back. Then, sweeping it across the deck, yelled, "This isn't even a fishing boat. I got no fucking nets and no fucking marlins here anyway!"

Using my fingertips to grip the glass shard, I began sawing frantically on the ropes behind my back. The angle was bad though, and I couldn't get much power into the cut, but what I lacked in strength I hoped I was replacing with adrenaline.

"You're not picking up what I'm laying down," I said, borrowing a line from *The Mod Squad*.

Still carving away at my bindings, I tried to think of a reason why any of what I was saying was even relevant. "The beauty of it is, the poachers don't use fishing boats to catch these things–the Purple Marlins. They're sailing up here on your average, everyday pleasure boats."

"Purple."

"Purple?" I repeated back.

Ozzy's shark eyes bore into me. "You just said *purple*."

"Any color boat," I said. "Blue boats, purple boats, red..." I knew I'd kind of fumbled a little about the color of the fish, but I still needed more time to get through the rope.

"No, asswipe, the fish! First you said Blue Marlin, and then you changed it to purple."

"No, no, you're still not get'n it, my man." With sweaty hands, the piece of glass was starting to slip through my fingers. "Don't you know anything about fish?"

"Only that your story stinks like one."

Caught up in the yarn now, the others' heads swiveled from Ozzy back to me.

"It's the Blue Marlin," I said definitively. "But when their gills get caught in the net, they can't breathe. That's why they call it a gill net."

Adjusting my grip, I was sawing harder now—nearly through one of the braids of rope.

"Again, who gives a shit?" Ozzy's impatience told me that my time was running out. It was a race to see which would give out first, my story or the rope?

"When they can't get oxygen," I said, "the fish change color. True fact. The Blue Marlin turns purple. That's how the Department of Fish and Game know that it's been caught with an illegal gill net and not with a hook."

"Fish and Game," said Ozzy as he brought the gun down to the top of my head. "First it's Coast Guard, then it's Fish and Game."

"Huh?" I felt the snap of one of the twines breaking free. "They're working together," I said. "Investigating as a task force, you know, because of overlapping jurisdictions. They look for lone Mexican men sailing back toward Mexico. If they profile you, they'll board the boat and ask questions. And they'll see that you're not even the owner. Then they'll ask more questions, and..."

He had tucked the gun away. "You want to know what I think, McKenna? I think your whole fish story is bullshit. Colored Marlins, gill nets, task forces... In about five minutes you're gonna be on the purple *fucking* bottom feeder task force."

Twang. Another of the rope's braids snapped free behind my back, so loud that I had to cover the sound of it with a cough.

"No, it's true." Everyone turned in unison toward Prowse, who hadn't said a word until now. "A fish task force."

I knew the guy was trying to help, but he sounded even more desperate than me. Prowse must have heard it in his own voice, so he reared back and threw a Hail Mary in order to gain credibility. "We should know because..."

No! I heard it coming before the words actually formed in the idiot's mouth.

"...because, we're both cops."

Ozzy stared at him, motionless and soundless. Then, slowly, as if all of the little fragmentary questions he'd had about me were suddenly being pulled together by a huge magnet. The answer was finally clear to him. At a fraction of normal speed, Ozzy turned to face me. This time I saw no trace of his wiseass grin as he studied me for a long moment.

Then he nodded, almost warmly. "I knew all along that there was something about you I hated. Knew it from the first minute I saw you, McKenna."

I glanced over at Doris, saw her jaw tighten as she glared at stupid next to her.

Meanwhile, Ozzy had made his decision—it was the end of the road for me. With a hand reaching behind his back for his gun, Ozzy spit the words: "La policía..."

CHAPTER 40

I gazed up from the deck just as Ozzy pulled his gun out to shoot me. Having successfully sawed through the final shred of rope, my wrists were now free. In my peripheral vision, I saw what looked like Doris rubbing Prowse's back. I recall being annoyed at what would probably be my final image.

Struggling to my knees, I heard Patricia scream something in Spanish. Her father jumped up, turned toward Doris and Prowse, and pushed them off of the bench. Somewhere in the back of my mind, I was aware that the only way Prowse could have been moved so easily was if Doris had untied his hands from the railing. *So, she wasn't rubbing his back after all.*

Ozzy swept his pistol in my direction, hesitating only slightly at the sound of Patricia's scream. It was distraction enough for me to launch myself across the deck. Torpedoing into the squirrely Mexican with the force of a younger Danny McKenna, Ozzy recoiled like the perfect tackling dummy. A tobacco-infused gust of air belched from him as I drove his spider monkey body into the aft railing.

A popping noise sounded, immediately followed by a sharp pain. I thought for sure I'd been shot, but it took only a minute to realize that it was my bum knee. Now equally pissed off at its notoriously poor timing, I lunged forward again.

Wrapping my arms around Ozzy in a bear hug, my goal was as much to keep myself from collapsing as to gain control of the gun. It was a clumsy, awkward embrace, not unlike my first school dance with Diane Musso.

From the corner of my eye, I saw Prowse on his feet—scrambling to shed his bindings and join the skirmish.

Patricia screamed something again in Spanish—this time ending with the word "*Papa.*" I realized that in Spanish, the word meant both father and potato. Unable to imagine why she would be talking about dinner at a time like this, the clever detective in me decided to go with *father.*

As I turned toward Mr. Uribe, I heard another pop. This one sounded more like a gunshot than a blown knee.

Something spun me around, tugging me backward with the violence of a feeding shark. Ozzy pirouetted with me, and so did Prowse—who had somehow managed to get behind us and was gripping Ozzy's neck. I suddenly felt like I'd been sucked into a black hole, as our spiraling, testosterone-fueled threesome tumbled over the transom into the sea.

We remained in a group hug, even in the ocean. As Ozzy struggled to get free, I saw both his gun and his cell phone slip from his grasp and disappear into the icy waves.

But even the nose-dive into the cold water didn't shock me as much as what I saw when I glanced back at the boat. There stood Mr. Uribe, like an older version of the Terminator, with a spear gun at his side. Minus the spear, I noted, which prompted a frantic check to find if I had been struck by it.

Cataracts having taken their toll on the old fisherman's aim, the harpoon had only winged me. It was a through-and-through wound to my Cal Bears sweatshirt, that had missed pithing me like a science class frog by only centimeters.

The spear had continued through Ozzy's blazer without lancing him either. Having skewered us all together like a kabob, the sharp projectile came to an abrupt stop when it buried itself in Prowse's fanny pack. The barbed tip was imbedded so far into it that Prowse couldn't dislodge it. Alas, the idiot's fancy little accessory joined Ozzy's gun and phone in Davy Jones' Locker.

Untying our feet in the roiling surf while at the same time untangling the harpoon line, proved to be an odd contradiction of hand-to-hand combat and collaboration. One person would lift an arm to untangle the line while the other two traded splashing punches. The whole scene felt like a three-way tug-of-war using one rope. I managed to get in a couple of swipes, at least one of which connected with the side of Ozzy's head—payback for cuffing me with his hefty ring.

By now everybody was yelling at everybody else. Prowse wanted to "hogtie" Ozzy using the thick fishing line we were in the process of untangling—as if we could calf-wrangle him under these conditions.

Ozzy pleaded for mercy, begging, "Don't let me die."

From the stern of the boat, Doris, screamed for us to "drown the bastard!" I'm fairly certain she was referring to Ozzy, but at that point she could have meant any one of us.

Patricia's frantic yet soft voice warned me to be careful.

And then there was Mr. Uribe, who sat silently on the bench—spear gun held at port arms, like a Roman sentry.

I was mostly leaning towards Doris' advice. Ozzy had beat me, drugged me, set me up, and threatened my family. Out of all of them, I had the most incentive to kill the son-of-a-bitch. All I'd have to do was swim back to the boat and let him sink in the ocean.

The current had pulled us away from the yacht, and I realized that none of those left aboard would be able to start the boat or steer it to us. We had drifted so far that a decision had to be made quickly, otherwise I wasn't sure I would have the stamina to swim back to it.

My concern for Prowse fell somewhere just above that of Ozzy... and I mean *just barely*. Doris' eyes frowned her disapproval from the back of the yacht—as if she somehow knew exactly what was going through my head. And then I saw it. About 200 yards out, in the opposite direction.

"Holly!"

CHAPTER 41

Platform Holly was the first California oil rig decommissioned after the Venoco Corporation went bankrupt. Now, the abandoned drilling platform loomed like the silhouette of a post-apocalyptic city.

"Get moving," I said to Ozzy.

Treading water now, he followed my gaze to the massive scaffolding behind him. "I don't swim so well." Ozzy's expensive suit clung to him, slick and shiny. He started to make another lame plea, but I cut off penguin boy before he could finish.

"Tell your story swimming," I said. "Float or sink, it doesn't really matter to me. Either way, you're not getting back on my boat."

Prowse looked at me with distain, as he began to object.

"Don't even!" I held up one hand while dogpaddling with the other. "If it were up to me, you'd be joining Ozzy on the oil rig." Then I turned away from both of the jerks and swam back toward the yacht. This time I didn't rely on a dainty backstroke to get me there.

The sounds of splashing behind me confirmed that Prowse was hustling to catch up—not willing to risk being left behind.

I glanced back as I climbed onto the boat, and saw that Ozzy had made good progress toward the platform. The asshole had been seconds away from killing me. Regardless of what the other passengers thought I should or shouldn't do to him, this was not about popular opinion. There was only one vote that counted on the good ship Bernice now, and it was the skipper's.

First thing I did was thank Mr. Uribe, who looked like it was his proudest moment. He had obviously absorbed more of the situation than I'd given him credit for. His dismal aim notwithstanding, the old man had saved my life—probably all of our lives.

Looking aft, I saw Doris and Patricia helping shit-for-brains into the boat. His lungs heaved as if he'd swum from Japan, though he still managed to snivel something about losing his fanny pack. And even though I was equally exhausted, I did my best to appear in Phelps-like condition.

"*Miles in Bello,*" said Prowse, raising a fist in the air. "It's Latin for soldier in battle--"

I interrupted, "If only Julius Caesar were here, I'm sure he'd be impressed. But nobody else gives a shit."

Turning to me with her hands on her hips, Doris said, "You should have taken the Mexican hostage!"

I squinted at her daffy notion. "Hostage for what?"

Patricia was still watching Ozzy from the back of the boat. "He made it to the platform." Her words carried a sense of relief, and I wondered if the woman actually was some sort of saint.

I started the boat's engines and put her into gear.

"Doris is right," said Prowse—his shriveled cojones apparently buoyed by his ineffectual aid during the fight. "We should have hung on to that Ozzy character, and turned him over to the proper authorities."

"And risk having him break loose?" I asked. "Possibly injuring one of us, or even taking over the boat again? No way, Prowse. I've seen this guy in action, he's a cat with nine lives."

At the helm again, I had us making 20 knots into the wind. It felt good to finally be free of the bindings and back in control.

"That's not what I'm saying." My wife wasn't letting go, which, by the way, is *so* Doris.

"What isn't what you're saying?" I asked over my shoulder.

"What he said." She motioned toward Prowse. "I don't care about handing Ozzy over to the police. But you should have kept him for--"

"I know, I know," I said mockingly. "...for a hostage. And to what end, Doris? You think we could ransom the asshole to his cartel buddies?" We'd passed a few more oil rigs by then, and I could see the lights of Santa Barbara off our starboard bow.

"No Danny, for a trade." She was still hanging on to it.

"A trade for what?" I asked, halfheartedly.

"For our daughter, who do you think?"

My annoyance was tempered by the nagging sense that I'd missed something. That somehow Doris was right, and that I was somehow wrong. "Now Doris," I said with dissipating confidence, "we both know that Bridget is safe with your mother in Pioneer. The place is so remote that it would be impossible for Ozzy's henchman to..."

I sputtered to a stop when I saw Doris shaking her head.

"She's not with your mother?"

Doris said nothing.

"But you told me..."

"Told you what?" She shook her head again. "I said my mother was taking care of Bridget for the week."

"But your mother never stays at our house." I hoped that my logic could somehow change the facts. "You and Bridge always go there."

"That's only because you don't like her. Look Danny, I'm not getting into all of this right now. Bridget has a math final she can't miss, so my mother came to stay at our house."

"And thanks to him..." I wheeled around, pointing a deflecting finger at Prowse. "*They* now know that our house is in Mill Valley."

My wife closed her eyes, and I knew she was struggling not to cry again.

"If I'd have known that Bridge wasn't..." I paused, then exhaled the last of my energy. "I wondered why you were so upset."

She cocked her head. "And I wondered why you weren't."

"Because I thought Bridge was safe."

"Doesn't matter now." She glanced behind the boat. "So, do we go back and get Ozzy or do we try to get to our daughter before they do?"

I suddenly felt like I was going to throw up. I slowed the boat to a crawl as my mind debated whether or not to return to Platform Holly. There were upsides and downsides to both actions, and Bridget's life hung in the balance.

CHAPTER 42

"No," I finally said, barking the word. "We continue northward up the coast."

An angry, one-sided argument ensued involving everyone except Mr. Uribe. They all seemed to be on the *go back and get Ozzy* side, and then there was me, the opposition, silently taking verbal punches. Doris was now in the hostage trading business, and her idiot boyfriend was all about "doing the right thing." Patricia, the patron saint of forsaken drug smugglers, took on the compassionate cause: "The man could starve, or get injured..."

"Do you people have any idea how big those drilling rigs are?" I'd slowed the yacht to a crawl. "They're like mini-cities. By now, Ozzy has probably climbed the footings onto the platform and could be hiding anywhere. It would take time, maybe several hours, to find him on there. Meanwhile, his assassin Sacacorcho is up in the Bay Area..." I left it at that, not wanting to mention, or even think about what he could be doing to Bridget.

Turning back toward the wheelhouse, I knew that at least Doris would be on my side now. The rest of them, I didn't really care about.

I pushed the controls beyond the recommended cruising speed until the speedometer registered nearly 30 knots. The jarring waves made it feel even faster. I knew, however, that even with favorable sea conditions we were still a good 18-20 hours from Alameda.

"The phones!" Doris suddenly cried out. "Ozzy put them into a canvas bag in the inflatable raft."

It was a good find, but it was unlikely any of them could get a cellular signal so far offshore. Which prompted another big debate: Do we waste time heading toward shore for a cell signal, or do we go for broke and continue north?

Again, I was on one side and my passengers were on the other. I asked, "At this point, what good would a phone call do?"

Doris wanted me to "pull some strings" and have a SWAT team sent to our house. If she only knew that I didn't have any *strings* left in my own department, much less in the Mill Valley PD.

I was guilt-ridden over having let my daughter down. Somehow, I had assumed or misunderstood that she was in the safety of Grandma Abrams in Pioneer. It wasn't a minor screw-up on my part, and I felt I owed it to Doris, if not Bridge, to capitulate on this one.

Turning Bernice toward the lights of Long Beach, I told the group to check their cellphones and let me know if anyone gets a connection.

Doris' eyes connected with mine in a way that needed no words; she looked both relieved and grateful.

"I think I have something," said Patricia.

"Me too," echoed Doris.

Prowse sat shaking his phone like a martini. "Still no bars," he said, probably eager to call the SFPD brass and plead his case.

Doris dialed the house, then looked at me with dread as the recorder kicked on. She tried Bridget's cell phone, and it too went to voicemail.

The shoreline lights became a blur and I felt a squeezing pressure in my chest. For the first time since this fiasco began, I really felt that Bridget's life was in grave danger. The image of what that animal, might do to my daughter was killing me. Then my mind started up: *What if it's too late and he's already killed my little girl?*

With my heartbeat crashing like waves in my ears, I turned the yacht northward again. I'd subconsciously pushed the throttle even farther forward, and now the yacht clattered and pounded into the waves. I had to get home. I had to try to save my daughter.

Just then I felt a gentle hand work its way across my back and caressed between my shoulder blades. She leaned in close enough for me to feel her warm whispering breath on my neck. "Don't worry, she'll be all right."

Doris hadn't touched me like that in years, and when I looked up I realized she still hadn't. Patricia's soft gaze dropped self-consciously along with her hand.

Doris blasted into the wheelhouse like someone late for a subway train. "I got ahold of the Mill Valley police." She paused, her feline eyes studying Patricia and me. "They promised to send a car out to check the house. Good news is they haven't had any calls there yet, and no record of contacting Bridget for any reason."

"Is there a bad news?" I asked, watching Patricia gracefully exit the enclosure to rejoin her father on the deck.

"Yeah, bad news for you that Patricia didn't finish your little back massage or whatever that was." Then, with a smirk, Doris added, "Sorry to have interrupted the tender moment."

I took a breath and let it out, not wanting to get into it with her. But I couldn't help it. "Better get an ice pack for Idiot Boy," I said with a nod toward Prowse. "I think he may have pulled a hammy trying to save the day back there."

She glared at me and I glared back. We could easily have gone back and forth like that for hours. The upside, if there was one, was the hint of jealousy in Doris' remarks. Boiling anger instead of cool indifference told me that she still cared.

Doris dialed her mother's number, but we'd motored out of range, and the call died.

I was consumed in thought as we bounced along the breaking whitecaps of the Pacific. At some point during the night, the starboard sky lightened to a smoky violet and I realized that I'd lost track of time. The sun would be up soon, and I knew my passengers would be hungry and anxious. They'd all gone below sometime during the wee hours, to warm themselves and get coffee.

Patricia suddenly appeared from the top of the companionway carrying a steaming mug for me. Though she said nothing, her eyes exposed the worry behind them. She had to be fearful of what she and her father would face once we made landfall. I was counting on my Customs friend to intervene for me... again. But I'd already used her name to get out of one jam, and I wondered how far I could push our friendship.

Mr. Uribe's head popped up from the opening behind her, gazing around as if the sunrise looked different in the United States. He said a couple of words to his daughter as he held out his cell phone to her.

Patricia gently ushered him back out of sight. "Something's wrong with his phone." She smiled at me sheepishly. "I bought it for him two years ago, but I'm not sure he's ever even used it."

Sainthood again. Even if my own dad would have appreciated a cell phone, I doubt I'd ever have spent the money to buy him one. Feeling the need to open up to Patricia, I was about to tell her what a miserable, depressed narcissist my father was, when Mr. Uribe emerged again—a little more insistent. He thrust out his phone to her, and this time whatever he said to Patricia reminded her that he was the father and she was still his little girl. I definitely recognized the shift in dynamics.

"¿Que?" Patricia's furrowed brow led the way to the top of the companionway, where she studied her father's phone. Then, turning to me she said, "He says this isn't his."

I scratched my head. "Well then, whose is it?"

"My father thinks it's your phone."

CHAPTER 43

The irony of Ozzy's bizarre tantrum was that he had inadvertently plucked the wrong cell phone from the pile, thinking it was mine. Picturing the episode rekindled a thought I had when it happened. Ozzy had been about to tie me up and shoot me anyway, so why had it been so important to disable my phone?

As soon as Patricia handed it to me, I had the answer—sort of. Ozzy had used it to place three calls during the time it was out of my possession. The first was to a number I didn't recognize, and lasted 27 seconds. The other two calls were more concerning, as both had been made to Bridget's cell phone. The first was 1 minute and 13 seconds in length, and the second lasted only two seconds. I hoped that one was Bridget hanging up on him. But it was the first call he'd placed to her that really bothered me—not only why he would call my daughter, but what kind of conversation between the two of them could take over a minute? Looking at the times of the calls, I realized they were placed only moments before he smashed my phone. Or, what he thought was my phone. Which meant that Bridget's hang-up was what pissed him off.

Doris was in the wheelhouse in a flash. "How did you miss that?" she asked in a preachy voice. "You didn't recognize your own cell phone?"

"Don't start with me, Doris. Obviously, these things all look the same. Even Ozzy was confused."

"No, Mr. Uribe's is a Samsung and yours is a--"

"Put a sock in it Doris, unless you want to swim home!" I shook my head in frustration. "Would you even care to know who Ozzy used my phone to call? Who he wanted to trick into thinking it was me?"

Doris paused, glanced at Patricia and Mr. Uribe, then back to me.

"He called our daughter," I said. "Twice."

Doris' eyes suddenly registered the same trembling dread that I felt, as her mind struggled to piece it together. "They haven't found her?"

"Maybe not, at least they hadn't yet." I was trying to reassure myself as much as Doris.

"Almost everybody's phone has some sort of geolocation feature these days," interrupted Prowse. "They'd probably use it to track her down. With the right equipment, they'd keep her talking long enough to triangulate her location via the cell signal. All they'd need is her phone number, which Ozzy obviously got from your contacts list."

Doris' eyes welled up and her shoulders dropped as if it was a foregone conclusion that our daughter was already dead.

I wanted to punch the guy, but he was still talking.

"Ozzy must have tried to scam your daughter into thinking he was a friend of yours or someone calling on your behalf," said Prowse. "Who knows what he told her?"

"I think we've all figured out that much," I said. "But thanks for upsetting Doris even more."

"Maybe your daughter didn't believe what Ozzy told her," said Patricia. "Perhaps that is the reason your daughter didn't respond when he called the second time."

I thought about it for a second and realized Patricia was right. "Yes, that must have been what sent him into a rage. Enough to want to crush my phone."

Now, Doris is the kind of wife that doesn't see things in a positive light. If I came home and announced that I'd won $100,000 in the Powerball Lottery, she'd ask how many numbers I got right and why I didn't pick such-and-such a number instead.

I could see that this was going to be no different. "Or..." said Doris, prompting us to all look over at her. "Or, the second call was successful. Maybe that triangle thing worked, and they found out where she was. That's why Ozzy didn't need your phone anymore."

She was as bad as her boyfriend. Taking a deep breath, I stretched the *Doris and Prowse knots* out of my neck. "No, I don't think so. He could have simply thrown my phone overboard. There was way too much frustration there. I'm going with *they didn't get what they wanted.*"

Doris continued to try her mother while I dialed Bridget's phone again. My call went right to voicemail, but it sounded like Doris had gotten through to her mother. I listened eagerly to her side of the conversation, and then slowly lost enthusiasm as Doris' responses got shorter and her expression darker.

Doris put a hand to her mouth as she dropped the phone. "They're not together. Bridget left."

"What do you mean, she left?"

Through watery eyes, Doris tried to recount the conversation. "My mom and Bridget were both at the house in Mill Valley, and Bridget got a couple of phone calls, and then..." Doris began sobbing.

"And then, what?"

Wiping her eyes with her sleeve, Doris said, "And then she told my mom that she was leaving to meet someone, and that it was okay for my mom to drive back to Pioneer."

Maybe Doris was right all along; this glass wasn't just half empty, it was all the way empty. There was no longer any other way for me to see it.

I suddenly wanted to strangle Doris' mother for leaving Bridget on her own. But Doris was inconsolable, so I decided not to start in about how irresponsible her mother was.

Patricia gently ushered Doris below decks while I stood in the wheelhouse, smoldering.

Alone again at the helm, I tried to reassure myself that Bridget would be okay. Having little luck, I mindlessly thumbed through my missed calls. There were three. One from my old partner, Linh Phú; the second from my Customs Inspector friend, Sarah Brooks; and the third from Shanay Moore—my secretary, or office assistant, or whatever she was. Of the three of them, only my ex-partner had left a message:

> *"Hello Inspector, this is Linh Phú calling. I did some additional checking on your neighbor's license plate—the Ford van. As luck would have it they're Drug Enforcement, apparently working a case in Alameda. The whole Cybernetic Systems address in San Diego is just a front, so at least now you know they're okay. Then, about the photo you texted me...Ozzy? However you managed to associate yourself with this guy, it can't be good. I ran the photo by some people on my task force, and he's a heavy hitter. Real name is Osvaldo Morales. Works closely with an assassin known as The Corkscrew, real name Manny Benítez-Garcia. Both major players in the CJNG—Cartel Jalisco New Generation. Both men wanted in Mexico, Honduras, and here in the U.S. Both have been Red Noticed by Interpol, and obviously, both extremely dangerous. Good luck with whatever it is you're working on, stay safe, and let me know if I can help."*

I had already found out the hard way about the two DEA agents, which reminded me that they were still expecting *their* delivery—one kilogram of real cocaine and 249 of fake stuff. And if I didn't come through, they would arrest me—which was by far the least of my problems at that point.

The identities and criminal records of Ozzy and El Sacacorcho, while interesting, was not surprising. Clearly, I already knew they were dangerous. And although I probably could have used Linh's help on some of what I was dealing with, I was too broken up about Bridget to think of much else. I didn't want to talk to my old partner just then, because I'd have to go into all of what had happened. So instead, I sent her a simple text: YOU'LL FIND OSVALDO MORALES ON ABANDONED VENOCO OIL PLATFORM HOLLY TWO MILES OFF THE COAST OF SANTA BARBARA.

The only thing left for me to do was continue toward home, and hope that my daughter was still alive.

CHAPTER 44

My daughter was missing, and the death threats against her could no longer be taken simply as abstract intimidation tactics.

I seriously considered returning to Platform Holly and doing exactly what Doris had suggested: taking Ozzy hostage and using him as a bargaining chip for Bridget. But I couldn't trust myself not to torture and kill the guy with my bare hands, and the pull to continue home to protect my daughter was stronger than logic or anger.

As I computed the distance to Alameda, Doris stepped into the wheelhouse. "Do you really think Bridget's alive?"

"I do." I reached up and put my hand on her shoulder. Seeing the surprise in her eyes, I realized I'd also surprised myself. Doris didn't recoil though, so I rested my other hand on the opposite shoulder. "She's is a smart girl." I leaned closer to look right in her eyes. "Our daughter has got the best of both of us, and I really think..." Choking back my own tears, I had to stop. In truth, I was just as worried and uncertain as Doris. We stood together in the same position for a few more seconds, both trying to get a grip on our heartbreaking anguish. Then Doris gave me a light hug and disappeared back down the companionway.

Whatever had just gone on between us was new, or at least it evoked memories of something so far back in our history that it felt new. It wasn't the words so much, or even the touch, but it was the feeling of partnership. Like, no matter what happened between the two of us, we will always be connected by the love we have for our daughter.

Feeling not only energized but a little more optimistic, I was suddenly buttressed by a moment of déjà vu. I'd been through desperate and seemingly hopeless situations before, and I've worked my way to the other end by doing what I do best.

Closing my eyes, I took a step back in my mind, imagining all of the jigsaw pieces laid out before me. I remember an old investigator once telling me, "Don't try to eat the whole elephant in one sitting, kid; slow down and take it one bite at a time."

So, my first piece of the elephant was the question of who killed Dylan Langdon. I'd initially suspected the guys on the drug boat or maybe even Dylan's wife, Teddy. It was now clear that Ozzy had either done the shooting himself, or at least ordered it.

Second piece: Why was Dylan killed? "Minor annoyance," was what Ozzy had said. In my mind it meant that Dylan had somehow become involved in the drug smuggling ring, enough, at least, to be seen as an *annoyance*. I was still at a complete loss as to how that may have happened. So, I put it aside for the time being.

Next piece was how Ozzy and Sacacorcho had learned not only where I lived, but the names of my wife and daughter. It's not something just anyone can look up; cops' names, addresses, and even driver's license information are kept confidential. I'd initially suspected Teddy. Not only had I talked about my family situation during dinner on their boat, but she was also the one who persuaded me to take her boat to Ensenada in the first place. But what was her motive?

Metaphorically taking another step backward, I tilted my head back and dug deep into my memory. Even though the conversation had been clouded by Dylan's strong cocktails, I couldn't recall telling the Langdon's those personal details. I'd told them I had a daughter in middle school, showed them a photo of her, and I might have even mentioned Bridget's name. But I knew that I had never told them my wife's name or where I lived... where I used to live, that is.

A wisp of a thought skirted through my head. *Could Teddy have somehow gotten a look at my liveaboard application?* That would have contained all of my personal information—address, family and personal references, even phone numbers.

More things came to mind. Inconsistencies that had seemed minor at the time, now stuck out like red flags. Teddy had originally told the police that she was below when Dylan was found in the water, but I had seen her topside when I slipped and fell on the dock.

And then there were her clothes, all of them still on the yacht that she had supposedly expected to sell.

I glanced at her Customs notes on the chart table next to me. There would have been no reason for her to leave returning instructions for me, unless she knew ahead of time that I was never going to sell the yacht in Ensenada.

And lastly, she hadn't answered or returned any of my phone calls.

All of this meant what, exactly? That Teddy's ditzy demeanor was just an act, and that she'd actually conspired with Ozzy and the drug cartels? That she had set me up to be used as a cocaine smuggler?

My thoughts ceased abruptly at the sound of someone coming up the companionway. "What is it, Prowse?" I said as he stopped, half in and half out of the wheelhouse.

"Just because I saved your life doesn't mean--"

"Wait, back up just a sec," I forced a chuckle. "Saved *my* life? I see you're already working on your narrative for Chief Dowd. And you didn't even bother to give poor ol' Mr. Uribe an assist?"

Prowse's dismissive hand flailed in the air. "That's beside the point, McKenna. I'm here to tell you that I've kept copious notes of everything you've done, and I'm prepared to testify against you in a court of law."

"Court of *law*," I repeated. "Glad you cleared that up, because I thought you were talking about a badminton court. Listen Prowse, you do whatever you need to do—I don't really care. My only concern right now is my daughter's safety."

Prowse stood in the opening, awkwardly shifting from one foot to the other. He seemed startled that Doris had come up the steps behind him and had evidently overheard everything he'd said. She shook her head in disgust before going below.

Prowse was about to go after her, when I grabbed his sleeve and said, "Forget it Prowse, it was only a matter of time until she saw what a pile of shit you really are."

I checked the chart again after he left. The weather was sunny and the seas were still calm. Making good time now, I figured with any luck we'd be in Alameda in another six hours—maybe around 5 p.m.

The idiot had sidetracked me from my brainwork, and now that I was alone again, my mind was having a hard time getting back to where it was. All I saw were dismal scenarios of what I'd be facing at the Buena Vista Yacht Harbor. I knew that Halliday and Rourke would bring charges against me once they realized there was no cocaine left on the boat.

Then there were the Alameda detectives, who probably thought that I fled the country after killing Dylan. And since Teddy had already set me up with Ozzy and the drugs, I doubted that she'd have any trouble implicating me in her husband's killing.

Either way, I knew that I'd be toast once the authorities found Patricia and her father hiding onboard. Especially when Prowse tells his story.

One thing I knew for certain was that the feds, or Alameda PD, or both of them, would most likely be waiting to pounce on me at the harbor. And that I'd be of no help to Bridge once they dragged me off to jail.

Calling down the companionway, I asked Patricia to bring her father up to the wheelhouse. A minute later they were crowded inside the space with me—Patricia's smiling face eager to learn why I had summoned them.

"Please translate for me," I told her. "I need to teach your father how to operate the boat."

CHAPTER 45

For the next few hours, Mr. Uribe stood at the wheel with me. Patricia leaned against the bulkhead behind us, watching and translating.

Cruising in the open seas wasn't a problem for the old guy, but I worried about him maneuvering the big yacht in the narrow confines of the marina. Drawing a crude map of the harbor for him, I penned a circle around the fuel dock—a long, wide pier with no tricky angles or obstructions. The layout was simple enough that all he'd have to do was pull straight in and cut the engines.

I didn't want any of the other passengers to know that I planned to abandon ship in the dinghy before we ever got to the marina. So I told Patricia that I was only training her father as a precaution, in case something happened to me. She seemed skeptical.

The other two stayed below deck, and it sounded like Prowse was desperately trying to explain his way out of the threatening overtures he'd made toward me.

Keeping them all in the dark about my planned escape was essential to its success. The longer they could go without knowing what I was up to, the better for Mr. Uribe and his crew. I would stay in the yacht as long as possible, but timing was everything. If I waited too long, anybody waiting for me at the marina could easily spot me.

The late afternoon wind had kicked up from the northwest, and we were motoring right into it. The pounding whitecaps made the ride uncomfortable, but I couldn't let up on our speed.

We had passed the south end of Monterey Bay, and off the starboard bow I could see the hump of the Big Dipper rollercoaster on Santa Cruz's Boardwalk. Checking my phone again, I noticed that I had picked up a weak cell signal.

Dialing the number of my Customs friend, Sarah Brooks, I yelled over my shoulder for Doris to give Bridget's phone another try. Prowse, who had come up from below a few minutes earlier, informed me that Doris was in the stateroom changing.

"Changing into what?" I asked.

Prowse shrugged. "I guess she found some women's clothes down there."

I shook my head, thinking that Doris will never be able to squeeze herself into any of Teddy's things. "Well, let her know that we're getting reception out here and she should try phoning our daughter again."

"Brooks," she answered.

"Sarah, it's me, McKenna."

She laughed. "Hey, Skipper. I hear that you've been a naughty boy. Where in the hell are you?"

Immediately, I felt a wall of reluctance come down. "Uh, on the water right now, it's a long story and my cell signal will probably give out before I can even get through the first chapter."

"Can't wait to hear it," she said. "Anything I can do to help?"

"Yeah..." I paused, realizing that, again, I was asking a lot of my friend. "Can you make it to the Buena Vista Yacht Harbor in Alameda by 5 o'clock?"

The call abruptly lost connection and the line went dead. I hadn't had time to explain why I wanted her there, and I wasn't even sure if she had heard the time and place.

My wife made her way up the steps, holding her phone in the air like an offering to the cellular spirits. "I'm not getting any bars," she said.

I noticed that she had changed into khaki capri pants and a white blouse—which, being Teddy's clothes, fit Doris surprisingly well.

Doris brandished an odd look at me when she saw the young woman and her father huddled with me in the wheelhouse, as if my proximity to Patricia had somehow devalued our earlier *moment*. It wasn't what I wanted Doris to think, but I couldn't tell her the truth about my planned departure. At least, not until the very last minute.

My phone gave a short buzz, and I realized it had picked up another missed call from Shanay during the brief period of connectivity. Nothing I could do about it until we got a signal again.

We were approaching Greyhound Rock, jutting sharply from the mostly barren coastline north of Monterey Bay. I felt like a racehorse jockey coming into the home stretch.

An hour later the yacht gnashed through the surf off Pillar Point near El Granada, and then around Point San Pedro soon after that. We were closer to shore now, and I recognized the endless string of white homes capping the hills in Daly City like rows of shark teeth. Finally passing the old Nike Missile site at Fort Funston, the yacht came abreast of the Great Highway. We had finally made it to San Francisco.

Slowing the yacht, I double and triple checked the charted hazards that lay between Point Lobos and Lands End. We carefully wove our way around Pyramid Rock—our final obstacle. Above us, the Golden Gate was tickled by the day's last fingers of light. The bridge's suspension cables glistened upwards into the fogbank.

From that point on, I felt my pulse quicken with each passing buoy. Besides being sick with worry about Bridget, I knew that my odds of getting away weren't good. A lot had to go right in order to succeed, and it would only take one thing going wrong to fail.

It was 5:04 p.m., which meant that we were less than thirty minutes from the marina.

CHAPTER 46

We rounded Yerba Buena Island and passed beneath the San Francisco–Oakland Bay Bridge. Off the port bow stood Oakland's busy shipping terminal with its dinosaur shaped cranes loading and unloading cargo containers. The knot already in my stomach grew, as memories of an old case I'd once investigated there flooded my head.

Handing the helm over to Mr. Uribe, I scanned the shore with my binoculars. I'd publicly made light of the whole co-captain thing to avoid arousing suspicion, telling everyone that other than shooting us with a spear gun, Mr. Uribe had yet to earn his keep on the yacht.

Nobody seemed to think it was funny, and of course the old guy had no idea what I was even talking about. Not that it mattered anyway, because the intent of my humor was only to set up my escape.

I was shaken by the sight of the rocky breakwater a quarter mile ahead, beyond which was the entrance channel to Buena Vista Yacht Harbor. It had come up quicker than I'd remembered, and I had yet to even unfasten the dinghy.

"Everybody on deck!" I yelled. "There's something I need to tell you all." I reached past Mr. Uribe and throttled the engine back. "Patricia," I called out. "Tell your father that we'll be turning the boat to the left just after this rock seawall."

She spoke to Mr. Uribe in a series of clipped monosyllable words, to which he responded with a nod.

"Where's Prowse?" I asked. Things were happening fast, and I wanted everybody's attention. "He needs to untie the inflatable."

"I'm right here." Prowse emerged from the companionway with a hint of a swagger. It was also in his voice, and I caught it right away. A smile spread across his thin lips, and I knew. Distracted by our entry into the bay, I hadn't thought to check for phone connectivity.

"What have you done, Prowse?"

His head bobbed with satisfaction. "I warned you, McKenna."

I followed his line of sight rearward and saw a helicopter coming in low and fast. It hardly mattered whether it was Coast Guard or the police that Prowse had called. He'd obviously screwed me good.

"Caught, *in flagrante delicto*." He flashed another satisfied grin.

"Son-of-a-bitch." I turned and gave Mr. Uribe a quick shoulder squeeze, then wished him luck.

On the aft platform, I unfastened the dinghy and tossed my binoculars into it. "This wasn't how I intended this to go," I said, as much to Patricia as to Doris. "But I guess Prowse always needs to get the last word, and apparently ruining my career and stealing my wife wasn't enough for him."

Holding the tether in one hand, I eased the inflatable into the bay. "Patricia, I appreciate everything you and your father have done for me. And I'm really sorry about your mother's remains..." I'd stopped myself before sticking my foot in it again. Her poor mother was still somewhere below deck, probably lying in a heap on the floor. *How could I ever explain that I had swapped out her mother's remains, and that it was cocaine, not her, that we'd scattered into the sea?*

"Where do you think you're going?" Doris asked as I climbed into the dinghy.

"I'm going to try to help our daughter."

Mr. Uribe increased the yacht's speed as I released the tether and started the dinghy's 5-horse outboard. Prowse hollered and pointed from the stern as the helicopter made lazy circles overhead. The pilot called to me over a loudspeaker, but whatever orders he gave were drowned out by my accelerating motor.

I tracked behind Bernice's wake until the yacht banked to port and disappeared behind the breakwater. Several police cruisers raced onto the flat area above the rocks, some of the cops jumping out with their handguns. It was a weak bluff though, since I knew that they could only shoot me if I posed an immediate threat. It was, however, a pretty good indication of how much trouble I was in.

Slowing just long enough to glance back, I saw that the cops had swarmed the yacht. I felt especially bad for Mr. Uribe, but I also knew he was tougher than he appeared.

I sped past the harbor entrance, south along the rocky shoreline toward a sandy clearing. It looked like a good place to land the dinghy, but I abruptly changed my mind when the helicopter started to set down right on the beach. More patrol cars poured into the area, so I kept a southward heading that paralleled a paved bike trail.

An apartment house stood along a road opposite the bike trail, and I thought about ditching the boat and cutting through it on foot. But there were too many cops, so I had no choice but to keep going. I hoped that the police would run out of light or real estate, and sooner or later they'd have to turn around. At which time I would beach the inflatable and make my escape on foot.

The sky was nearly black, but the roadway was illuminated by the shoreline park. Police cruisers kept coming, paralleling my route on a street that seemed to have been designed for chasing a guy in an inflatable dinghy. I had only lived at the marina for a couple of months and was still unfamiliar with Alameda's surface streets. The vague idea of where I was heading was confirmed when I saw a commercial aircraft ascending steeply into the smoky sky. Oakland's international airport being so close, meant more trouble for me.

Even though the helicopter would pull off once we neared the runways, I would become a much bigger security concern. Since 9/11, commercial airports have been ground zero for law enforcement resources. They'd have ready access to all the big acronyms: DHS, TSA, FBI, in addition to the local police, sheriffs, and highway patrol. I knew that the troops would be coming out of the woodwork.

Suddenly the road next to me ran out. The parade of police cars abruptly turned away into a residential neighborhood. To my left an estuary ran eastward about a quarter mile to what looked like a drawbridge. In what I thought was a good open field head fake, I changed course and turned the dinghy into the estuary. But when I was already fully committed, I saw the line of emergency vehicles winding their way up and over the draw bridge like a strand of Christmas lights.

Quickly banking the inflatable toward a stand of pine trees, I ducked into the mud and reeds before they could spot me. Killing the engine, I shoved the boat into some shrubs next to a sign that read HARBOR BAY CLUB, and tucked myself under a low-hanging tree. A helicopter lagged overhead with its spotlight illuminating the ground around me. Without moving a muscle, I stayed face down in the dirt for a good twenty minutes after it had left.

Skirting along the club's fence line, past tennis courts and a pool, I eventually emerged into a tidy residential neighborhood that ran along a shallow lagoon. I could no longer hear the helicopter, but police sirens still reverberated in the evening air.

The night had drawn a breeze off of the bay, yet a few people were still out walking. I didn't want to appear frantic, desperate, and overwrought—all of the things that I was—so, I slowed my stride and tried to act casual.

The sirens eventually faded to a distant hum, and I knew that the cops had no idea where I'd gone. They would likely cast a wide perimeter in an attempt to contain me, and then begin an organized search. Hopefully, they'd still be looking for a big white guy in an inflatable boat.

Having zig-zagged several blocks, I found myself at a small park next to an elementary school. Glancing around first, I pulled off my beloved Cal sweatshirt and tossed it into a trash can.

"Hey, that's a pretty nice sweatshirt." The voice was low and jaunty and unthreatening.

I turned to see three young men walking from the direction of the school, the tallest and skinniest of whom had made the comment. He held a skateboard under his arm, and wore a disarming grin. His two brothers—judging by their similar features—trudged along on either side, the oldest of them giving the skateboarder a shepherding nudge. The more serious of the three stood on the opposite side, continuing to regard me with a face that was born for high stakes poker.

"Hey, can you guys tell me where I am?" I asked.

The tall kid maintained his grin. "Uh, Alameda?"

"Are you lost or something?" asked the older brother.

"Yeah, sort of."

The poker player pointed past me. "If you keep going a few more blocks, you'll come out on Mecartney. There's a fire station on the corner if you need help."

They watched me as I walked off. Having heard the sirens and having seen me toss the sweatshirt, I wondered if they suspected my involvement in whatever was going on. Just then my cell phone rang, and I ducked behind a hedge to answer it.

"Yeah?" I was afraid to even say my name.

"Is this Danny McKenna?" asked the woman's voice.

"Who's this?"

"It's me, Teddy Langdon."

CHAPTER 47

One thing I absolutely hate is trying to trust someone that I don't trust. In this case, however, I had no choice.

"Teddy..." I paused, immediately wondering if she was helping the cartels track my phone. "Why are you calling me?"

"Wow, somebody's a snappy little turtle," she said. "I'm actually returning your call."

"I mean, why are you calling me right now?" I hunkered further into the shrubbery as a police car sped past. "I've called you several times during the past few days, but you never answered or called back. So, why return my calls now?"

She was quiet. "I just saw that you'd phoned me, and until now I didn't--"

"*Just* saw? C'mon Teddy, what kind of fool do you take me for? You're telling me that you just now noticed my missed calls?"

She paused again. "The police had my phone, Danny."

Now I was silent.

"I picked it up only a few minutes ago."

It made sense that they would check her cell phone as part of the investigation. I wondered what they had found; possibly calls or text messages from Ozzy. But those would mean nothing to the detective. The calls from me, however, in *Mexico* and on *her* boat, those would definitely mean something. *No wonder I'm a wanted man.*

I asked, "How did you get it back?"

"They were done checking it, I guess, along with my laptop." She sounded confused by my accusatorial tone. "Detective Grassi just said I could come pick them up, so I did."

Teddy's story answered one of my questions, but other suspicions remained. "Are you alone?" I asked.

"Yes. I just left the police station."

"The cops will have seen calls from my number, and they'll suspect that we were involved in this together."

"But why would they..."

I popped my head up, glanced past a soccer field to the empty street, and then to a wooden sign posted on the corner. "You'll need to do exactly as I tell you. First, do you know where Tillman Park is?"

"No, but I'm sure I can find it."

"Good, now make certain that you're not being followed. I'll be under some trees near the corner of Kofman and Aughinbaugh."

"Sounds mysterious," she said with a giggle. "By the way, the money for the boat was never wired to my account. What's up with that?"

My eyes closed as I shook my head. Hers was either a really good act, or she was one of the dumbest women I'd ever known. Somehow though, Teddy came across as authentic. "Long story," I said. "We'll talk when you get here."

As I waited for Teddy, two more police cruisers crept by with their spotlights shining into the park. I ducked behind a hedge, praying that Teddy didn't show up while they were still sniffing around. No sooner did the cops leave when a sleek, cream-colored Lexus pulled to the curb. I couldn't see into the car, but it certainly fit with Teddy's stylish mien.

Hoping it was her, I ran to the passenger door and jumped in. The sweet scent reached me before the light even hit Teddy's face, and I was transported back to the night on their yacht. *Get your head out of the clouds and focus, McKenna!*

My eyes darted around. "You're sure you weren't followed?"

She shook her head, then glanced down at the phone in her hand. On its screen, a mapping application showed a pulsating blue circle around Tillman Park.

"Let me have that." I snatched her phone. "They're probably using it to track you. I quickly shut it off, pried open the back panel, and popped out the battery. Still angry and distrustful, I emphasized my point by opening the car window and chucking the battery as far as I could. I immediately regretted the infantile display, but at least I had her attention. "Now drive."

She stared at me as if I'd gone mad. "Where to?"

I didn't want her to know we were going to my house in Mill Valley, at least not until I had more answers. Instead, I directed Teddy onto the freeway, through Oakland and Richmond, and across the bridge. The forty-minute drive gave me time to question her further.

"So, why do the police think I killed Dylan?" I asked.

"I don't know that they do. Grassi hasn't really told me much of anything. But he did get worked up about you leaving the country."

"Well, did you tell them why I left?" I turned in my seat. "Did you let him know that it was *you* who asked me to sell your boat in Ensenada?"

"Yes, of course I told them." Her words were confident, almost stern. "Which brings us back to the question, where's my money?"

"I didn't sell the yacht," I said. "That guy, the supposed buyer, your friend, Ozzy, had other plans."

"Wait a minute, what? Who's Ozzy?" Teddy seemed legitimately surprised.

"C'mon, drop the BS." I watched her expression. "He's the one behind the drug smuggling."

"Drug smuggling?"

"Yeah, and he's also the guy behind Dylan's murder. And, by the way, he nearly killed me. And now he's going after my daughter."

Teddy grabbed ahold of my arm. "Listen to me, if this is all true, you've got to tell Detective Grassi. You have to believe that I didn't know about any of it."

"Then why did you say that you were below deck when Dylan's body was first spotted in the water?"

"I don't know. Did I say that?" Her eyes were lost in thought. "Danny, that morning, in fact that whole day is still a blur to me. Yeah, maybe I got the timing wrong, but even now, I don't remember all of it."

I recalled back to my training on the force; how traumatic shock affects witnesses and victims' memories. It's not uncommon for stress to warp the mind's perception of time and sequence.

"Do you remember when I slipped and fell on the dock?"

She shook her head. Which, was a good thing because I must have looked pretty clumsy. "Why? Did you fall?"

"Oh, no," I said. "I was just testing your memory. Anyway, what about the clothes you left onboard? The only reason you would have done that is if you knew ahead of time that I was never going to sell the yacht."

We came off the Richmond—San Rafael Bridge to a maze of red taillights. I told her to take the Sir Francis Drake turnoff toward Mill Valley.

"Where are we going?" she asked again.

"Never mind that. What about the clothes?"

Teddy let out a sigh. "I used to be a little heavier than I am now. Probably all the beach parties and Margaritas. It took a lot of work to drop those pounds."

I frowned, still not getting it.

"The clothes on the yacht are two sizes larger than I wear now," she said. "I didn't want or need them anymore, so I just left them on the boat."

"Hmm." *No wonder Doris fit into her things.* I was starting to realize that I'd missed a couple of subtle clues. "What about that colorful little sundress?" I asked weakly. "You also left that onboard and *it* seemed to fit you just fine."

"You noticed." She grinned. "That dress was one of Dylan's favorites, too. But after wearing it that last night on the boat with him, I never wanted to see it again."

I scratched my head, frowning at the bulk of the elephant that still remained on my plate. The abandoned clothes now off my list of questions, there were still things that didn't add up. "If what you're saying is true, how do you explain this Ozzy guy? How do you know him, and why did you put me in contact with him?"

We turned onto Walnut Avenue and I motioned her toward the curb. "Number seventy-five," I said, pointing up the street. "The beige one with brown trim. Just park the car here."

Teddy turned on the dome light to check her lipstick in the mirror. I quickly reached up and flicked it off.

Just then my cell phone rang, and I saw that it was my Customs Inspector friend. I answered, "Brooks?"

"Yeah," she said, a hint of irritation in her voice. "Tell me you're not smuggling dope and trafficking illegals like they're saying."

"Don't listen to that idiot, Prowse."

"It's not just him," she said. "I've got two DEA agents ready to arrest you on federal drug charges."

"Yeah, I know." I looked up the block to see my house completely dark. Didn't look like Bridget or anyone else was there. "And I've also got the Alameda cops after me for murder."

Brooks was quiet for a second. "Not so sure about that one," she said. "They told me they're looking at a Mexican national for killing your neighbor. Guy by the name of Benítez-Garcia."

"The Corkscrew," I said, taking my first real breath in a while. "They figured out that it's him? That's the first break I've gotten in a long time. Did they catch him yet?"

She got quiet, and I suspected it had something to do with my daughter. "They're still looking for him," she said. "Pretty sure he's in the area though."

"And Bridget?" I asked.

She hesitated.

"It's all right Brooks, you can give it to me straight up. If you know anything at all--"

"Nothing." She said it with a conviction that I knew I could rely on. "Your girl hasn't turned up yet, but on the negative side, nobody has seen her in a few days. Local cops checked her school and interviewed all her friends, but still nothing."

I took another breath, though this one was not as restorative. "What do you think?"

Another long pause. "I'm thinking you need to turn yourself in. Get this thing cleared up before it doubles back on you. As for your daughter and this Garcia asshole, leave it to the local PD. They actually seem to know what they're doing."

Sitting in the dark car with Teddy, I leaned my head back and tried to loosen my mind. I knew there was no way I'd surrender until I found Bridget. "Let me think it over," I said. "And I almost forgot why I asked for your help in the first place. Is there anything you can do for the two Mexican nationals on the yacht? The woman and her father are good people, and they had no intention of coming across the border with us. That was all on me."

"I can do that," she said. "Not a problem. We can transport them back, and I'll make sure it's not in an INS bus."

"Thanks, Brooks. I'll explain the rest of it--" Teddy nudged my arm and I stopped talking. Her eyes were fixed on my house. "Sarah, I'll have to get back to you."

I shut down the phone and the car's interior went dark again. "What is it?" I asked.

"I don't know." Teddy leaned forward in her seat, squinting against the glare of the streetlamp. "I thought I saw a light come on for a second, but then it went off."

"Stay here." But as I started to get out of the car, Teddy grabbed my arm.

"I don't want to stay in the car alone," she said. "I'm coming with you."

CHAPTER 48

Our home sits back from the street behind an upward sloping lawn—which, I couldn't help but notice had recently been mowed. I guessed that Doris had taken it upon herself to hire a gardening service, or perhaps the brownnoser Prowse had insinuated himself into my old life even more than I'd thought.

The houses on either side were well lit, making mine stand out like a black hole in the middle of the block. Stopping short of the driveway, I took a minute to watch and listen. No cars out of place, no unusual sounds, and no lights—as Teddy had claimed to see.

We crept beneath the shadows of our four Quaking Aspen trees. Leading the way to the end of the driveway, I felt Teddy coiled around my arm like a python.

At some point during our approach, I realized that I'd left my house key aboard my sailboat before departing for Mexico. But there used to be, as I recalled, a hidden key above the sliding door in the backyard.

As we started down the narrow walkway next to the garage, a floodlight burst on—illuminating me and Teddy like a couple of stage performers. It wasn't the first time I've been busted by a sensor light, either. I thrusted Teddy around me, past the spotlight and up to the side gate.

"That's the light I thought I saw from the car," she whispered.

The gate was already unlatched, and I noticed that the patio door was ajar—which meant that someone had taken the same route only moments before us.

I leaned close to Teddy and said, "Someone's inside." Her hair smelled really nice, like Herbal Essence. Then, realizing that I was losing my focus again, I suggested for the second time that Teddy wait outside. Her response was an even tighter grip on my arm.

Pushing the sliding door open a few inches farther, I made a mental note that whoever had squeezed through the space was thinner than me. I imagined Sacacorcho's squat, fireplug of a body trying to get through the space. *Doubtful.*

A black silhouette shot across the dark room, and I felt my arm jerk backwards. Besides pulling me off balance, Teddy's horror movie elbow clench had included a loud gasp that had probably alerted the intruder.

Too late for being covert, I broke loose of Teddy and started after the guy. I must have been unconsciously taking in data and adding it up as I ran through the dark house. Whoever I was chasing was more nimble than the stout Mr. Corkscrew, who would have been charging toward me rather than running away.

The intruder quickly disappeared into the darker recesses of the house. Thinking that he had moved like a scared cat, I was suddenly reminded of my description of Ozzy—a cat with nine lives. *Could he have somehow made if off the oil platform and gotten to Mill Valley ahead of me?*

Starting down the hallway, I was building an angry head of steam. I had decided that he was not going to leave the house alive.

I paused at the intersection of our kitchen and a hallway that leads back to the bedrooms, and listened. The dark house was filled only with an eerie silence. Glancing back, I saw that Teddy had taken refuge in the family room, flattening herself against the wall behind my recliner.

"Call the police," I said in a hoarse whisper.

"I would if my phone had a battery."

Touché, I thought. These women must have all graduated from the same school of sarcasm. I fumbled with my phone, lighting myself up in the process, only to see that the battery was nearly dead again.

The sounds of movement drew my attention back to the hallway, and I continued edging my way along the wall. Recognizing that I would be in a much better position if I had my handgun, I found myself thinking that the Alameda cops should have finished testing the ballistics by now.

A metallic clank sounded behind me, in the kitchen that I'd just passed. I froze in my tracks like a petrified fossil. Knowing it hadn't come from Teddy, I also knew it hadn't come from the person I was stalking down the hall. Which meant that there were two of them—one ahead of me, and the other now behind me. There was only one scenario that would explain it: Ozzy *and* Sacacorcho.

I yelled, "Teddy, get out of the house!"

"Dad?" came a familiar voice from the blackness at the end of the hallway.

It took a second to percolate into my brain. *Bridget?*

The lights came on, startling and blinding me at the same time. I spun around toward the second threat behind me, while trying to imagine a situation where my daughter and the killers would be in the house at the same time. I imagined that they'd taken Bridget hostage and had tied her up somewhere down the hall.

I stepped back to the kitchen doorway and cautiously glanced in. There was my secretary, or assistant, or whatever she was— straightening from a crouched position behind the butcher block island. Gripped tightly in her hand was an enormous carving knife.

She set the knife down. "What the hell you doin', McKenna? You almost got yo'self stabbed."

Teddy appeared behind me just as my daughter materialized from one of the bedrooms in front of me. I scooped up Bridge in my arms and hugged her tightly. She was still shaking with fright, and didn't let go for a long time.

Shanay eyed Teddy. "Who's she?"

"Teddy Langdon," she said with a warm smile. "I'm a friend who lives in Mr. McKenna's neigh--"

Shanay tilted her head. "Hashtag: Rich lady who sent McKenna on goose chase."

Teddy raised her palms. "Guilty as charged."

Shanay turned to me. "And why you didn't return my calls?"

"It's a long story," I said. "Bridget was in danger, and a very bad man threatened to have her killed."

"Short Mexican dude with a soup bowl hairdo?" Shanay nodded. "Yup, he been sniff'n around. Came to the office axe'n a bunch of questions. Matter of fact, someone been callin' Bridget from your phone." She motioned to the counter where Bridget's cell phone sat— its battery lying next to it.

"Thank God," I said. "You disabled it so they couldn't track you."

Bridget took Shanay by the hand. "She said that the man who called wasn't a friend of yours, Dad. If it wasn't for Shanay, they would have gotten me and Grandma for sure. Actually, being without my phone was like a death sentence anyway."

I forced a laugh.

Shanay gave me a lofty smirk. "I tol' you I'd be check'n on Bridget. Lucky thing I called her right after that dude did. Put two and two together and told her to send Grandma pack'n and turn off that damn phone."

"Where have you been staying?" I asked Bridge.

"With Shanay and the baby, but we had to come back here tonight to get the notes for my math final."

I'd never seen Shanay's apartment, but if it was anything like where she used to live in Hunter's Point, I knew that my daughter had gotten a real eyeful. Still, I was amazed at how well the two of them had managed to survive on their own. And, once again, Shanay's keen street sense had prevented what could have been a terrible tragedy.

"Remind me to give you a raise," I said to her.

"Hah! We still ain't got no pay'n jobs."

She had a point, but we had other things to consider—the first of which was that Corkscrew was still outstanding, and presumably still after my daughter.

I watched Bridget plug the battery back into her phone. My first reaction was to tell her not to, but then an idea came to me. If the killer was still looking for my daughter, then it made sense that he might still be trying to track the location of her phone.

"Can you bring Bridget back to your place, Shanay?" I then said to Bridge, "Only for one more night, but I'll need to take your phone with me."

CHAPTER 49

The connection had to stay open in order for Ozzy's boy to track it, but I didn't have the technical knowhow to figure it out.

Shanay programmed the phone to continuously redial Teddy's number over and over—activating the cell towers, which they would triangulate, and which would hopefully lead them to Bridget's phone.

I hated seeing Shanay's car drive off with my daughter in it, especially after finally having had her safely in my arms. But Shanay had kept Bridge alive so far, and my instincts told me that it was the most prudent thing to do. Remaining with me would have only put my daughter in greater danger.

"That young woman who works in your office," Teddy said as we got into her Lexus. "She..."

"Wasn't very nice to you?" I said.

"...she's very loyal to you," continued Teddy. "It's important to have people in your life that you can trust."

I nodded, not sure what Teddy was getting at. She just gazed out the window as she drove.

"You're talking about Dylan and you," I said, finally taking a stab at it.

Her eyes welled up and I knew I'd gotten it right.

"We were loyal to one another," she said faintly. "Dylan was my best friend."

It was true. The relationship I'd witnessed that night on their boat was no act. Sadly for me, there was probably no substance to Teddy's flirtatiousness or provocative banter. Apparently, theirs had been a unique companionship in which trust transcended every other thing. Which told me something else about Teddy—there was no way that she had anything to do with Dylan's murder.

That realization only added to the questions in my head. I wanted to know how she knew Ozzy, and why she put me in contact with him. But Teddy had slipped into the depths of wistful remembrance—holding Dylan's sainted image to her bosom—and even I wasn't boorish enough to intrude on that. But maybe I could go about it another way.

"So, the sale of your yacht..." I started. Her eyes took on a wary look, and I knew I hadn't fooled her. "Never mind."

I mulled over the facts as we silently headed back across the bridge into Richmond. Teddy's connection to Ozzy and the cartel was still the most glaring of the unanswered questions. I knew that the key was hidden somewhere in the small, seemingly insignificant details— it always was.

Clearing my head, I tried to think beyond the personal biases and subjective impressions that may have colored my thinking. I found my mind hovering around my personal information, and how Ozzy managed to get it.

"Sorry Teddy, but I just need to come out and ask... Did you tell anyone that I had a daughter named Bridget?"

"No, of course not." Her eyes showed disappointment. "Whyever would I?"

I ignored the question. "Did I ever tell you where I lived?"

"Yes."

"I did?"

"You don't remember? She glanced over at me. "Less than an hour ago when we turned onto Walnut Avenue, you told me to 'park near number seventy-five.'"

"No, no, before that," I said. "Did I ever mention it to you and Dylan that night on the boat?"

She shook her head.

"Did you ever look at my liveaboard application?"

Teddy shook her head again. "Never."

A hazy notion skirted through my mind, too fast to grab it—a loose piece of the massive elephant. Something about the application, I mused. And then I had it again. *Clifford.*

The nosy harbormaster at the Buena Vista marina was the only person who had access to all of the information about me. A few pieces fell into place as I mentally plugged him into the scenario.

"What about Cliff?" I asked.

"What about him?"

Closing my eyes, I thought back to the dinner on their yacht. "Didn't you and Dylan say that Cliff had introduced you to the idea of going to Mexico?"

She thought for a minute. "He was the one who told us about the Baja Ha-Ha. But it's mostly for sailboats, so we always did the cruise group trip with--"

"Sure," I interrupted, "but it was Cliff who first pointed you guys in that direction."

Another detail suddenly shook loose. When we were at the harbor in Puerto Salina, Ozzy had ordered me to take the boat to Oceanside instead of Alameda. "*My guy* says things are too hot up there right now," were his exact words. So, if Ozzy's original cocaine buyer was in the Bay Area, and by "too hot" he meant because of Dylan's murder, then who in the hell is it?

It was another damning indictment of Clifford.

"Why did you tell Cliff that I was going to take your boat down to Mexico?"

She frowned. "I didn't."

I frowned. "The day before I left, Cliff said he'd heard I was leaving to sell Bernice in Ensenada. How else would he know that?"

"I've no earthly idea," said Teddy. "But it didn't come from me. Why? Do you think Cliff had something to do with Dylan's murder?"

"Not sure yet."

Tiny fragments swirled around my brain as I gazed across the bay toward San Francisco. From a distance, it was a beautiful city; the colored lights, rolling hills, and picturesque skyline. But the close-up view from Sunnydale, Reardon Heights or the Tenderloin was a different picture. Kind of like ol' Cliff, I thought. He looked pretty good as a suspect from where I sat, but on closer scrutiny I wasn't so sure. Cliff was close, maybe, but still not a perfect fit.

A pair of headlights silhouetted us from behind, and I was forced to mentally change gears. I'd somehow drifted away from the here-and-now, and the car behind us was a reminder that Bridget's cell phone being tracked still loomed large. If Corkscrew had honed in on the signal as I'd hoped, then he could be closing in at any time. I slunk down in the seat, realizing that he would expect Bridget to be the passenger.

Teddy glanced into the rearview mirror, but didn't say anything. We were still fifteen minutes out, so I took the opportunity to explain that a large shipment of cocaine had been stashed aboard her yacht while I was getting drugged and beaten.

Expressions of shock and concern took turns on her face, then finally a look of discernment.

"What is it?" I was crouched next to her.

"We never should have bid on that boat."

"What do you mean 'bid'?"

"We bought the yacht at a government auction in Southern California," Teddy said. "Dylan always joked that it had probably been seized from a drug person. Maybe the cocaine was there all along, like someone left it there by accident."

I shook my head. "It was no accident."

But something she said stuck inside of me, choking my thoughts like a quarter in a nickel machine. It took a minute or two to dig it out, and then I recalled the previous owner's information. I'd seen it on the old transfer of title paperwork Teddy had left for me. Suddenly, things started to click.

I had first heard about SRRA Group during a homicide case I investigated in The City. A couple of stolen 40-foot cargo containers had been recovered, and were later sold at public auction by SRRA Group. *Seized, Recovered & Remarketing Auctioneering Group* in Riverside has a contract to auction vehicles, vessels, and other large asset forfeiture seizures by federal agencies on the West Coast.

"The auction house," I said. "Who first told you about it?"

Before Teddy could answer, she glanced in the mirror with a look of dread. Her eyes grew wide in the light, and then wider.

"Oh my God," she screamed. "Look out!"

CHAPTER 50

The car lurched forward from the impact, whiplashing our heads against the seatbacks and sending us careening across the freeway. Shattering tail lights, twisting metal, and Teddy's high-pitched scream all blended into one concussive eruption.

To her credit, Teddy hung on, maintaining control of the Lexus as it pitched sideways across the road then fishtailed back plumb again. But then she turned on the emergency flashers and pulled into the breakdown lane, as if we were now going to exchange driver's license information.

"Don't stop!" I yelled, "You need to step on it!"

The engine roared as she accelerated back onto the highway. Headlights reflecting in the rearview mirror gave me a pretty good gauge on how close the other car was. *Close!*

Still ducked down in the seat, I wished that I was behind the wheel instead of Teddy. Wrestling the phone out of my pocket, I saw that my battery power was only at 4%. Maybe enough for one call, but it would have to be a quick one.

Teddy was driving much faster, but I saw on her face that she was no speedster. Her little sedan was meant for style, not eluding armed assassins. I thumbed through my numbers until I found *Linh Phú*, then hit *dial*.

"Who are you calling?" asked Teddy, her faltering voice seconds away from a full-fledged sob.

"My former partner."

I ventured a quick peek over the dashboard to see a massive freeway interchange directly ahead of us. One branch veered West to San Francisco, another swung East toward Berkeley, and the third continued South. "Keep going straight," I said. "And then take... uh..." I was still out of my depth on this side of the bay.

"I know the way back to the marina," said Teddy. "On a different note, can I ask why you are calling your ex-wife at a time like this?"

"She's not an 'ex'—at least not yet. And I wasn't calling her."

"Oh. You said former partner, and I just thought--"

Had it been under different circumstances, I might have laughed. I took a glance out the rear window and was blinded by flashing high beams. They were right on top of us. Teddy suddenly jerked the wheel, slamming me against the passenger door and hyperextending my bad knee. I closed my eyes, silently wincing at the pain. When I opened them again, we were halfway down an exit ramp—dropping away from the freeway and into the shadows of a shoddy industrial area in West Oakland.

"*Partner,*" I said, "as in, we were teamed up together on the force."

We rumbled over the potholed 5th Street, bounding along like *Daytona 500 meets the lunar rover.*

Teddy's astonished expression was too authentic to fake. Not knowing that I used to be a cop was another point in the *Teddy's not involved* column, otherwise she would have seen it on my liveaboard application.

But I already knew that the application hadn't been used to find my address, or my wife's name, or Bridget's name for that matter. Still piecing it all together, I knew I was getting very close.

The rectangular light of the mirror had faded from her face a bit, and it seemed like Teddy's little maneuver onto the off-ramp had bought us some distance.

"Force, as in police force?" she asked.

I nodded. "Uh, yeah. Didn't I mention that?"

"No." She glanced at me again, this time with a spark in her eye. "So you have a gun then?"

"Uh, well, no. It's kind of a long stor--"

The phone suddenly picked up. "This is Linh Phú."

"Linh, it's McKenna. Where are you?"

"Hi, Inspector. Still at work, I'm afraid. Just finishing up some paperwork at the task force office downtown."

The light on Teddy's face grew brighter, and I knew the car was on us again.

"I need your help, Phú, and I need it quick."

A sharp crack suddenly sent us headlong through the intersection of 5th and Market. Teddy's Lexus skidded sideways up onto the curb and through a cyclone fence. Teddy screamed again, as she struggled to gain control of her car. We spun a full 180 degrees, kicking up a cloud of rocks and dust and coming to rest inches from a group of homeless people huddled around a barrel fire. There was a sputtering sound, and the engine died.

The freeway roared above us, and I saw that our rear window was gone. Getting my bearings, I realized that the other car was now perpendicular to us.

"Go, go!" I yelled, watching as the pair of headlights bore down on Teddy's side of the car.

The starter chugged for a second, and I clenched my teeth in anticipation of a horrific crash. The engine caught and Teddy dropped it into reverse—lurching us abruptly backwards and surprising both me and the other driver. The van jetted past our front bumper, missing us by a breath.

Teddy's mouth dropped open as she recognized the vehicle and its driver, but I had figured out that piece of the elephant already— since shortly after leaving Mill Valley.

"Linh!" I bellowed into the phone. "You still there?"

"Yes, Inspector."

"I need you to posse up your team and get over to the Buena Vista Yacht Harbor in Alameda."

"Right now?"

"Right now!"

CHAPTER 51

Tents and bungee-corded sheets of plastic lined the street, fluttering in the dark wind. An entire community living beneath the freeways among the noise and rats and filth. A few of the homeless people stooped there in the shadows of the overpass, barely even glancing at the death defying chase that was unfolding just a few feet from their bedrolls.

"If we get out of this alive, I'd like to hear more about your cop job." Teddy's eyes darted between me and the mirror. "It's too bad," she added. "Dylan would have loved talking to you about it."

"If we get out of this alive, I'll probably be going to prison." I flashed a wistful smile. "But we can talk about it on visiting day."

She looked like she didn't know how to take me. "Hold on tight," she said. We veered sharply left, and I suddenly felt like a bowling ball in a concrete sewage line.

"Where are we now?" I asked, hoping that our pursuers still believed that Bridget was Teddy's passenger.

"Webster Street Tube."

I'd driven through it a few times since moving to the East Bay, and knew that we were only five minutes out. Taking a quick glance over my seatback, I saw two silhouettes inside the white van. The DEA agents were right on our tail.

Halliday and Rourke would have figured out that we were heading to the marina, I thought. And, assuming that the Alameda detectives were still hanging around the harbor, the two federal agents would have to run us off the road and kill us before we made it there.

I peeked back again and saw that even though the van was keeping pace with us, the agents were laying back a bit now. Oddly, they didn't appear to be making another run at our rear bumper.

We were getting close, only a few more streets to go.

The marina's lights came into view, and then the sailboat masts pitching gently in their moorings. Praying that the police hadn't wrapped up their stakeout and gone home, I strained to spot at least some activity on the docks.

We hit the parking lot entrance at warp speed, launching Teddy and me airborne with an excruciating thump. Looking back, I saw that the van had entered the lot with equal gusto. These two weren't taking any chances that we'd beat them back to Teddy's yacht, and I finally had a pretty good idea why.

This was going to be a footrace for our lives, and I knew I'd still have to code in through the locked gate. That few seconds would be the dicey part, because it would give them time to chase us down. In a worst case scenario, none of the cops inside the marina would see what was happening in the parking lot. The two rogue agents could conceivably force us at gunpoint into their car and spirit us out of the area without anyone even noticing.

"Hit the horn," I said to Teddy. "Keep doing it, and flash the high beams too."

She did, and we flew across the parking lot like a Rose Bowl float gone wild. Then I saw the pedestrian access gate. Like the morning Dylan's body was found, it had been propped open to allow the police access. Which meant that the cops were still there.

"Get ready to make a run for it," I said. "Don't worry about the keys, just throw it into park and jump out sprinting." Preparing Teddy was the only way I knew of to ensure that she'd keep up with me. I wasn't going to leave her behind, but on the other hand, I wasn't about to let myself get caught by these guys.

Teddy aimed the Lexus straight at the pedestrian gate, and for a second I thought she was going to crash through it. But she jammed on the brakes when we were only a few car lengths away from it. Skidding to a smoky stop, we bolted from the car.

She had timed it so well that I wondered if she'd done it before. Regardless, we were easily going to win this horserace by a furlong.

I slowed to let Teddy through the opening before me. But as I turned to start down the ramp behind her, I felt the hot searing pain in my knee. I'd done it again.

Teddy didn't hear my stifled yowl as I collapsed against the ramp's railing. "Keep going," I called out, trying to be chivalrous even though she was already well ahead of me and probably wouldn't have stopped anyway.

Somebody yanked me hard from behind, and I felt an arm slip around my neck. Immediately, the cold, unyielding barrel of a gun dug into the center of my back. The noose-like grip was so tight that I could neither turn nor resist without fear of pressing harder into the gun, possibly causing it to fire.

My feet flopped like a marionette as they fought to gain purchase on the wooden slats. I tried to stay upright and yell for help, but both efforts were futile. The tightening vice of the arm was crushing my larynx like a paper straw.

Suddenly, an untimely memory edged its way into my mind, and I found myself reliving a scene from thirteen years earlier. I was a police academy rookie, learning how to apply the *carotid restraint* control hold. The instructor kept repeating, "You're not executing the hold correctly if the person can't breathe."

It was the last thought to go through my mind before flickering lights drained from my periphery, and everything went dark.

CHAPTER 52

"Let him up."

They were the first words I heard when the lights came back on. The dark fog in my head inched slowly upwards, and I realized that I was on the ground. The dock shook to the sound of running footsteps, and suddenly four men in suits stood before me.

"You've got no cause to choke him, he's not even resisting." The one doing the talking stood ahead of the other three. "I'm only going to tell you one more time, let him up!"

The guy giving the orders seemed increasingly familiar, but my head was still in the clearing stages. Trying but failing to stand, I felt the weight of a man holding me down.

Like a duel at twenty paces, the leader of the small group in front of me reached into his blazer and pulled out a handgun. Though it seemed to be pointed at me, I realized it was aimed at the guy on my back.

I felt a slight easing of weight, and looked back to see Agent Halliday brandishing his pistol over my head toward the men on the dock in front of me.

"Drop it!" shouted the head guy, and with that came recognition on my part. He was the detective investigating Dylan's murder.

In a weak voice I croaked, "Detective Grassi, hi."

Grassi ignored me, as if I were a salmon waiting to be gutted and cleaned. With the suddenness of a lightning strike, the three men with Grassi drew their weapons as well. The term *Mexican standoff* sprung to mind, which might have been amusing if I hadn't been lying directly between them.

"I'm a drug enforcement agent," said Halliday. "This man is in federal custody on charges of 21 U.S. Code 952: International importation of a schedule one controlled substance—cocaine."

The Alameda detectives lowered their weapons. At that point, I saw that it was only Halliday behind me—which was a bit of a shocker. I couldn't imagine a circumstance in which Rourke would have stayed back at the car.

Then I spotted Rourke about 50 yards to my right, standing on the fuel dock next to Bernice. I immediately wondered how long I'd been out. *Was it enough time for Rourke to get from the van to the gate, pass by me, and make it all the way to the fuel dock?*

Trying to catch up, I gazed around the dock. Crime scene tape had been strung around Bernice, from her bowsprit to her stern. My Customs friend, Sarah Brooks, was there, standing with her boss, Tim Sanchez, on the dock near Rourke. Also on the fuel dock were Doris, Mike Prowse, Patricia, and Mr. Uribe—all of whom sat comfortably on plastic chairs.

Teddy, I noticed, had made it down to the bottom of the ramp before I was choked into unconsciousness, and she was now cowering behind Grassi and the other Alameda detectives. Everything around me seemed to be at a tense détente. The local cops and the federal agents faced one another like soccer teams preparing for a penalty kick. Someone had to break the stalemate.

"Walk McKenna down to his wife and the others," ordered Grassi. "And get him a chair." Grassi stood firm on the wavering ramp, waiting for Halliday to holster his gun and comply. After a few uneasy seconds, he finally did.

With the scruff of my neck still in his grasp, Halliday ushered me down the ramp to Bernice. My former passengers regarded me like a newcomer to their little club. I couldn't tell whether or not they witnessed me being choked, but it seemed that they wanted to distance themselves from the federal fugitive—me.

Finally, Doris asked, "Is there any news about Bridget?"

"Yeah," I nodded. "She's okay. She's safe."

"With who?"

I glanced at Halliday, who by now had taken out a pair of handcuffs. "I'll fill you in on that later." I wasn't about to tip the agents as to where my daughter was hiding. Especially when it seemed like I was about to be arrested.

Doris looked confused, but the wrinkles on her forehead eased and she simply nodded.

"We can add charges of interstate kidnapping," said Rourke. He motioned toward Prowse. "This guy says that McKenna held them all captive on the boat against their will."

Halliday smirked beneath his surfer boy hairdo as he clapped the cuffs on my wrists. Grassi watched without showing any reaction, and though his body language revealed discomfort with the situation, he wasn't ready to take a side.

I had finally gathered enough pieces to make a run at the rest of the elephant. If my hypotheses were correct, I could provide Grassi with enough information to solve Dylan's murder. But if I had somehow gotten it wrong, I'd be spending the rest of my life behind bars.

Turning to Agent Halliday, I asked, "If you're charging me with drug trafficking, then shouldn't you have evidence?"

My wife, Prowse, and the Uribes tilted their heads to hear the answer. I glanced at Brooks, realizing that she's seen me in this situation before. She knew that I wouldn't have asked the question if I didn't already know the answer.

Ready to lay all of my cards on the table and call the hand, I was suddenly distracted by muffled voices floating down from the parking lot. This development threw a temporary monkey wrench into my planned discourse.

Halliday abruptly turned toward the entry gate. Detective Grassi's eyes followed, and then the rest of the group looked over. Heavy footsteps of a half dozen people trudging down the ramp vibrated all along the pier. My ex-partner led the entourage to the fuel dock where we curiously waited.

Grassi let out a long sigh. "And you are?"

"Inspector Linh Phú." She extended her tiny hand. "San Francisco Police Department."

Grassi glanced around with open arms. "This is Alameda. What business do you have all the way over here?"

She motioned toward her team of officers. "We're actually part of a Bay Area wide drug task force, and we'd like to have a word with Inspector McKenna."

"No can do," Halliday said. "He's in *federal* custody."

Phú said, "And you are?"

He flashed his credentials at Phú, then brusquely introduced his partner, Rourke.

I could see that Halliday was trying to make it sound official—like it was all super-secret, high level DEA business, well above everybody else's paygrades. But by now, I had pretty much figured it out. These two agents were a couple of dirty birds, and they were about to shit all over themselves.

Heavy wheezing drew everybody's attention to Cliff, chugging across the dock. "Do all these people have permission to be in here?"

"We're all police," said Brooks. "And you are?"

"Clifford Phillips, the Harbormaster."

I was about to continue my monologue when a stoutly built woman with a clipboard appeared at the open gate. She clopped her way down the ramp, and I immediately recognized her as the family court case worker from Marin County Family Services. The woman stopped to take in the scene, including me in handcuffs. "Did I catch you at a bad time?" she asked.

"No," I said. "You're more than welcome to stay."

Grassi tilted his head until it was nearly sideways. "And you are?"

"Claudette Higginbotham," she said, handing him her card.

I turned back to Halliday. "Now that we've all gotten acquainted, how about answering the question?

CHAPTER 53

I had gotten everyone's attention. "What evidence do you have that I'm involved in drug trafficking?"

Halliday turned to Rourke. "Did you search the yacht?"

"Yep," Rourke said. "Nothing there."

Another piece fell into place. Rourke hadn't had enough time to search the boat and string crime scene tape around it, all while I was unconscious. He had been at the harbor the entire time. *So, who's the second silhouette sitting back there in the van?*

Rather than disappointment or frustration at not finding drugs on the boat, Halliday simply shrugged. "Well, no matter. We know the cocaine was in your possession, and that's enough to bring charges."

Sarah Brooks and Linh Phú both knew the law, and saw the flaw in Halliday's logic. Chomping at the bit, Brooks got the words out first. "Excuse me, but isn't a warrant required to search someone's boat?"

Rourke dismissed her with an adolescent shrug. "Nobody was here to claim ownership. Since there were no drugs found, the whole Fourth Amendment thing is a non-issue anyway."

"And we're seizing the yacht," added Halliday.

"Based on what?" I asked.

Halliday bristled. "Based on our observations when it was under your control, McKenna. Based on the cocaine we took off of the boat as evidence in Southern California."

Another piece slipped into place. *It wasn't Southern California, in fact, it wasn't even the United States.*

"Humor me for a second," I said. One of the cops set a chair down for me, but I wanted to stay standing. It was about to be my fifteen minutes of fame, my final performance, my only chance to speak from the pulpit. And the minister doesn't sit during his own sermon. "You searched the entire boat?"

Rourke nodded.

"And you're sure you checked everything? No drugs anywhere?"

Rourke frowned. "I searched it from top to bottom, stem to stern. I said there was nothing."

"We're federal agents, McKenna. I think we know how to conduct a search," added Halliday.

A smile inched across my face as I realized that I had them both, right where I wanted them. "But you're still going to seize the yacht?"

"Isn't that what I just said?" Halliday's annoyance was obvious. "Yes, we are seizing the boat." He grabbed me by the shirt as if he was about to drag me off to prison.

I twisted away to face my old partner. "Linh, why don't you and your team go in and search it again for them?"

Halliday came to an abrupt stop, his eyes bulging with anger. "You already heard my partner, McKenna. It's empty! There aren't any drugs onboard!"

"The boat is in our custody now," said Rourke. "And the Customs agent said it herself, the boat can't be boarded and searched without a warrant."

Unable to hide my grin any longer, I nodded to Phú.

"Not so fast, Rourke." She stepped over to Teddy. "You're right, a search warrant is required... unless the owner gives us permission."

I winked at Teddy. "Are you the yacht's legal owner?"

"Yes, I am."

"And do you give Inspector Phú your permission to enter and search your yacht?"

Teddy smiled at all the attention. "Yes, I do."

Halliday's face went pale as the six task force members stepped onto Bernice.

The Alameda detective rubbed the bridge of his nose. "You want to tell me what's really going on here, McKenna?"

"Sure, Grassi." I wanted to use my hands for better effect, but they were still cuffed behind my back. "As Mrs. Langdon has already told you, she asked me to sell the boat for her in Ensenada. But what she probably didn't think to mention, and I didn't know until earlier tonight, was who put her in touch with the supposed buyer in the first place." I pivoted toward Teddy.

"It was them," she said, pointing at Halliday and Rourke. "The morning Dylan's body was found, they told me that the marina wasn't safe and that I shouldn't live on the boat alone. They said they knew of a buyer in Ensenada."

"And if I'm right," I said, turning to Cliff, "It was also Halliday and Rourke who told you that I was taking the yacht to Mexico."

Cliff cleared his throat. "Yes, that's right."

Grassi shrugged. "What's the significance, McKenna?"

"The significance is that there was never any buyer. The two agents set the whole thing up. Their phony buyer was Osvaldo Morales, a cartel guy who drugged and beat me and then hid 250 kilograms of cocaine onboard the boat. They assumed that I'd sail the boat back here, at which time Halliday and Rourke would sneak the shipment off of the yacht."

"Uh-huh," said Grassi. But I could tell he was still uncertain as to where this was all going.

"I found the drugs hidden behind a false wall," I said. Not wanting to complicate the story with irrelevant details, I glossed over my naiveté in carrying a kilo to the embassy and being arrested. "Anyway," I continued, "Halliday and Rourke contacted me in Tijuana, saying that they had confiscated the cocaine as evidence, and had replaced it with flour. But as it turns out, they never logged the cocaine into evidence."

Grassi scratched his ruddy face. "How do you know that?"

"Two reasons," I said. "First one is that the yacht was moored at the Coronado Islands when they supposedly seized the cocaine. The Coronados are in Mexican territorial waters, and by Halliday's own admission, the DEA has no police powers in Mexico. In fact, had the agents taken the cocaine to the Imperial Beach CBP Station as they had claimed, they, themselves, would have been guilty of bringing the drugs into the United States."

I glanced at the faces of my former passengers—all of whom were doing their best to keep up with the story. Patricia's eyes told me that she never doubted me, but Prowse looked like he still didn't believe a word of it. Doris sat quietly, as if she was seeing me through a new lens.

"The second reason," said Brooks, "is that no cocaine ever made it to CBP's Imperial Beach station. A co-worker of mine in San Diego verified it with the section chief."

Grassi's eyes narrowed, and his men quietly moved to either side of the two DEA agents. Grassi nodded. "Go on, McKenna."

"So, I knew that the fake drugs were just a ruse, and that the real cocaine still had to be somewhere onboard—which is why Halliday and Rourke were so adamant that I return the yacht directly to them in Alameda."

I was reading the agents' body language, and I could tell that they were feeling the heat. Halliday's tight jaw and balled fist were a dead giveaway. Rourke's eyes darted around the marina like a rat about to jump ship.

Grassi asked, "Why wouldn't they have left the cocaine stashed in the hidden compartment? I mean, why replace it with fake drugs?"

"Because there's no honor among thieves," I said. "They didn't trust their supplier—and for good reason. Osvaldo Morales tried to sell the flour to someone else down in Oceanside... which didn't go too well."

Brooks rolled her eyes. "I had a feeling that was you."

Grassi frowned. "I hope you're able to prove all of what you're telling me, McKenna."

Just then, Phú and her task force cohorts popped up from the companionway. Her eyes connected with mine, and I saw an almost imperceptible nod.

I turned back to Grassi. "If Halliday and Rourke are so convinced that there's no cocaine onboard, then they'd have no reason to seize the boat." I let that hang in the air for a second before continuing. "The real reason they want to seize the boat is to get it out of our hands before we find their stash. But, I think it's too late for that..."

Linh Phú joined us on the dock. "Just like Inspector McKenna says," she motioned toward Bernice. "We found the load of cocaine down in the engine room."

"That's ridiculous," said Halliday. "If there *is* anything onboard, my partner probably just didn't see it."

"Didn't see 250 kilos?" said Phú. "It's the size of a Volkswagen. And I'm willing to bet that when the crime scene technicians get out here, they'll find your prints all over it."

She nodded at her team, and they promptly drew down on Halliday and Rourke. Phú relieved the agents of their sidearms and cell phones, and then her people handcuffed them.

Grassi had listened patiently, and now watched as Phú placed Halliday and Rourke's personal property into evidence bags. Finally, he turned to me and said, "It sounds like you've put together a strong trafficking case against these guys. Since most of it involves the boat belonging to my shooting victim, I'm guessing he was also involved in cocaine." Grassi lifted his eyebrows to make it more of a question. "So, what part does Dylan Langdon play in all of this?"

I unconsciously glanced at Teddy. Her eyes welled up, but she looked as hungry for answers as Grassi. It convinced me that Teddy had no involvement in any of it.

I answered, "If my hunch is correct, it was Halliday and Rourke who steered Dylan to the federal auction house to buy the yacht in the first place."

Teddy nodded.

"And it was the same two who first introduced the Langdons to the idea of traveling down to Baja on the boat."

She nodded again. "They even told us where to go in Ensenada for a good meal. The agents were kind enough to set up dinner for us at a friend's restaurant. Complimentary drinks, too."

"I'll bet." I let loose with a chuckle. "Which would have kept you off of the yacht for at least a couple of hours, right?"

Teddy nodded.

To Grassi and Phú I said, "It was enough time for Ozzy and his people to hide cocaine onboard without the Langdons' knowledge. And when the yacht returned to Alameda, Halliday and Rourke bided their time until Teddy and Dylan left the boat. Fifteen minutes to retrieve the load from behind the false wall, and they were done."

Teddy looked shocked, broken, and resigned. "Did they do this each time me and Dylan took the yacht to Mexico?"

"Probably." I shrugged. "But we may never know for sure what went wrong with their little racket."

The question on everyone's mind remained what Dylan's role was in all of it. Even though I had a hard time believing he was involved, the cops' expressions told me that they thought otherwise.

Grassi eyed the two agents before turning to me. "Do you have reliable evidence that *they* killed him?"

"No, but who else could it have been? Either they did it, or they had one of their Mexican henchmen do it." I turn to Phú. "Any update on the info I gave you about Ozzy?"

"Sheriff's got back to me earlier today." She pulled a small notebook from her pocket. "Their air support unit dropped a SWAT team onto platform Holly last night at 2130 hours." Glancing at her notes, she said, "Found Osvaldo Morales, wet and shivering on one of the bracing beams beneath the main platform. He was suffering from mild hypothermia, but he's warming up in the Santa Barbara County Jail as we speak."

"That's one possible suspect," I said to Grassi. "The other one is hiding inside a white cargo van right up there in the parking lot."

Sarah Brooks said, "If the guy in the van is another illegal, I can place a detainer on him for you. It'll give you time to question him."

Grassi quickly ordered two of his detectives to accompany Brooks and a couple of Phú's task force guys. They hustled up the ramp into the lot, and though I anticipated gunfire, I heard none. After a while, I began to worry that I'd been wrong. But the ad hoc arrest team finally returned with Manny Benítez-Garcia, also known as El Sacacorcho—the human corkscrew.

"He wasn't in the van," said Brooks, "but we checked the area and found him hiding in some bushes."

While searching Sacacorcho, they recovered a 9mm handgun, which Grassi took for ballistics testing and comparison.

Rourke and Halliday denied knowing Benítez-Garcia, and the Mexican killer wasn't talking. I knew that the connection between the agents and Corkscrew would be difficult to prove—now that he'd been caught outside the van.

"Check Benítez-Garcia's phone, Phú." I struggled to point with my manacled hands. "Hopefully his text messages and call logs will show that they were all working together. They may also tie them to Dylan's murder."

Grassi unlocked the handcuffs, and then glanced over at Prowse. "I hope it's all right with you that I'm releasing McKenna."

Prowse missed the sarcasm altogether. "No, it most certainly is not all right. You still have four kidnap victims here, all of whom are ready to swear out statements."

Patricia whispered something to her father, who walked over and shook my hand.

"My father and I were not kidnapped," said Patricia.

Prowse's wide eyes turned to my wife. "Doris?"

She's shook her head before he even got her name out. "You just don't get it, Michael. *You* caused half of the problems that you're complaining about."

With my chest puffed up, I strode over to where they all sat. I took a second to relish the moment before leaning down to Patricia. My face was almost against hers as I inhaled the sweet bouquet of her skin. "I'm sorry that you and your father had to endure all of this," I whispered.

Patricia's warm almond eyes gazed back at me.

I leaned closer. "And if it's okay with you, I'd like the chance to--"

"Hey!" It was the task force officer that Phú had left aboard the yacht to guard the cocaine. Stepping onto the dock, the guy held up an oblong package wrapped in duct tape. "Hey, I found this under some blankets in the forward stateroom."

"Another kilo of cocaine?" asked Phú.

"I don't think so." The guy scratched his head. "Wrong color and consistency. It looks like a bunch of fireplace ashes."

CHAPTER 54

Patricia stared at the cop holding her mother's remains in the air like a loaf of bread.

I hit the pause button on my sweet little talk and switched into damage control mode. Trying my best to explain why I had to swap Mrs. Uribe's ashes for a kilo of cocaine, I realized that Patricia was no longer looking at me in the same tender way.

"You let us believe that we were scattering my mother's remains into the sea," she said. "And the whole time; our eulogy, our blessings, our goodbyes, they were being spoken to an urn full of drugs. How can I forgive that?"

It was a fair question, but it sounded so much worse when she said it. Unwilling to look over at Doris or meathead, I stood there stuttering like Elmer Fudd as I tried to come up with a plausible answer.

Sarah spared me further embarrassment by stepping in and ushering Patricia and Mr. Uribe to her boss's Town Car.

I followed them all the way up to the parking lot while Sarah explained her plan to them. She had booked a flight from SFO to San Diego—arriving at 1:10 a.m. Brooks' CBP coworker would pick up the Uribes at the other end and deliver them to the PedWest border crossing in San Ysidro.

I apologized again to Patricia, hoping to segue into the two of us getting together sometime in the near future. Telling her that I wanted the opportunity to make it up to her, I also wanted her to know that even with my distain for travel, I'd be willing to meet for an intimate weekend in Cancun or Cabo.

"Goodbye, Mr. McKenna," she said, extending her hand abruptly. "My father and I wish you well."

I gave the rigid hand a lifeless shake, then watched her get into the car. Glancing over at Sarah Brooks, I saw that she had witnessed the entire encounter.

"Sort of blew that one, McKenna," said Brooks. "Couldn't have looked much worse if you'd smoked her mother in a crack pipe."

By the time I got back to the dock, things were winding down for everyone except Phú and her team. The task force had brought in portable lights and tables, and called a forensics team to help with evidence processing.

Teddy was told that she'd have to stay the night elsewhere, but could take back custody of her yacht sometime the following day.

She mouthed a silent thank you to me before she headed up the ramp and drove out of the lot. I wondered how thankful Teddy will be once she gets a load of the bathroom door, the ravaged radio system, and all the bullet holes in her wheelhouse.

Prowse sat upright, glancing around like he was still waiting for someone to take his statement. Doris looked disgusted with the whole lot of us, and my pandering to Patricia was probably the icing on the cake. I wrote down Shanay's number and handed it to Doris like a peace offering. "You can get in touch with Bridge at this number."

A few minutes later, a taxi cab arrived and Doris left without a word to either me or Prowse.

Overcoming the tinge of ache in the center of my chest, I projected my raw emotions onto an easy target—the idiot. "Hey Prowse, hope you have a good pair of shoes. Because you'll need them for that long walk back to Long Beach to get *the Jag*."

"Like you did any better with the Mexican girl," he fumed.

"We got it all straightened out in the parking lot," I lied. Not only did I want to save face with him, but I hoped that he'd pass that on to Doris—if she ever talked to him again.

Prowse stormed out of the harbor and into the dark parking lot alone. I thought about calling out one last insult, but it probably would have been overkill. Besides, the guy was right; I hadn't done any better with Patricia.

Grassi waited until Halliday, Rourke, and Benítez-Garcia were carted off to jail, before turning to me. "I'll need some time with you tomorrow," he said. "Most of the charges against these scumbags hinge on your testimony, so we'll have to record your statement."

We made plans to meet at 10 a.m. in his office.

Stepping aboard Wanderlust felt as good to me as getting into a hot shower. My little sailboat felt cramped compared to Teddy's yacht, but it suited me better. I was exhausted, and I fell asleep without eating or unpacking. After dozing like a hibernating bear, I emerged from my den hungry and stiff. I stopped for a chorizo breakfast burrito and coffee on my way to Alameda PD, and demolished them in the parking lot before going in.

Grassi took me into a conference room, where he interviewed me in the presence of a police videographer, a representative from the District Attorney's Office, and two stiff suits—a man and a woman. Turns out that they were from Drug Enforcement's Office of Inspections—DEA's equivalent of internal affairs. They were attempting to build a case against Halliday and Rourke for internal policy violations, as well as a host of other federal charges.

As I was leaving the room, one of the OIS suits mentioned to the other that the charges against their two agents appeared to be "circumstantial at best."

I realized that they were right. It would be my word against the two corrupt agents, unless someone came up with physical evidence— such as digital phone data, fingerprints, DNA, ballistics, financial records, or corroborating witness testimony. I left the police station with a cloud of dread hanging over my head.

The next morning, Grassi called to tell me that the bullet that killed Dylan Langdon matched the 9mm handgun taken from Corkscrew. Although it tightened the murder case against him, it did nothing to implicate Halliday and Rourke.

Grassi also asked that I return to Alameda PD for another series of interviews. At 11 a.m. I met with two City of Oceanside detectives and walked them through the incident that took place at their marina. Although I provided detailed suspect descriptions, they already seemed to have a handle on the players' identities.

At the conclusion of the questioning, and once they shut off the recorder, the detectives filled me in on what I didn't know about their investigation. Two men had been injured during the Oceanside Harbor shootout: an innocent bystander and one of the drug traffickers—later identified as a member of the Las Moicas Cartel. According to the Oceanside detectives, the ¼ ton cocaine transaction represented an uneasy alliance between Las Moicas and Osvaldo Morales' Jalisco Cartel.

In any case, lingering distrust between the two organizations was like pre-existing explosive material, and the fake drugs is what lit the fuse. I just happened to be the one holding the bomb.

On my way out of the building, Grassi told me that the case against Halliday and Rourke has taken another bad turn. "Forensic work on their phones came up dry," he said. "The agents were apparently smart enough to communicate with the cartels using burners—which we're unlikely to ever find."

Evidence collection aboard Bernice was just wrapping up when I arrived at the harbor with the Oceanside detectives. The crime scene techs had removed the yellow tape and were stowing their equipment.

I asked the scene supervisor how it went, and she shrugged. "Aside from yours and Osvaldo Morales' prints, we haven't recovered any other latents from the cocaine packages—only shiny smudges, which are consistent with a synthetic lubricant. Whoever moved these drugs to the engine room probably wore polymer-based gloves."

The Oceanside detectives exchanged looks. I realized that without a clear nexus to the drugs or the cartels, Halliday and Rourke would walk free. What's worse, I'd look like a complete fool and there would be no real justice for Dylan's murder.

Teddy hadn't returned from wherever she was staying, so I quickly escorted the Oceanside guys aboard the yacht to take their photographs. When they saw the gunfire damage inside the stateroom, they told me that I was "unbelievably lucky to be alive."

My final interview was with Linh Phú and Sarah Brooks. Since both women were my close friends, we agreed to meet on my sailboat.

Brooks' paperwork was mostly Immigration forms relating to the Uribes' transport back, and the detainer placed on El Sacacorcho. Linh's questions were specific to the cocaine; who touched the packages, who had access to them, and how long the drugs were out of my sight. Although chain of custody had to be documented in order to nail down criminal charges, I was increasingly doubtful that the case would ever see the light of a courtroom. As it stood, there was more forensic evidence against me than the two rogue agents.

Phú and Brooks finished the questioning around five o'clock, and though I offered to buy them dinner, both still had work to get done.

After they left, I thawed a couple of frozen hot dogs in the microwave and warmed a can of baked beans. It was an easy meal that we called *beans-and-weenies* as kids. Then, I sat on deck watching the sun set as I ate my paltry dinner. It was Friday night, and I was alone, but at least I was home on my boat in one piece. And most importantly, my daughter was safe.

My rucksack still sat near the companionway where I had left it two days earlier. I hadn't had the time or energy to take my clothes and toothbrush out, but I knew it wasn't going to empty itself. When I finally got around to it, I saw the bottle of Cabernet Sauvignon I'd snatched from the yacht on my way down to Ensenada. My delight was quickly doused by the guilt that I'd returned the boat to Teddy unsold and in a shambles. Not to mention, minus a bottle of wine. *What a louse!*

I set the bottle on the counter, making a mental note to give it back to Teddy the next time I saw her.

At the bottom of the rucksack was Dylan's book, *Sadhana*. As it flopped onto the table, a folded piece of paper slid out from between its pages.

Blinking hard, I stared at the handwritten words on the backside of the note. *Can I be seeing this right?*

DAN ~ PLEASE MAKE SURE THAT TEDDY GETS THIS LETTER.

CHAPTER 55

It was just before 10 p.m. when I walked across the dock to Teddy's boat. The moon's unbroken reflection on the slack tide looked like a painting. Gazing at the spot where Dylan's body was found only two weeks ago, I was struck that there was nothing to mark that it ever even happened.

A U-Haul truck pulled up to the gate, and I watched the marina's newest resident—a young woman—struggle through with an armload of clothes and a table lamp. To her, our quiet little harbor probably seemed like a haven from the outside world. I wasn't so sure that I'd ever get that feeling back.

Making the turn onto Teddy's dock, I stopped to take in the slip where the DEA boat was once moored. The feds had seized the 63-footer, leaving only an empty slip—another harsh reminder of how life goes on.

For the second time in as many weeks, I found myself nervously standing outside Bernice with the same bottle of wine in my hand.

"Knock-knock," I called out. "Teddy? It's me, Dan."

She greeted me at the top of the companionway, her damp hair brushed back like she'd just showered. Over black stretch pants, Teddy wore an oversized jersey—which I imagined had belonged to Dylan.

She gave me a sisterly hug and then stepped back to regard the wine with a quizzical look.

"I came to return a couple of things that belong to you," I said, handing her the bottle. "The first is this wine, which I lifted from your yacht when I thought we were selling it."

"Come on inside." Teddy laughed as she took the bottle and led me into the main salon. "What's the second thing?"

"You may want to sit down for this." I took the folded letter from my pocket and set it between us on the table.

Teddy's expression grew in intensity as she recognized Dylan's handwritten instructions to me. After glancing between me and the note, she donned a pair of reading glasses.

"*My love.*" Teddy's eyes welled with tears as she glanced up once more before burying herself in her husband's final message. "*If you are reading this letter, then they have already killed me...*" Volume slowly seeped from Teddy's words, until only her lips were moving. When she finished reading the letter, she looked at Dylan's instructions again, and then turned it over to read it a second time.

I pretended that I hadn't already read the note, even though I had. *Who wouldn't?*

Teddy let out a long sigh, then set the letter down and removed her glasses. She closed her eyes, and finally a smile of contentment came onto her face. "He knew," she said. "Dylan knew how much it would upset me, and he tried to deal with those guys himself."

I nodded, realizing it was pretty much a given that I'd already read the letter. "Sounds like he figured out what Halliday and Rourke were doing," I said. "Dylan probably approached them about it."

She stood and got a corkscrew out of the drawer. I let the irony of the *corkscrew* pass as I watched her open my wine. After pouring us each a glass, she slid onto the settee and put her feet up. Raising her glass, she said, "To Dylan."

"He was a good man." Unable to wait any longer, I asked "What was that he mentions about gathering evidence?"

Teddy shook her head. "No idea. And I don't understand why he wouldn't have spelled it out in the letter."

After a minute, I thought I'd figured out why. "Maybe he believed that by the time we read this, we would already know what the evidence was."

"But we don't." Teddy took another sip. "Do we?"

I examined the wording again. "*...Evidence of the crime that started all of this,*" I read aloud. "That could mean something written, or recorded, or even a photograph." I snapped my fingers. "Where is Dylan's phone?"

Teddy had no idea. Said she hadn't seen it since before he was killed.

It took twenty minutes for me to get through to the night shift watch commander. Another five minutes of badgering the guy before he reluctantly agreed to call Detective Grassi at home. Teddy was pouring the last of the wine into our glasses when Grassi called back.

"This had better be important, McKenna."

I told Grassi about the note, which seemed to capture his interest. But when I mentioned the possible existence of video evidence, the other end of the line went quiet.

"If you're going to ask me about Langdon's cell phone, I'm afraid it's bad news." Grassi cleared his throat, and I realized that he'd been asleep. "Our divers found the phone in the water near where we think he went in. It had been submerged for more than 24 hours, and saltwater had corroded the internal components."

"Aren't there ways to recover the data?"

Grassi groaned. "Forensics people tried. They rinsed it, packed the circuit board in silica gel, gave it a new battery, and did whatever other technical mumbo jumbo they do. But when they ran a recovery scan, they got nothing. And FYI, the victim's laptop was clean, too—nothing worth a damn on any of the drives."

Disheartened, I ended the call and sat staring into my glass. "You know what this means, don't you?"

Teddy seemed to have gotten the gist of the news. "You thought that Dylan had proof on his phone, right? And now his phone doesn't work?"

"Yeah, sort of." I barely had the energy to explain that it's much worse than that. "It means that nobody's ever going to know for sure that Dylan was innocent. Sure, you and me know he wasn't involved, but the cops are always going to wonder. And not to paint too gloomy a picture, but those asshole DEA agents are going to walk free."

"How do you know that?"

I was too wrapped up in my own disappointment to pick up on her emotion. "Jurors won't want to believe that Halliday and Rourke were capable of doing these kinds of things—working with the cartels, smuggling drugs, brutally murdering innocent..."

Her face saddened, and I realized that my filter had slipped loose again. I offered Teddy an apology, and we finished the wine in silence. A few minutes later she stood, letting me know that it was time for me to leave. But I was in deep thought, staring at the table and focusing on what was anchoring me to the seat. Another wisp of an idea, I realized.

"What about personal effects?" I asked.

"Halliday and Rourke's?"

I tried not to roll my eyes. "No... Dylan's."

"I got rid of most of it," she said. "It was only two boxes of clothes. We had already downsized when we moved onto the boat."

"What about another phone?" Then before she had the chance to ask, I clarified. "Dylan's."

She shook her head.

"A camera?"

"Nope." Teddy leaned against the bulkhead, yawning. I knew that whatever the past two weeks has been for me, it had been far worse for her.

Finally, I stood to say goodbye. My bad knee nearly gave out from sitting so long, but I played it off like my leg had fallen asleep. I was on the deck, still replaying everything in my mind when it hit me. Turning around, I asked, "You said that Grassi took Dylan's computer along with your cell phone?"

She frowned at the question. "No, it was my laptop."

"They didn't want to look at his?"

She thought for a second before shrugging. "Maybe it was his laptop that they asked for. Oops, my bad. I must have given them mine instead."

CHAPTER 56

Shanay wasn't happy to hear from me at 7:30 on a Saturday morning.

"You want me to be at the office when? You gotta be joke'n with me, McKenna. I'm eat'n breakfast with my baby right now."

"It's important," I told her. "I need your technical expertise." The last part was a bit of an overreach, but it hooked her. In truth, she did know more than me about such things, but what I really needed was to tap into her street smarts. Somewhere in Shanay's lengthy criminal resume, there must have been something about computer hacking.

Twenty-five minutes later, I walked into my office—a 749 square foot unit near Jack London Square. The second floor suite has no elevator, but it's got what the rental agent called a "peek-a-boo" view of the estuary.

Shanay and her daughter were already there, sitting on a blanket next to a space heater. Teddy Langdon arrived a minute or two after me, with her husband's laptop tucked under her arm.

"I know Dylan's email address," she said, "but I have no idea about his password."

Teddy and Shanay exchanged acknowledging nods, but I knew that Shanay still blamed her for sending me down to Ensenada and getting me into the mess in the first place.

Briefly explaining the situation to Shanay, I showed her the note that Dylan left. "So," I said. "It looks like there might be evidence out there somewhere, that would prove Dylan's innocence and put away the two corrupt agents."

"What about his cell?" said Shanay. "That's what I'd use."

Shaking my head, I explained the saltwater damage from the bay.

"So you think I'm gonna break into the man's computer and find this stuff?"

"It's our only hope," I said. "Dylan may have transferred it from his phone to his laptop."

"Could have." Shanay handed me her daughter then took the laptop from Teddy. "But only if he had a backup app or program. And y'all gonna need his password for them. Or unless he loaded it all onto a disk or thumb drive."

Teddy shook her head. "I didn't find anything like that in Dylan's things."

The baby fussed a little, so I rested her head against my chest. It reminded me of when Bridget was a baby and the resonance of my voice would calm her.

On the evidence front, I was beginning to think I had misjudged Shanay's cyber proficiency. "Don't people get hacked all the time?" I asked. "I even read about some celebrities who got their naked selfies stolen."

"Professionals did that," said Shanay. "They know how to get that stuff off the cloud."

"You know any professional hackers?" I asked, half kidding.

She slowly closed and then opened her eyes. "Nobody knows them, McKenna. You can't just drive on over to Hackers-R-Us. These dudes live in the darkest places of the internet, and be usin' names like *Fetish, Oblivion, Neurosis.* They get paid in Bitcoin, too, so ain't no way to track 'em... But, yeah, I can hook you up with this dude I heard of called *Frat Boy.*"

Shanay's baby had fallen asleep, so I kept rocking her in my arms. The more I thought about Shanay's hacker friend, the worse it seemed. "Well, I don't have any Bitcoins."

Shanay laughed and shook her head.

"...and furthermore, having some shady hacker recovering important evidence would screw up the whole case. We'd have to document the chain of custody, and if it ever went to trial I doubt this *Frat Boy* would testify."

Staring at a blank login screen, Shanay asked Teddy, "So, you think that your man *scwabbed* with the drug-sling'n agents?"

"Scwabbed?" Teddy looked at me and we both shrugged.

Shanay shook her head. "Squared up? Jumped bad? You know, did he challenge 'em?"

Teddy nodded. "Yes, I think my husband might have told Halliday and Rourke that he had evidence of what they were up to. Especially if he wanted them to back off and leave us alone."

Shanay looked at me, and I suddenly understood where she was going with it.

"You're thinking that Dylan would have known they might come after it," I said. "So he would have backed up or copied the file, or photos, or whatever the evidence was."

"But didn't we already know that?" asked Teddy. "Isn't that why we're here?"

"Yes," I said. "But if Dylan knew they were coming after him for the evidence, he would do everything he could to keep it out of their hands. Which would add a wrinkle, because he would have to hide it from them in such a way that we would still be able to find it."

I carefully grabbed Dylan's note off of Shanay's desk without waking the baby. "It's got to be here somewhere..."

Teddy leaned around me to view her husband's letter. We read it separately, but together, in a harmonizing mumble.

"Bernice!" We both said it at the same time.

Shanay quickly typed the name into the password box, and the screen changed to a rotating hourglass. Within a second or two, the screen changed again.

"It's a video," said Shanay. "The date stamp says he recorded it on January 8th."

"Two days after we got back from our New Year's trip to Mexico," said Teddy. "I bet those two A-holes put drugs on *our* boat then, too!"

"And Dylan found out about it," I said.

Teddy and I leaned over Shanay's shoulder as she pulled up the video. We all watched in silence, orienting ourselves to the undulating dock where the filming was being done. The grainy view across the Buena Vista Yacht Harbor was of two men—DEA Agents Tommy Halliday and Jonas Rourke—covertly carrying armloads of kilo-sized packages off of Bernice. They used the marina's dock carts to ferry the load over to their yacht. The video wasn't the best quality, but the men's identities were unmistakable.

The wobbly clip lasted only 32 seconds, and there was almost no audio—except for the very end when Dylan Langdon's voice could be heard saying, "I'll be damned, they've stashed something onboard my boat and now they've come to get it."

Teddy was already on the phone with Detective Grassi as I watched the video for the third time. Shanay had taken over rocking her baby, who had awakened hungry. The two of them were back on the blanket in front of the space heater, and the little girl drank contently from a bottle.

"That was good work," I told Shanay. "You'll have to remind me to give you a raise."

"Yeah, you said that before." Shanay pursed her lips. "Except you ain't got money, 'cus you ain't had no pay'n jobs yet."

"True enough." I nodded as I gathered my things and set them next to the door.

"But…" Shanay lifted her daughter onto her hip and adjusted her bottle. "*If* you had got paid, you would'a split it with me, right?"

"That's a big *if*," I laughed. "But yeah, I'd have split it with you."

"Serious?"

I shrugged. "Sure, why not?" It was all hypothetical anyway.

"Good," she said. "B'cause I forgot to give you a message."

I stopped. "A message, you say?"

"Yep, it's from your friend." Shanay ripped a page from a message pad on her desk. "Sarah Brooks." Shanay handed me the note.

EPILOGUE

I looked out at the blanket of gray hanging overhead, enveloping the marina like a soundproof cloak. The peace and tranquility of my little yacht harbor was finally starting to come back to me.

The Spanish-speaking operator came on the line, and I waited as she connected me to the manager of Jardìn Carrizalejo. Patricia Uribe's recorded voice message asked me to leave a detailed request. My request was to be forgiven and to be allowed a second chance, but this was my fifth unreturned message and I didn't think that it was going to happen. I hung up.

My second call was to Sarah Brooks, and thankfully she answered. "Congratulations, McKenna. I read in the paper that your two corrupt DEA agents are going away for a long time."

"Ten years for the drugs, and another forty for conspiracy to commit murder." It was a great relief to have it behind me. "I wasn't even subpoenaed to testify."

"It was a slam dunk," said Sarah. "And your two cartel friends were given life sentences."

"Yeah, but they were both deported instead."

"Well, yeah, there's that." Sarah chuckled. "They've been turned over to the Mexican government, and who knows? That might be worse than if they'd stayed in prison here."

She had a point. Then again, Ozzy and The Corkscrew might pay off some prison guard, and both of them could end up living in a beachfront villa. *Whatever, I'm done with it.*

"And you heard about the reward," she asked. "Pretty nice hunk of cha-ching in your pocket, I dare say."

"I got your message about the reward money from my secretary, or office assistant, or whatever she is." Then I smile to myself. "Shanay managed to hoodwink me into splitting it with her."

Sarah let out a hardy laugh. "Good for her."

We talked awhile, and I thanked her for smoothing the way for Patricia and her father back to Mexico.

"Oh yeah, speaking of which..." Sarah fumbled with the phone, and I heard the crinkling of paper. "Miss Uribe asked me to give you her new cell phone number."

Sarah read the number to me before ending the call. It was the shot in the arm I needed, maybe even better than the federal reward money. I was about to try Patricia's number when I heard the familiarly annoying voice calling from across the marina.

"Mr. McKenna!"

I glanced over to see Cliff Phillips, the harbormaster, huffing and puffing across the dock in my direction. He seemed a little too spry for the early hour, and I imagined that he wanted another favor.

Stepping over the dockline and up to the side of my boat he said, "I need to talk to you about our newest tenant—single lady over on dock twelve. Just moved in the other day, and there's something that's just not right about the woman. Can you do me a favor and run a check on her?"

Other books by this author:

San Francisco File
Danny McKenna Series – Book #1

It's Only a Badge
Police Memoir – Book #1

Barkers & Bones
Police Memoir – Book #2

Malfeasance
Police Memoir – Book #3

Sadhana
Family Saga Novel

www.ingramcontent.com/pod-product-compliance
Lightning Source LLC
Chambersburg PA
CBHW060323260626
47160CB00007B/2667